More praise for
People of the Whale

"In her remarkable new novel, Hogan . . . explores themes of love and loss among the A'atsika people of Washington State. . . . [Her] style is both dream-like and realistic, with a nonlinear narrative that loops back on itself as more and more is revealed." —*Library Journal*

"Deeply ecological, original, and spellbinding, Hogan ascends to an even higher plane in this hauntingly beautiful novel of the hidden dimensions of life, and all that is now imperiled." —*Booklist*

"This book brings you deep into the realm of a people who have ancient, complex ties to the natural world . . . through a compelling and insistent narrative." —*Tribal College Journal of American Indian Higher Education*

"This is a fine story that embraces the worthy subjects of modern American Indians, the Vietnam War and the importance of family." —*Rocky Mountain News*

"In telling a story of the fictional A'atsika, a Native people of the American West Coast who find their mythical origins in the whale and the octopus, Hogan employs just the right touch of spiritualism in this engrossing tale . . . with a powerful, romantic crescendo." —*Publishers Weekly*

"With her unparalleled gifts for truth and magic, Linda Hogan reinforces my faith in reading, writing, living."

—Barbara Kingsolver, author of *The Poisonwood Bible*

"Hauntingly wise, beautifully written, and fiercely tender, *People of the Whale* goes between realms of animal and human, between Native and non-Native, between the radiant world as it once was and still might become. This book is a bridge, a revelation, an open heart."   —Brenda Peterson, author of *Build Me an Ark: A Life with Animals*

"*People of the Whale* is pure magic—and pure truth. It's as perfect as a smooth stone."

—Sy Montgomery, author of *The Good Good Pig*

PEOPLE of the WHALE

ALSO BY LINDA HOGAN

PEOPLE of the WHALE

A Novel

LINDA HOGAN

W. W. Norton & Company
New York · London

For information about permission to reproduce selections from this
book, write to Permissions, W. W. Norton & Company, Inc.,
500 Fifth Avenue, New York, NY 10110

For information about special discounts for bulk purchases, please
contact W. W. Norton Special Sales at specialsales@wwnorton.com
or 800-233-4830

Manufacturing by LSC Harrisonburg
Book design by Charlotte Staub
Production manager: Julia Druskin

Library of Congress Cataloging-in-Publication Data

Hogan, Linda.
    People of the whale / Linda Hogan.—1st ed.
        p. cm.
    ISBN 978-0-393-06457-5
    1. Indians of North America—Fiction. 2. Vietnam War,
1961–1975—Veterans—Fiction. 3. Culture conflict—Fiction. I. Title.
    PS3558.O34726P46 2008
        813'.54—dc22

                                                        2008025040

ISBN 978-0-393-33534-7 pbk.

W. W. Norton & Company, Inc.
500 Fifth Avenue, New York, N.Y. 10110
www.wwnorton.com

W. W. Norton & Company Ltd.
15 Carlisle Street, London W1D 3BS

7 8 9 0

For the healing of the oceans,
for the healing of our veterans
coming home from all the wars,
and for my brother,

        Larry Henderson.

CONTENTS

PROLOGUE

We live on the ocean. The ocean is a great being. The tribe has songs about the ocean, songs to the ocean. It is a place where people's eyes move horizontally because they watch the long, wide sea flow into infinity. Their eyes follow the width and length of the world. Black rocks rise out of the ocean here and there, lending themselves to stories of sea monsters that might have consumed mere mortals. Several islands along the coast are tree-covered green jewels. The nearby fishing towns are now abandoned, as is the sawmill in disrepair, the forest missing. Down the beach a ways to the south, white piles, shining piles of clam and oyster shells were left behind by the earlier people, the Mysterious Ones, who were said to have built houses of shells, perfectly pieced together. These places truly existed, the secret places where houses were made of shells. Royal ships once anchored there; those who kept journals said the houses were made of pearls. No one sees them now except as a memory made of words. One man passing by at sunset wrote, in 1910, that they were made of rainbows, but of course no one believed him. This was also the year the deadly influenza arrived with the white whalers. The houses of shells were covered in a mudslide that same year.

Even the land gives in to history.

Out in the water, in the uplift of black stones, caves are left open and revealed when the tide is out, but there are caves on land also. A *pile of treasures still remains in one cleft in black rock where once, not long ago, the old revered man, Witka, used to enter the cold sea naked and converse with whales, holding his breath for long periods of time. "Stay away from there," the mothers tell their children, making it all the more enticing, and when no one looks, the children go through the offerings left there, tobacco, black shining stones created when lightning struck sand, a glass float from the other side of the ocean. On some beaches are the broken bones of long-ago boats, skeletons of carved wood, even with ribs, that are broken dreams of poor men's labor. Almost everything from the boats that could be used has been taken years ago. Old and porous whalebones were also used inland as grave markers for the last generations, now as fences for flower gardens, and for occasional carving.*

To the north, there is an old rubbing beach where the whales used to come out of water and flop awkwardly about. "Wake up," a sleepless person would say back then. "Come." And others threw on their coats in the early morning to watch the whales rub their backs into sand and stone, to scratch and remove the barnacles that lived on their skin. The whales looked joyful and happily clumsy when they did this, heaving themselves about with great breath and effort. They were sights to behold, and were watched with awe and laughter. The whales have always been loved and watched, their spumes of breath blowing above water, their bodies turning, rising.

Sometimes this is a turbulent place. Two rivers reach the sea here, sometimes in a muddy rush away from the land. When there are storms, waves reach far heights and water crashes against the rocks, still smoothing them through time.

Sometimes, too, it is peaceful, the water calm. Then the people go out on the still water and fish, or sit on the beach drawing pictures or sifting through the gray sand. They talk with their friends and eat sandwiches. On summer days the sand is warm against their backs and they rest on its heat.

Across the bay are whitewashed buildings. They look as if they've been painted with milk. The old people, the traditionalists, live there.

It is a secret place, this world. You could say it is in Washington but that is too far north, by degrees and fathoms. I keep it a secret, the place, the people, though the world will soon hear about it.

But place or time or season, it doesn't matter to the man who turns his back to the sea. No one knows if he will turn toward life again. They wonder if it is hate he feels, or remorse, or merely human grief. After a while, some forget he is over there.

PART ONE

PART ONE

OCTOPUS

The infant Thomas W. Just was born on July 2, 1947, to much happiness and many pictures of his mother smiling down at him. It was the day just before the octopus left the water, walked on all eight legs across land and into Seal Cave. Sometimes young people made love in that cave. Sometimes boys escaped school and smoked cigarettes there.

But on this day, the day after Thomas was born, the octopus walked out of the sea and they watched it. Every one of these ocean people stood back, amazed to see it walk, the eye of it looking at them, each one seen, as if each one were known in all their past, all their future. Its skin paled at the sight of men smoking cigarettes and women in their cardigans pulled tight, with their dark windblown hair. One child stepped toward it as if to speak before his mother grabbed his arm and pulled him back to her, claiming him as a land dweller and no communicator or friend of any eight-legged sea creature.

None of them, not even the oldest, had ever seen an octopus do this and their people had lived there for thousands of years. It scared them into silence, then they talked about it. They knew it meant something. They didn't know what. Four fishermen in dirty clothes wanted to kill it and use it for fishing bait. "It's only practical!" they argued. "It's the best thing that could happen to us." They could take it, undigested, out of the stomach of flounder and halibut and use it again. For days they talked about it. They quarreled. They cried about how blessed they were. A few wild-haired men, afraid of its potent meaning, wanted to throw kerosene in the cave and burn it.

But one of the powerful women stepped up. She believed it had a purpose for going into the cave and that the humans, a small group of lives beside a big ocean, should leave it alone. Others agreed. Its purpose was a mystery. Or perhaps it was sick or going to give birth. It turned a shade of red as it reached the safety of the cave. And so the people thought it was holy and they left gifts outside the entrance to the black rock cave. Some left sage and red cedar. Some offered shining things, glass smoothed by the sea, even their watches. As for the infant Thomas, his mother, whose own infancy was fed on whale and seal fat, was one of those who thought it was a holy creature and its presence at the time of his birth granted to Thomas a special life. She came from Thomas's birth at the place of the old people and stood before the entrance of the octopus cave and held her kicking baby up to it, to be seen by it. "Here is my son. You knew his grandfather. Watch over him." They were poor people. She had little to leave but the pearl she inherited from her father, Witka. She rolled it into the cave. She was convinced the octopus would be the spirit-keeper of her son, because she thought like the old people used to think, that such helpers existed and they were benevolent spirits. An older man named Samuel left his silver ring at the entrance to the cave; it was his finest possession. Not to have given something they cared about would have been no gift at all, so, following his example, others left sparkling glasses, pieces of gold, beads, all the shining things the octopus people love in their homes beneath water.

For the time it dwelt there, they brought offerings, even the first flowers of morning. The treasures built up like small middens. Even the children didn't take the treasures, although

they did go look at them and marvel at what they found, until
their mothers grabbed them away. The younger children tasted
them and found them without flavor except the salt from
the air.

Those who were afraid the octopus was created by magic or
called into being by some force on land not benevolent kept an
eye on how it stood in the back of the cave. But it sensed their
emotions and formed itself to fit beneath a ledge. It could shape
itself to fit into anything, a bottle, a basket. That was how they
were caught in the old days, by baskets lowered into the water
at night and lifted in the mornings, the creature inside it. Yet,
that quality scared people who knew little about them, but had
heard much about shape-shifters and their deceits and witch-
ery on humans, always with poor outcomes for the mortals.

Nevertheless, the mother of Thomas, in a plain white dress,
took the baby Thomas daily across the sand to the cave when
the tide was out.

Then, one night, without any sign, the octopus disappeared
from human sight and went back into the water.

As closely as they watched, no one saw its return to the ocean.
It must have been three in the morning, they decided, because
early each morning the old people were on the beach singing
powerful, old, and still-remembered songs. They sang around
four each morning when the atmosphere is most charged with
energy. They could say this now that they lived in measured
time. Also, they could remain and pray and watch the reflected
red of dawn on the rocks and sky. Drinkers might have seen it
at two in the morning as they sat on the beach drumming and
singing their newer songs. Of course, they may have missed it
while kissing a lover or, like Dimitri Smith, the man who never
tucked in his shirt and slept often on the beach, while gazing
only upward at the sky, searching out and naming the constellations: Whale. Sea Lion. Octopus. Yes, that was one of them.

With the departure of the octopus went their gifts. The octopus, by accepting the Smiths' gold ring, Witka's pearl, gems,

the pieces of silver, even a pair of glasses, knew it was loved by them and it would help them as it went back under the sea and stayed there, maybe giving them good fishing or good deer hunting, whaling money, love medicine, all things desperately wanted by humans and shifting in their value day by day, moment by moment, depending on their needs.

Thomas's grandfather was the well-known whaler named Witka. He was the one who told them what gifts the octopus loved. He was the last of those who could go under the sea holding his breath for long times and remain, so he had a great deal of knowledge about the ocean and all sea life. He was the last of a line of traditional men who loved and visited the whales to ensure a good whale hunt, along with his friend, the great-grandfather of Dimitri Smith and a man named Akita-si who could also remain beneath water for briefer times than Witka, but long enough to sew a whale's mouth closed when they killed a whale. This sewing was important so that the lungs wouldn't fill with water and the whale sink to the bottom of the ocean.

Witka's wife lived most of the time in the white town. His other women lived in the wooden houses that used to be up against the mountain before the tidal wave washed the places away, but he himself stayed and dreamed much of the time in the dark gray house he built on top of the thirty-two-foot-high black rock where his grandson, Thomas Witka Just, now dwells, thinking of his grandfather, whose watch on the sea had been constant, that man who spoke with the whales, entreated them, and asked, singing with his arms extended, if one of them would offer itself to the poor people on land. He beckoned and pleaded when the people were hungry. The rest of the time Witka watched their great numbers passing by, spraying or standing in water to look around, or rising and diving, their shining sides covered with barnacles. The infant whales were sometimes lifted on the backs of the mothers. They were such a sight for him to behold, the man who lived between the worlds and between the elements.

Water was not really a place for humans, but Witka the whale hunter had courage. He had practiced holding his breath from childhood in preparation for this role. Only for this. He was born to it and his parents were unhappy about it. When he went beneath water, they stood in their clothing woven of sea grass and waited for him to surface. But they couldn't hope away his destiny. He was born with a job set out for him and his life was already known to them. He wore white cloth that set him apart so the others would know and remember what and who he was. That way they would treat him well. He learned the songs and prayers. By the age of five he had dreamed the map of underwater mountains and valleys, the landscape of rock and kelp forests and the language of currents. He had an affinity for it. He saw it all. At night he dreamed of the way it changed from day to day. They were beautiful dreams and he loved the ocean world. "You should see the circle of shining fish," he told his mother.

"Oh my," was all she could say in return, creasing her embroidered handkerchief, wiping her eyes.

Later, as a man, he visited the world he dreamed. He traveled there. A person could always think of the old man in any way they wanted, but usually they saw him in their mind's eye as the old whaler who went underneath the water, white hair flying in the currents, old dark face even more wrinkled from the salt water, the man who was a medical oddity, a human curiosity, a visionary, a hunter and carver, and a medicine man who could cure rheumatism and dizzy spells.

His knowledge of the ocean was so great that scientists came to question him. Scientists and anthropologists then wrote papers about what he told them. Doctors from as far away as Russia came to find out how he held his breath and stayed beneath water for as long as he did with no ill effects, how he could remain in a hibernating state without breathing. "He's like those men in India who do yoga," said one of them, thinking if they could learn it what a weapon it would make.

Once Witka remained for part of the time with an octopus. It was a larger one, a fifteen-footer all stretched out, Witka caressing the tentacles. Of course, he could have exaggerated. Who would ever know? The octopus, who had the gift of feeling its way into small places, searched out his pockets and took several coins. It then worked the wedding ring off his hand. That was how they knew what the octopus loved. Witka told them all about it, laughing, his missing tooth showing when he laughed. His left hand he held up for display, naked of the ring. "And not a single tentacle print did it leave!" he said.

All this was in the days when the women would sing the whales toward them. Witka's wife, too, was a chosen one. That's how they came to be matched. She was one of the whale-singers. As for whaling in those days, nothing except the women who sang the whales toward them was more serious than Witka's knowledge of the sea. When he walked into the cold depths of the ocean, or slipped so carefully out of the canoe, he began in earnest a hunt for the whale. When Witka went into the ocean, everyone and everything on land was still. The town stopped living. No one labored. No one bought or sold. No one laughed or kissed. It was the unspoken rule. All they did was wait, the women singing, eerily, at ocean's edge. They were solemn and spoke softly and they considered this the great act of a man who sacrificed for them. All they did was think of him out there in the sea and of the whales that would approach. For them. The people of the water. People of the whale.

When he entered the water, his wife, by spiritual rule, went underground. Even when she was very old and stooped, she dug the hole herself. With a small shovel and with her own thin, wrinkled hands. This was the way it was always done. She dug a hole, like a bear den, deep inside the giant roots of a tree. She covered herself with skins and she stayed under the earth, eyes closed, visions in her head of what her husband was seeing inside the water. She was beneath ground; he was beneath water. Maybe she breathed for him. People wondered if they were that connected because it was known that in the cold and dark they were as one.

With his mind and heart, Grandfather Witka told Mary, her catholic name, "My hands are swollen and cold," and about a flotilla of plankton he'd just passed through. He said, "It's like a snowstorm," and as he talked she saw it, too, as far away as she was. She asked the water to have mercy on the old man she'd known as a child when he climbed trees, laughed, practiced holding his breath, and hunted his first seal. "Look," he'd said, his first gift to her, smiling, a tooth missing. "It's for you. I want to marry you someday."

She smiled. "Only a seal? I'm worth more than that." She laughed and walked away, looking back at him once or twice over her shoulder.

Mary sang to the whales, *onio way no*, loving them enough that one of them might listen and offer itself to her people. Entombed with the smell of cedar, curled like an infant newly born, even though her hair was gray now, her face bony, she was suspended and stiff. And then together, when he saw a whale, the two of them pleaded and spoke. *Look how we are suffering. Take pity on us. Our people are small. We are hungry.*

It was said the whale listened mostly to the woman because who could ignore her pleading, singing, beautiful voice?

The last time Witka entered the sea he did not return. Worse, a storm arrived. They all feared that this time, at his age, his heart failed and he would not come back to the air world where they lived. His daughter, the mother of Thomas, was little more than a child. She didn't know where her mother had buried herself in the trees. Out of grief, she pounded the gray sand beach with her fists. She was such a thin girl, too. She stood by the black rocks in her nightgown looking out into the dark water, watching in vain. She held hands with one of Witka's girlfriends and together they cried and hugged each other and grieved for the lost old man.

Then, when all had given up and some turned toward home, someone yelled, "Look," and he came out of the dark underwater cave where he had anchored himself and rolled out of the green swells of the waves onto the sand, coughing. When he surfaced, the water rolling off his head and face, he took a great breath. He dragged himself up, skinny with age, wrinkled, and walked out from the sea with kelp still on him, looking anything but dignified. A fish caught in the kelp escaped his hair and dropped back down to the tide. He walked like a stick, stiff from the cold, and his face was nearly blue. He walked straight over to his daughter and said, "Girl, do you want to scare the whales away, hitting the ground so hard? I heard it all the way out there." She ran off, ashamed, while he laughed. Everyone waited for his pronouncement. This time he said, with smiling eyes, "Yes, tomorrow. It is the right time for us to bring a whale back home," as he looked with great joy at the green land and sunlight and his wife walking—no, floating—toward him, earth and twigs still clinging to her hands and clothes and hair.

His brother and his best friend called the other men and they went to prepare the wooden canoes. They brought the harpoon, the floats, drinking water, for they might be gone four days or more. When they hunted, the women would be quiet the whole time the men were out. Everyone had to be pure in heart and mind. By then the whale would be coming gladly toward the village.

"Oh brother, sister whale," he sang. "Grandmother whale, Grandfather whale. If you come here to land we have beautiful leaves and trees. We have warm places. We have babies to feed and we'll let your eyes gaze upon them. We will let your soul become a child again. We will pray it back into a body. It will enter our bodies. You will be part human. We'll be part whale. Within our bodies, you will dance in warm rooms, create light, make love. We will be strong in thought for you. We will welcome you. We will treat you well. Then one day I will join you." His wife sang with him.

When Witka truly died, his wife, best girlfriend, and daughter held on to his body longer than they should. They couldn't be sure he was dead just because he wasn't breathing.

Those were the grandparents of Thomas Witka Just. They were the grandparents and mother, on one side, of Thomas, the man who had been missing in war, the man who now lived in Witka's gray hut on the craggy rocks. Thomas, the man who'd won the Purple Hearts and nearly the last Medal of Honor and other shining tokens of actions that should have made him feel esteemed.

When Thomas was a boy, he, like his grandfather, always watched the water. As if keeping with the old traditions they'd all heard about, he and his friends, Dimitri III, Dwight, jealous of the abilities of Thomas, and the others would see how long they could hold their breath underwater. "It isn't funny," Thomas's mother said when she thought, more than once, that he had drowned and she pulled him up to air by the back of his shirt. The last time, the shirt, an old Arrow, ripped off and Thomas nearly drowned, laughing.

Custer died in an Arrow shirt. That was their joke.

Later, as his grandfather had gone under the ocean, his grandmother under the land, Thomas had taken to the sky, a most unnatural thing for a human. On his way to war, the first plane crashed and he was the sole survivor. Before he could even protest or tell the story of what he'd seen, they put him on another plane. After that, he believed he was saved for a reason.

But now he hopes he has an appointment with death and all he wants to do is wait for it. He has turned his back on the sea.

It's a secret to the rest of the world where Thomas lives, as he wants it to be. If it were known, people would come searching. They would find him. He is a war hero missing for over five years after the war was declared over, until he was found by the army, then, after a stop in Hawaii, he was lost again in San Francisco, named for Saint Francis. Now he is missing from himself.

If you knew about him, you would want to go talk to him and tell him it's not his fault and you'd tell him to live, or if he is dying, or wanting to die, he should at least do it without closing the doors of the world. But your words would tire you out. Even more, they might convince him out of spite or frustration to go into the water and never come back, or to leap off the high rock where he sits, and throw himself to earth from one side of the rock like when he was ten and made wings and jumped off this very rock cliff. For one moment the air took hold of his sewn wings and he flew for just that moment before he landed, scratched and bruised on the ocean sand. What a moment, that second in air.

Now you look at him and think he never had a boyhood or wings.

Now at night he never lights his grandfather Witka's kerosene lamp. He doesn't even have a wick for it any longer. Just as it is for him, what ignites and maintains the fire is missing. He doesn't want light and some people hear voices from the place at night so they stay away.

Thomas wishes that, like the octopus that came to land when he was born, he could place himself inside something small and pull the last stone over the opening.

During the daylight hours he travels, without wanting to, the inside passage of his own self, a human labyrinth of memory,

history, and the people that came before him. Witka's grandson, his dark hair unwashed, his face still one of handsome
angles, sits in the dark of the old house like an octopus in a
dark corner, is in trouble, not with the law, not with other
people, but within. What lonely creatures humans are when
they thread through these passages. It is an inner world, one
of disasters and whirlwinds, unknown islands, and he must
journey them all alone. There are circles inside the mind of a
man, circles a man can't escape because each time he comes
to a conclusion, it is the same place and it begins over again. It
courses hard. And Thomas harbors too many secrets.

Death would be beautiful for him, but he's destined, miser-
ably, to live. He owes a debt to life. It's as simple as accounting,
as hard math. He owes something. Maybe he will understand
what it is now in the dark at the place where the old man
Witka once watched for whales. The sea is beautiful, but he
looks at it not at all, not even for whales. Soon his clothes grow
too large for him. Inside the sleeves and collars and legs are
memories inside the body that can't be forgotten.

Like the octopus from 1947, the one that could have gone
into a basket to hide, the one that portended good things for
this child, Thomas is contained in small things, the gray house,
cups and cans, packs of cigarettes.

DEATHLESS

Here is what happened, how the man was lost. Here is how he lived through death, how he came to live on the dark rock and to pass memories through his heart.

First there was the war and it was in Vietnam and few of our people had ever heard of that small country before. They knew little of the war except small things on the news. This is a small reserve, village, or town, as some prefer to call it, one with old houses staggered here and there on the flats and on hillsides or near the river. Nothing in Dark River is given to straight lines or planning. The roads curve up one hill and down another. The roofs are of faded blue material on some of the small wooden houses, the blue that was once brighter than sky or water. Other homes are covered with red, also pale so that the colors look like those of dusk and dawn. The houses, sitting here and there, hold people who have grown together, all with the same histories like one tree with the same roots and fallen leaves. They have ancestors in common, most of them. Even the dogs running after food together or sleeping in the winding roads look like they descended from the same Adam and Eve of dogs.

· · ·

Then there was Ruth, the woman Thomas Witka Just had married in a tribal ceremony on the beach. What a wedding! All their friends were there. It was even said the fish attended, making the water shine with their silver leaps and splashes.

Ruth and Thomas had known each other all their lives and it was inevitable, all thought, that they would marry. As a woman, Ruth inherited a well-boned face, the kind that is beautiful photographed but looks sharp in person, like she was carved by the winds that blow there. As an infant, Ruth was born with gill slits. It had happened before, children being born with gills, but her mother, Aurora, said, "It's an omen. I don't know what, but I don't like it. She's bound for water, this one. Like her father." She was afraid her daughter might die. In or out of water, at first it seemed she wouldn't live either way. The midwife had to keep the baby girl in a zinc tub filled with water so she wouldn't drown in air before they took her to a doctor in town. The gills were right in front of her ears. The doctors were baffled and it took many weeks to sew the gills together and keep Ruth Small breathing through her lungs. Later it seemed she heard things others didn't. She heard through water, schools of fish and the whales before they surfaced.

Ruth Small, granddaughter of Akita-si, Witka's friend and the other beneath-the-water man, was anything but small. Large in spirit, strong in hand, big in heart, she was a tall girl, taller than Thomas until he caught up and finally outgrew the leggy young woman, and then one night kissed her and their love was sealed, lip to lip.

The night of the wedding there was a full moon and Ruth's dress, painstakingly made by her mother, had shells and abalone buttons and other things that shine sewn on it. It looked like the reflections of moonlight on the ocean itself. Ruth wrapped herself with a shawl that was also shining. She looked as if she were a spirit that could walk the ocean pathway made by the moon on water, like the woman in one of their stories. In this story, the woman and moon together created the cycles of growing plants, the movement of tides, and the falling rain.

That night, barefoot, Ruth was not only shining with her dress of shell and bead and white ribbon, but she was glowing from inside. The happiness of the two, who were always meant to be together, was visible to all, especially to Ruth's father, who married them with words in their own language. All noted how much Ruth and her father resembled one another, their bony good looks, their golden skin tanned from sun, their long fingers. They even fished together, and it was hard work. Their muscled arms showed it. All day they fished and their long fingers and hands had calluses. They would have fished into the night except for the collision they once had with a fisherman named Vince Only. At the wedding, Vince, always a fisherman, watched the sea.

"What a smart man you are," someone said to Thomas after the wedding. Thomas smiled at his new wife. "I know it."

Linda, Ruth's friend, her hair curled for the first time, said, "You two have always been married anyway."

It did seem that way. Ruth and Thomas were, even as infants, two people who had grown together, who were meant for one another, who sat together as infants in their cradleboards watching the adults fishing, gazing at the world around them, and at each other, talking in their own language. Ruth's stitches had been removed and she could breathe. Yet she did, even then, long for the water at times. Together they had watched his father carve masks for the dances, frightening ones, raven masks, ones that made the children laugh. At night the older people danced, sang, and played old gambling games for stones while the babies watched, the ocean shining in moonlight. They saw all this from the time they were children and they saw one another as if they were one person sharing the same world, the same thoughts.

After the marriage, they moved into a small place by the river and painted it green from top to bottom because it had been the only paint available. They called it "Fruit Box imported from California." It was where they began their life as a married couple. It was over by the Salmon River. Naked they lay together in the breeze from the windows. Outside was what had once been a fence made of willows, but the posts miraculously took on life and now, in spite of being cut and buried, they bloomed and leafed out, light green, held by wire that Ruth, with her long black hair, set about clipping, calling out, "The liberation of the trees!"

She painted on each end of the house, CALIFORNIA ORANGES.

Thomas adored her. They were people of scant resources. Ruth helped her father fish. She could hear where the fish traveled beneath water so they had a more or less successful business. Her hands were hardened from the ropes and wires. Thomas worked beneath cars, adding parts, tightening screws, fixing tires. His nails were black. And she was tired. Her father had grown old. That, and he was called on any time of day or night to help people with their ailments. Her mother went with him but only to tell him if the man on the bed should have his leg removed because of diabetes or if it was something that Indian medicine could cure.

Not far from them was the Shaker church many belonged to, but not Thomas and Ruth who belonged to the age of Aquarius, as they laughingly put it when making love.

Sometimes at night they swam naked in the sea, plankton on their bodies lighting them when they surfaced. Thomas was a weak swimmer, but like his grandfather he could hold his breath for long times.

The young couple had no everyday routine except for work and that varied. Sometimes no one brought in a car. At times there were no fish. Even old Vince with his whiskers didn't go out, unless he went to the deep sea.

. . .

Still, the war finally came to the village. It was on a day Ruth was wearing sea-blue. For some reason, they would both remember that. She looked like a mirage to Thomas.

"What?" she was surprised. "You have joined the army? You are going to boot camp and we've barely been married? Don't you love me?" she'd asked him when he had enlisted. "Why? We're just starting together!"

He loved her. He didn't know why he enlisted. "We just all did it," was his only reason. "Together," he said. They'd been drinking, "the boys," as she called them. They believed in America. They did. They were patriotic. "I'm not just an Indian. I'm an American, too."

"You were drinking with them! That's why."

She turned her back to him so he wouldn't see her cry. After a while she left the small bedroom in their rented place, the green walls and ceiling they'd once laughed about, that only paint they could find, which now seemed pitiful. And she put away dishes, quietly, carefully. He wished she would slam cupboards and silverware. Later he went to her, stood behind her and held her. She didn't forgive him, not then. Not really until years later when she realized how men were so influenced by their peers and governments. This was something Ruth, a woman who could stand alone in the world, would never understand.

Thomas was sent away before the others.

He argued with the recruiter. "But the army promised us the buddy system. We'd go together. We were supposed to go together. We wanted to fight together for America."

"The army promises a lot," said the man at the recruiting station in the little shopping center next to the post office. "Don't worry. You'll all catch up with each other." And maybe Thomas knew he lied, but it was too late. Now he was owned.

On the day Thomas left, Ruth was torn in half. The two of them, who'd always laughed together, floated in the water and talked together, who saw with the same eyes, were now separate. She wept when he left and she couldn't stop for days. Then she set her lips in tight resignation, more akin to sorrow, and went about her life of fishing.

Soon she moved onto their boat, an old Trophy, a Cadillac of boats, she'd always been told. It had a decent enough living space. Besides, she of the independent spirit and born with gill slits had always wanted to live on the water, and now she and her father would always be ready when the salmon came down from the north.

She was pregnant when Thomas left for war. She didn't know it until it made her sick to fill the boat with gas, too sick to head toward the salmon run or out deeper to the halibut, as they sometimes did. Her father watched her vomit over the back of the boat and said he'd go alone that day. He sent her home on his worn-out little excuse for a dinghy. She barely made it, and then her mother looked at her and said, "You don't even need a doctor to tell you that you are having a baby. I give you seven months."

Evenings, or early mornings, drenched in salt water, loneliness, an infant inside her growing by division she thought, not multiplication, she brought in the nets, counted the fish, sometimes only eleven trying to leap from net into water, both shining.

She already saw the child she was going to have and so she named him Marco Polo, the infant with black hair who was going to do what she'd always wanted and travel the world. Oh, he'd see camels and deserts and silks and people wearing orange and red robes. He'd see temples and monkeys and paintings and hear sounds of the world she'd never heard, jungle sounds, and he'd see the far north.

Guess what? she wrote to Thomas. *You would have loved it today. I saw the bald eagle nest. Remember it? It has grown. They added another room. But even better, I saw an octopus in the water.*

Thomas, best of all, we are going to have a baby. Yes, a baby. He is
a boy. I can see him. He looks like you. My mother will be so disap-
pointed. She swears he will look like Dad.

That same day she mailed the letter. After she talked to the
gossip Carlene, who worked at the post office, she was followed by a scrawny spotted dog. "Go home," she hissed at him.
But no amount of stomping her foot, of saying "Shoo," turned
the dog back away and when she went to the water, the little
thing stood at the shore watching her leave, howling like a
baby wolf, until she turned back. "Okay, come on." He hopped
in the dinghy with her and, to her amazement, climbed onto
the boat like a human, a few steps up and then a leap. A master
at boats already.

That day she had to fix a pending leak in the boat where
she lived, fix the hatch, and decide how to make room for a
baby and for a dog. She looked at the dog and thought of the
words *poop deck*, and how she would have to train him. She
looked about her small room and thought about where the
cradle would go, then the crib, then the bed. As it turned out,
she didn't have to wonder where the dog would sleep. The
little spotted dog slept with her and she loved the warmth of
his body.

Even without Thomas, it became a happy time. Hoist, as
she and her father named their little canine assistant, dragged
nets in with his teeth as if to help, making them laugh. She
would always remember her father's face as he laughed that
first day, red and happy. Hoist also chased his tail. He leaped
over waves, biting the top of water. Everyone loved him, even
the customers at the NO DOGS, and SORRY WE'RE OPEN café. And
the baby was moving, turning like a butterfly growing wings
in a cocoon.

It's salmon season, she wrote Thomas. *They are so beautiful. I*
hate to kill even one. But I only sell what we need to. I almost have to
divine what the restaurants will use. Sometimes I throw a few back. I
wish you would write me more about what life is like over there. Your

letter about how green it is made me curious. I wish I could see it. The baby is growing!

Thomas laughed when he read the letter. But there were two laughs, one about the baby, one about the idea of Ruth seeing the world over there, not worth laughing about, a world taken apart, bodies, fear, and the smell of death. But then, it was the beginning of many lies, how could he tell her the truth of his life there.

Ruth left out some things, as well. She didn't tell him when her father died and how they'd had a traditional service and his body was taken to the island where once they kept the dead. The mourning songs and the crying would have made a mountain weep. He was left for the vultures, according to tradition which was so rarely kept now. Her mother went into mourning, painting the part in her hair black.

Nor did Ruth write to Thomas about how his own father had attacked her at the corner of the schoolhouse one night. He'd been drinking. She begged him to stop as he pulled her blouse open, then held her arms with one hand. There were some men nearby smoking and laughing. She called to them for help. They didn't come to help her, even though she knew they heard. They walked away. Worse, they laughed. With her strong arms she had to break his hold herself and leave him bruised, drunk, and angry enough to tell everyone he "got some" from his own daughter-in-law. He was known for his handsome charisma, and some might have believed it if they hadn't known Ruth. More than one person saw him with a black eye underneath his sunglasses.

When he was born, Marco swam out of the birth canal hands first, like a diver. The doctor at the hospital was worried when he saw the small wet hands, as if a small replica of the woman was reaching, grasping from within herself. One hand even took hold of the doctor when he was feeling for the head and the baby began to pull himself into the world of light and air.

Marco managed to swim. Ruth looked at every part of him, his perfect brown fingers. Then his toes. She laughed. "Well, no wonder, Doctor! Mother, look, he has some webbed toes! Of course he came out swimming." Webbed feet were not unknown around those parts, but no one liked to admit it. Besides, in Marco's case, there were only a few. And Aurora had never told Ruth about how she had been born with gill slits. They were a family not bound to land, that was for sure, Aurora told her own sister, who lived farther north. Like the whales who were dependent on land, in many ways they lived in two elements.

One morning after a long silence from Thomas, Ruth sat on her mother's couch eating a Popsicle. It was an old couch, worn velvet or horsehair—she never knew which—and slightly rough. The lovebirds in their white cage in the corner of the room were cooing. Hoist always watched them with strong alertness and snapped up their fallen feathers. Ruth had her eye on the sea. It misted outside. She was looking toward the ocean trying to see through the mists and drifts of fog when a black car pulled up the dirt road to the drive. A man stepped out with clear plastic covering his military hat. Strangely, Hoist did not bark. When the man knocked, Ruth knew why he was there. "Don't open the door, Mom." Ruth went to it and spoke through it to the man she would always call Mr. Death. "No one lives here," she said. As if that was not loud enough, she said, "Death, you have never heard our name. Go away."

He, like everyone, was merely doing his duty. "I have a message to deliver. Mr. Just sent me to you." There were two men. One remained in the car.

"Ruth, don't be rude. Who is it?" Her mother, with her white hair and dark skin, always gracious, dish towel in hand, opened the door to the stranger. Ruth was already on the floor, fallen as women have done before, so often, some doubled over, some on their sides, some shaking with sobs, some staring

at linoleum because at least the floor was not the dread face of
human truth.

Aurora, the mother of Ruth, knew why he was there. She
pitied her daughter, but she let him in and he removed his hat.
"I'm Sergeant Green," he said. Then, slowly, he bent toward
Ruth. "May I?" He looked at the older woman. She nodded.
It was clear he was experienced at this and he was strong, as
if they only selected men with arms that could hold women,
chests that could be hit by them, backs that could lift them. He
picked Ruth up carefully, her black hair cascading down, and
laid her on the sofa with doilies on its arms. Her beauty was not
missed by him. Ruth, as she had done as a girl, cried without
crying, water spilling from her eyes, and the man never even
had to say, "I regret to inform . . ."

The baby Marco, who already had watching eyes and showed
signs of difference from other children, slept in the next room.
He was a calm child, and the voices did not wake him. Or they
did and he listened and understood.

"Here." The messenger spoke to Aurora. "Her father-in-law
told me to give this to her. I'm sorry, ma'am. We didn't even
know he had a wife. It wasn't in our records."

"No," said Ruth's mother. "It was a tribal wedding. It's in our
own records."

He took something out of his pocket and handed it to the
older woman. It was a dog tag, a single one. It fell into Aurora's
hand on its snake chain. "Thank you," she said. Ruth heard the
chain and metal. Dog tag and chain. Dog, that was a man in
war. Dog. He had to follow orders. He had to sniff for danger, be
willing to die for his owner. He had to hate strangers, be wary,
be nothing, be kicked and hungry and still obey. He needed
madness. Dog, what Thomas and so many others had been.
The president had said about war that it was proof there was
still madness in the world, only Ruth always wondered who
the mad ones were. Anyway, even if she often thought he was
one of them, the president's words were the truth.

Anger and sorrow grew together in her like a single tree. Sorrow had knocked her down, but anger lifted her to her feet.

Standing tall, Ruth looked at the man. "He's not dead."

He'd heard the same thing so many times before. "I hope you're right."

The car backed away and left the way it had come.

"He's alive, Mother. I feel it."

"You're probably right." She took her daughter in her arms and held her. "You usually are." She, still grieving her own man, smoothed down Ruth's black hair.

Nevertheless, it was the end of laughter for a time.

The love between Thomas and Ruth was a love that existed in another dimension, just as Witka, the grandfather of Thomas, and his wife had a love that communicated from earth all the way through elements to the depths of water. Ruth had seen through space and time across this world through her own eyes and heart. Through distances across the ocean, with its pulsing jellyfish and swaying kelp forests, flying manta rays, sea turtles coming up to breathe, across all that and heavy clouds, too, she had seen him in her twilight sleep. Once there were firestorms. She had seen him encircled by fire and, like a salamander in the forest, surviving it by staying down in the wet earth, beneath it, breathing through a wet brown rag, not running like others. She saw him leap into a ditch. Once, more recently, he was standing at a brown river in a green world, and he was fishing, his black hair in a ponytail as he threw out fishing nets in their tribal fashion. But then, Ruth's spirit had never remained in the hiding place of her body. It always traveled. "Last night your father was drunk," she said to Thomas once when they were children. Tommy, as he was called then, nodded, accustomed to her and how, even shy and quiet, she knew things. He had looked down at the ground where they sat. She said, "And I know why." She pulled at her braids. "Because he aches inside, because he will never be like your grandpa."

Now, at night, she pulled her dreams and memories into a net like a school of silver fish. There was the time she dreamed a short-haired Thomas eating with a tribe of people. They wore faded blue and brown clothing, and so did he. They talked rapidly and laughed. They ate fish and rice.

But after the man in the shining car arrived, there were times she doubted herself. "What if he's sharing food with the ancestors? Or fishing for them and not for earth people?" she asked Linda.

Linda, who owned the only restaurant on the reservation, said, "You always know things, Ruth. Trust your feelings. Your intuition is always right. Yeah. He's alive."

Linda was thin from moving all day and her hair was dyed too dark now. She wore it in a bun when she worked, although no customer would complain to Linda about a hair in the food. Some had, and she had merely removed it and said, "There you go."

"Sit down for a while," she told Ruth, and poured her some coffee. "For one thing, the ancestors don't catch fish at rivers. They fish the clouds. They only eat ground acorns and flowers. Like the people of the past."

But when Linda put her arms around her, and Ruth was an armload of grief, Ruth knew Linda didn't believe her. She felt it. Linda was thinking, after all, they had the dog tag. And Ruth had it in her pocket, constantly fingering the chain, the cheap metal that should have been gold. Throughout the day, she caressed and felt and read it with her fingertips, that thing which had touched his chest, his sweat.

After Death had come to her mother's door, Ruth began staying awake on the boat where she lived with Marco. She watched

Marco sleep, his lips parted, his skin smooth, eyelashes like his father's, his eyes already with lines at the side as if he'd spent a lifetime laughing. He was an astute child. Born an old man, was what people said of him. He was also a quiet child. Still, he had a sense of humor from infancy and he was set apart by his inborn wisdom. He was the incarnation of an ancestor, the elders said, those who still believed in such things.

Like his father, like Witka, the boy began to go into the salt water of the plankton-filled ocean and not come to the surface for a long time. Ruth, unable to bear the thought of losing him, waited in tears and then reproached him. "It scares me. I wait for you to be alive. Don't you understand?" She had already lost her father, her husband.

Marco didn't. Every day he stayed longer, telling his mother, "I can't help it. Something else makes me do it."

Over the next years, Ruth's visions were a wave that flowed from her bed on the boat and floated her out to the waters of another world. She merely floated, her body lying on the bed moored to her place on the sea as she journeyed. Now and then she had a dream of Thomas with a little girl on his lap like a spirit child.

Out loud one night, she said, "He's standing in water," waking her son. Hoist licked her face.

"My father?" Marco asked, half awake.

"Yes," was all she said. "But it was only a dream."

"No. He is there. He's walking across a field of grass."

Ruth stared at him in the moonlight a long time. "I think it's rice," she said.

"Me, too." As if he'd know what rice looked like.

So, she thought, the boy saw these things, too. So she told Marco the stories about his father as a child, the time he tried to fly, how he also, like Marco, tried to hold his breath until it scared his mother, until she pretended to die of fear and Thomas came up one day gasping and found her lying down, her hands over her chest, posed like a corpse waiting for vultures. They laughed.

When she said the word *vulture*, she thought of her own father, over on the island, his body on a platform in the trees. But there was her son, and as time passed, Marco grew into a beautiful child. He helped her when he was not in school even though she worried about him getting hurt. Fishing was dangerous business. For a time, she began shore fishing. It suited them better. Marco, like her, hated to kill fish.

One chilly day Aurora rowed out to Ruth's bay in her own dead husband's dirty old rowboat as if rowing was still natural to her skinny old arms.

"Ruth!" she called out as she tried to change boats.

Hoist, with damp fur, licked the old woman's face, barking happily as the exhausted old woman climbed aboard.

Ruth went to see what the noise was.

"Oh my God, Mom! You rowed all the way out here?" She helped the older woman up the ladder, grabbing her waist with her strong arms, lifting her, really, the skinny old legs finally touching wood. "Hoist, get back!"

In between breaths her mother said, "You were right! He's alive, Thomas is. You were right all along."

She'd been called that morning when a few flakes of snow began to drift down. He'd been found living in a village. "He was held by the enemy, brainwashed or injured, they think," she said. "I'm freezing. I wish you could get a phone out here."

Ruth wrapped her mother in a quilt that had been stitched of men's old suits, ones they wore after the Catholics had converted them.

As the snow melted on Aurora's hair, Ruth heated coffee water, hardly able to lift the kettle.

"You knew it all along. You were right and I'm sorry, but sometimes I didn't believe you. And now they say he is coming back."

"I know." Ruth leaned across the table, smiling at her mother. She put her hands on each side of Aurora's face and kissed her. "It's okay. No one did."

"Except me!" Marco, who had been studying snowflakes, jumped up and down, not his usual style, but he said, "I could see him. My father!"

They all laughed. "Cocoa, Marco Polo Just?"

The morning Thomas was to return, Ruth braided her hair down her back, undid it, brushed it again, and braided it until it was perfect. She wore jeans and a dark green silk shirt and sat up straight. Marco insisted on wearing a traditional woven men's skirt over his jeans. He had gifts for his father, a wooden cedar box which held a bald eagle feather and a carved and painted canoe paddle. And he had himself, already with an air of authority. They waited. It was eight and Thomas was not due in until nearly ten, but Ruth was anxious.

He had been found, she was told, quarantined, hospitalized for examination, questioned by the army, and honorably discharged. But she'd heard nothing from him and she was puzzled and concerned. She had been waiting for a century even though Marco was only nine. The war had been over, at least for America, but she had never given up hope.

She and Marco sat in the small airport and looked out the window. Planes arrived and left on currents of heat and air. Light crossed their faces. It reflected off moving things, a woman's pocketbook clasp, a van outside by the planes, silver on the luggage.

"Here, young man." A stewardess gave the boy a pin with a pair of wings. He sat with it on his lap and waited. Ruth pulled him toward her and touched his hair. She watched him. He had, for some reason, lost his excitement about his father coming home.

The sun moved past where they now sat.

Ruth looked at her hand, then at her arm. Muscular and

lean. It was hard work, the fishing boat. She looked in a mirror at her face, wondering how much she'd changed in these years, if he would recognize her, love her, if she was still beautiful as he'd once thought.

They had warned her that Thomas would be changed. Maybe in ways incomprehensible even to himself. The one witness to the massacre said he'd been hit in the head by something flying, something large. That one witness, the survivor, young Michael, said he'd seen Thomas fall. The last thing he himself recalled was that he panicked and ran to the water, turning toward it in the smoke of burning people and trees and land and then the fog, too, as he reached the water and jumped in so he wouldn't burn. He was picked up from the water by a navy boat. "What luck!" said the man who found him. "And timing." The boy was in shock. The words seemed cold after what he'd seen and told them. "Undress, soldier," they said, and gave him dry clothes. He believed at the time that Thomas had died, or if not, desperately needed medical attention. He had every intention of getting help to him, but he could only cry. He cried when he told them the story and they had to keep moving away. Then he heard on the boat that city after city had fallen to the communists. For the first time he wondered what a communist really was.

The countries fell quickly, easily, to the north. Soon Saigon was invaded. They said the Americans were leaving the country. The army then had used nerve gas wherever they thought soldiers either had defected or were caught by the enemy. To keep them from suffering at the hands of a more cruel enemy, they said. He thought of Thomas. Sarin. Nerve gas. He wondered for years where they had dropped it. It occupied his daily thoughts. So did his guilt, his fractured conscience. He was thinking of it the day they found him and he'd think of it for a long time after, about the man, Thomas, who must have died that day, at least his name was on the Wall in DC along with the others.

• • •

Ruth's mother arrived at the airport just before the plane, her hair in a sheer pink scarf, for it had become windy. She removed the scarf and fluffed up the white hair which framed her dark face with a circle of light. Ruth looked at her mother's dark, ropy hands, her radiant skin. She carried flowers for "the soldier," as she called him, and sweet rolls for Marco and Ruth. The flowers were red, white, and blue. Ruth could not look at them, still thinking of the soldiers as America's dogs not cared for as much as she cared for Hoist. Then came the old friends of Thomas. Ruth did not sit near them or acknowledge them. She knew them. They were the men who wouldn't stop a rape. Dwight. Dimitri. Cyrus. Dark men, not necessarily in skin color, for two of them were mixed, but of heart and spirit. She could see through them. And they had taken Thomas away. Them and their beer, or whatever it was. Ruth always thought that if there was justice in the world, one of them should have been the one who didn't come back. Then she disliked herself for thinking it.

There was a smell of sugar and cinnamon, but the sweet rolls went untouched.

Ruth combed Marco's hair as the plane arrived. Aurora, still the mother, patted down Ruth's hair. "Do you remember before he left for the war? Your wedding. It was so beautiful." She smiled, recalling the wedding on the beach, the firelight that night, almost the entire village there, even old Vince, the fisherman.

Years had passed since he'd been gone and Ruth's hair still shone blue-black, with only a few gray strands. She still looked like her father. She thought of Thomas's face. It was wide, and his eyes crinkled when he smiled, even when he was a child, even when confused. He had a sweetness about him, and an Asian look. She had teased him about his ancestors coming from China across the Bering Strait even though the people knew they had come from the caves out in the ocean, come out on strands of seaweed, some carried, with their stories in their arms and on their backs or carried on the fins of the water animals, and the story of the whale, their ancestor, was one of these. All their stories clung like barnacles to the great whale, the whale they loved enough to watch pass by. They were people of the whale. They worshiped the whales. Whalebones had once been the homes of their ancestors who covered the giant ribs with skins and slept inside the shelters. The whales were their lives, their comfort. The swordfish, their friends, sometimes wounded a whale and it would come to shore to die, or arrive already dead. It was an offering to the hungry people by their mother sea and friend, the swordfish.

Ruth thought of the octopus in the cave when Thomas was born. He was to be special. Now he was decorated by the army and coming home.

When the plane landed, Ruth stood up, watching, nervous. One by one, the passengers departed. Then there was no one. She waited. Perhaps his bag was in the back. Finally, an employee went over to them and said, "I'm sorry. Everyone is off the plane. Your passenger was not there." Thomas's disappointed buddies said nothing to Ruth. They walked out, their pants too low, their walks too arrogant for almost-poor men who spent their nights at the bar. Knowing she disliked them. Knowing why.

A garbled announcement was made for a town whose name no one could understand.

"There must be a mistake." But Ruth already had a feeling he would not be there. Still, trying not to cry, she asked, "When does the next plane come in?"

Ruth went to the window and looked at the plane. She noticed the fingerprints on the glass, handprints, and thought of them as the ghosts of people who had been there and gone. In the reflection, she watched families meet, happily. Lovers kissing. People parting, reaching out to touch one last time.

She waited.

At four he didn't arrive, either. She looked at their son, who had never met his father. He was pinning on the wings. He'd seen the pilots.

She looked at her mother in despair. "Why didn't he call? He could have let us know. I don't know why he hasn't called. I want to hear his voice. I just want to hear him. He could have even called us earlier." Her face was pale and tired. "What's happened to him that he'd do this? Treat us this way?"

Aurora, thinking he'd broken Ruth's heart once again, saw her daughter sway. "Come on. Let's leave. It's no good here."

They drove past water and land, logging trucks.

"You don't know. Anything could have happened." But Aurora also knew he would not be coming home.

"Why didn't he just call?"

Marco watched his mother cry. He knew his father was there, somewhere. He'd return.

Hours. Days. Years. Who knew how long?

BODY LIES

Thomas didn't call. He was a lie. His cells were all lies and his being was made up of lies. Lies couldn't call out the way truth does. They feared discovery. They were constantly confused and had soft edges that overlapped. Thomas was walking, thinking, My body is made of lies. There are lies on my tongue. He no longer knew the truth.

But lies are the first recognition of truth. He wouldn't think this, he wouldn't know it for many years. He would think, instead, My ancestors had purity and purpose. They had songs for everything. They were honest, even in their treaties, which in truth they called entreaties.

Had he gone home, he would have been surrounded by human faces that believed the lies about him and he would have had to act as if they were true, so, in his civilian clothes, he walked away from the airport, carrying only one bag. The other had gone along without him.

Shaking coins in his pocket now and then, he walked toward the city in the morning, feeling also the bundle of bills from the overdue pay he'd collected in Hawaii. Some of it should have gone to Ruth, he thought. He bore the realization that she had worked all those years. He had given little. The army didn't know about her.

The distance from the airport was deceptive and by the time he saw buildings, he was tired.

He was cold even as the fog lifted and his feet had new boots on them, the ones they gave him in Hawaii when they questioned him on how he'd been treated. Now he had blisters.

When the officers questioned him, with their gray unyielding authority, he'd said, "Fine, I'm fine," but his eyes were swollen with uncried tears, his face red. He thought they would want him to go to the brig for years.

The strange men said, "'Fine'! That word is the typical reaction. Did you know that?"

He didn't. So, everyone said fine. What else would they have said? The truth?

The war was like an ocean, an ocean where everyone burned or drowned, and only a few could swim it.

He missed the real ocean. He'd never thought of the future in that ocean. Only of swimming and holding his breath.

As he walked, his feet hurt, but he was glad to hurt, glad his tooth hurt, also. He changed his bag to the other shoulder. He felt a pang of missing home. He saw Ruth's teeth, how small they were when they bit into a piece of fruit, and he missed her. He wanted to touch her, but this was the decent thing, he told himself, the right thing, not to go back. He had two lives. Now they both seemed as if they belonged to another man. He'd been taken away from both of those lives. He was a stolen person. What remained was not him. It was just his body walking, the body of dishonesty. He was a taken-away human being. Right now the only earthly connection he felt to anything was this walking away from everything in his new boots, hurting and stiff. Miles he walked, miles a long way for a man who was a rice-grower, accustomed to standing in water, bending over, a man with a back that showed his labor, too. And a fisherman he had been until he was found. He saw the brown sea grasses as he walked, then the green of the plants on the side of the road. He was in a different world. He was from a different world. It was a long distance between the two. He thought it would never be crossed.

When at last he reached the city it was in warmth. People passed by, foreign to him, pale, everything about them strange. The sun watched him from the sky. He set his bag down on a bench.

Before he began his third life, he lay down on the bench that said THE HARTFORD with an elk on it, loosened his boots, and fell asleep beneath the antlers, dreaming his head was in a woman's lap, not on his bag of earthly possessions.

After the last plane, after the arrival of buses, after days and sleepless nights, Ruth realized he was not coming, maybe he was never coming, that he had gone somewhere she didn't know. All her hopes dropped to the ground and deeper, past the soil, deeper than sand and rock. She was afraid to go out on the water even though she lived on the boat and was a fishing woman. She was afraid because she was heavy and sinking and the weight would carry her down even farther than an anchor and she would drown in darkness and loneliness and cold. She would drop to the bottom of the ocean and maybe the boat, too, with its beds and pots and pans all falling, floating, dropping. She had thought this day or this night that she would hold Thomas, touch him, be held in his smooth dark arms. And his son would be there, and now Thomas would not sit with Marco and look at his face so like his own. Finally, she fell into a sleep at her mother's house on the side of the hill. To the dismay of Hoist, Aurora covered the lovebirds' cage so they would not wake her.

And so the man whose body was dishonest just by living woke and went into the city and found a place for himself on a turn to the right, not far from a highway, a room with an entrance through a crooked alley. It had a bed, a table, and two chairs. He thought it looked like the painting of Van Gogh's little room because the floor was painted wood, red in color and scuffed, the bed was wooden and made a sound when he sat on it. The chairs and table were in a corner, the walls were blue. Even though it smelled like an old man, he rented it. Around the corner was a fruit and vegetable stand. He bought apples the next day. For a few days he felt free. But at night when he went to bed, if he fell asleep, they searched him out and found him, the people he'd been forced to leave. Ma. He'd always laughed at her name. Lin, their daughter, his daughter, with the body thin as rice grass, his girl. Maybe they came through the worlds and found him because they were the dead and the dead could travel easily. She could be in the spirit world with her mother. She could be exactly the same as when he left. If she was alive, Lin could be anything now. She could be an enlisted child in the communist army. He saw the old man Song with the goatee weeping at the end before he, Thomas, had been taken away, Lin crying for him, running toward him on her precious skinny legs. He looked back down at her as the helicopter flew him away and he wanted to jump. He should have, he thought.

The faces of the shot men also came to him. Lizards came, and the rubber trees he saw in the shadows that one time, trees the French had wanted. The heat descended on him like a blanket. He saw faces that emerged like ghosts from the canopy of the jungle and then disappeared back into the trees. In his closed eyes men climbed ladders into the red dream night sky as if they were spiders climbing their strands of shining silk. American men slept with limbs of trees for pillows, their guns in their arms like women, or they wrapped themselves around a tree as if it were safer, the nights cold, days hot, telling stupid jokes, fighting with each other, then stopping to fight an enemy and trying like hell to help one another live. Mikey, as he had called the blue-eyed boy whose life he tried to save; he came toward him.

. . .

In Hawaii the hospital had been filled with men who had vacant eyes or worse, mean ones, or the ones with gentle smiles and silence as if they'd been through nothing. At that hospital the doctor asked Thomas questions in a room with a mirror that was a window. Thomas said to the mirror, "Why don't you just come in and sit with us?" because there were faces behind everything. He was ignored.

"Do you remember how long you were unconscious?"

"I wasn't unconscious that I know of," he said, then paused. "Sir." He hadn't said it in a long time. Sir. It was foreign to him now, years later.

"Did you have anything to do with the communists? Did they hold you or question you or wound you in any way?"

"No, I only worked. They didn't think I was an American. The way I look, you know, being who I am. I mean, what I am. I never talked. I kept quiet like I was mute or had been shot in the mouth or throat. I grew rice." There had been times, too, when he had hidden in dark tunnels forgotten then by those who had tried to build them too close to the water and so they'd mostly collapsed except for the reinforced entrances. Or he'd hidden in food containers. "I just grew rice."

"Did they try to indoctrinate you in any way?"

"Sometimes I fished, too."

He couldn't explain to those who thought everyone an enemy how he'd been hidden all those years, but even so he wasn't against the communists. They were for their own people. They would have killed him, though, and strange as it was, he would have understood. Of course there had been no Khmer, not yet, and he had no idea that later it had all come to an end.

"I never even knew where I was."

This was almost true in the man made of lies because he was a map lover. It was in the South, he thought. They'd been sent on a special ops mission. There was the tea-colored river. He thought it must flow into the Delta. They were rice-growers. They were treated well. There was a shortage in Saigon. People, even the army, were hungry. Ma, it was a Thai name, it was so unusual, packed rice in baskets and helped haul it to the road where the Others would pick the baskets up, always kind to her and leaving her with special treats—ginger, lemongrass, or cloth.

He could still hear the sound of rice flowing into baskets like strong rain. He still saw her bending, filling the baskets with grain, the lines of her neck and shoulders, the concaves of skin and veins, the line of jawbone, small and delicate.

"How long were you unconscious?" the doctor asked.

"I don't know." He thought he was unconscious now, on his bed.

The faces of the alive haunted him, too, Ruth and the ghost child, Marco, the son. He had loved Ruth all his life. But then, in his second life, he loved Ma and Lin. He was two men. He told himself love had no limits. For him there was divinity in both his worlds. It was made stronger by knowing he was a doomed man and sooner or later he would be killed by one army or another. That's what he had told himself until now. He was alive, or something like it. Maybe he'd go to prison.

He didn't say to the doctors—because his body was a lie—that he'd lived with a tribe there and he wanted to stay and his only fear had been of the Americans. Even now. Instead he cried. For one of very few times.

"That's healthy," the doctor said, his brown eyes warm beneath his graying brows. "You'd be surprised at how many men can't cry."

Thomas hated the doctor and his all-knowing understanding of men like himself, but he couldn't show it. The questions were over for then. Only then. With his extra-keen hearing, he heard the doctor in the next room say, "Keep a record on him. We'll need to keep track of him." Thomas wondered how long Dr. Christmas, as he called him, had been in war. Dr. Tannenbaum.

Outside in the blue tropics of Hawaii as he thought about

what it all meant, the dolphins were leaping all together like one being. He himself was an island of a man surrounded by water, mystery, and being returned to a country he no longer knew or wanted. He was not a part of it, he in his hospital cloth scuff shoes and blue robe, watching the blue ocean.

THE WIFE OF MARCO POLO

No one wrote about the wife of Marco Polo, the first journeyer. As far as anyone knew, no one wrote about the women who were left at home when their husbands were at war or searching for other worlds or traveling out of pure longing. The wife combs her hair. She takes on a job, a mission, a love, or she becomes weak with sadness.

After Thomas did not return, Ruth knew another kind of sorrow, but a calm also set in, as if the solitude would give her over to her own self. Ruth took Marco to the sea and showed him the fish that lived with dolphins. They sat on the wet beach and wrote his name in sand as if it would last. They peered into the morning tide pools. Ruth was a tide pool, full of life that awaited the return of its element. Perhaps explorer Marco Polo's wife was also a creature in a pool, she thought, awaiting the return of her beloved. She didn't know that the women gods on all the islands Odysseus visited awaited any traveling sailors around the Mediterranean, to keep them from returning home.

When Thomas went to war, Ruth had never felt so abandoned. On television she watched the casualties, searching every face for his. They promised mail. At first the envelopes arrived with the APO numbers and then they dwindled. Ruth missed her hand touched by his.

Like all the women left behind in wars, she was young but old, both at the same time. Wars amputate the minds and souls of waiting women in different ways than they do the armless, legless bodies in khaki and olive drab or the children stepping on land mines. But it is an amputation all the same. Watching the bullets, the men surviving fire, the dying children, what the women saw on television gave them some truth and from then on American wars were not on the television because people would rise up against their own government if they saw what they had done.

Then the back of this world, all across the land, began to break. Ruth herself heard the sound of its back breaking, almost inaudible, but she could hear it, for her ears could even hear the fish and the whales. It was to that she owed her fishing success. Hearing the country break, she knew nothing would ever be the same.

Oblivion, she thought. That was the world she lived in. It was what they should name some countries, towns, and places.

What she cried over was nothing. Chipped plates. Another form of oblivion. The Mayans knew the concept of zero. Most other cultures did not. A parrot, they say, also knows it. She lived at Zero and thanked god she did not have to pay rent on it, yet she had to add One to it, and keep a life for her son Marco until she knew they would come for him. She knew because it was in his face at birth. He was a full number, a whole one. He would lead people, so calm, so laughing. And so singled out. At an earlier time he would have worn only white. Always the ones who would be singers wore white, to show their place, but now he wore a T-shirt that said MARINERS or DOLPHINS or one that said POWERED BY JUNK FOOD. Ruth bought him one that said U.S. OUT OF NORTH AMERICA, but he didn't wear it because he didn't want to be treated badly by anyone.

· · ·

Marco, her son with Thomas, had been an unusual child. He smiled when he heard the sounds of birds and he blew feathers into the sky with his breath. He laughed his first laugh at three months, an adult laugh they said sounded exactly like Witka's. Not only was he watched by all; he watched everyone, everything, but he especially watched the ocean with great care and told Ruth what he had seen beneath it.

Once he said, "I see tiny jellyfish in a forest."

Ruth looked at him, thinking, Who are you? but she said, "That's wonderful, my boy."

"I see a school of silver fish woven into a ball."

She knew he was right because she heard them. And when he held his breath at night, she said, panicking, "Marco," and shook him. She realized he dived into the water in his sleep, and then he did it in his waking, too, and she would keep watch to make sure he surfaced. She wished his father could know him. He was chosen.

"You need vitamins," Aurora told her daughter, placing an amber bottle of pills in front of the young woman.

Ruth took a pill, then said, "We're going out for a while."

She and Marco went to the river where she once lived with Thomas and showed him their CALIFORNIA ORANGES house. It had never been repainted. It was faded and in disrepair.

Then she took him to Witka's up on the black rocks. It would, after all, belong to Marco one day although it might have been hers. She loved it there, her eyes constant on the sea. They sat at the table near the old stove in the corner and listened to the ocean below them.

"He was a great man, your grandfather Witka," she told him. Just then, as she said it, they felt something there. Someone walked with them, inside. They both heard and felt it. Perhaps it was the old man, Marco's ancestor. The back of her neck grew cold, the hair starting to rise in the old animal way. Dragonflies came in the window she had opened to the sea and floated in the air around them, blue and shining. A soft knock on the door. She went to the door. "No one is there," Marco said. "It must be the wind," but they both knew better because it was a calm day. She knew there were many spirits and felt the air move, spirits one after the other related to the child, come to see him, to infuse him with the world that was his, that he belonged to. Belonging. It has so much significance. So few have it. In his grandfather's place of many spirits, she brushed Marco's hair. Both of them knew the spirits had been there, waiting, some human, some the same as in a tide pool, a small octopus with its powerful eye, a starfish.

"Don't be afraid, Mom. I feel them, too."

That day when Ruth and Marco returned, Aurora looked up from her knitting of constant afghans that sat on the back or were folded neatly on nearly everyone's sofa. She guessed where they had been. "You were born prematurely," she said to Ruth. "Maybe that's why you need more vitamins." She handed her the bottle again. "You look pale. Did I ever tell you about the gill slits? When you were born I never even went into labor. You wanted to come into the world and the moment you could walk, you went to the ocean. You walked into it. We yelled and chased you. We were mortally scared. Here, take some more of these vitamins."

"Gill slits? What gill slits?" Sometimes Ruth wondered if her mother was slipping.

"You were born with them. I was sure you knew that. Didn't I tell you? At first you had trouble with the air. The midwife put you in water, she told me later, and you lived through it. But then we had to take you to a large hospital in the city where the nurses were very worried, even afraid, I'd say. They never did see such a thing. You choked when the doctor stitched them up. You were a fish even then, my child. They had to open them up again. Then they experimented and put you in water and you didn't drown. They wanted to call in other doctors to look at you. I wouldn't hear of it. They even wanted to write about it. I could hear them talking."

Ruth knew about her mother's good hearing. She had it,

too. It seemed Thomas did, as well. But hers was like sonar. She didn't believe her mother. "What happened then?"

"You can ask the midwife. I wouldn't lie about something like that."

"Why didn't you tell me this before?"

"Oh, I thought you knew. I guess I thought it would upset you. Oh, I lost a stitch." She stopped talking and counted the threads.

"It's upsetting me now." Ruth held her voice down, but there was tension.

"I already thought you were a force to be reckoned with, but they got them closed so you looked like everyone else and began to breathe through your lungs. You've never had trouble since then. Just those little scars." She looked up. "Do you want to play Bingo?"

"No. No, I don't. What did the elders say?"

"The doctors said it was a genetic throwback or something like that. Anyway, the elders said they had known of this. It's happened before. Destiny is water for her, they said."

There was an old story about a girl who came from the sea. Not just the sea of a mother's womb, but really *from* the sea, to make the People into what they were to be. She had a hard life, for she had to live in water so much of the time. There was no modern medicine then, so she would have drowned in air. Every morning she rose from the sea and went to a bed where she looked like a normal human coming out of the house. But from the sea she brought knowledge. She came in with the sounds of the ocean and she sang them to the people. That's how they learned the whales' songs and also the ticking of coral. She protected the sea and the animals. The people kept her wet.

"You remember the story. She was a lot like you, always protecting the sea life. She could hear the fish from land. When she died, which unfortunately was too early, she returned to the sea cut in pieces, and each piece was eaten by the sea ani-

mals so the songs and the animals would continue. Not like
Sedna up north where her fingers became the animals. It isn't
that old of a story. Could you get my green jacket? Are you
sure you don't want to go play Bingo?"

Her mother was lying, Ruth was certain, but too casually.
Ruth took the jacket off the hook, noticing that the wall around
the hooks was dirty with years of the touch of hands Aurora
didn't want to wash away. Hands of people who no longer
existed.

"That's about all I know, but I figured it explains your behavior. You always were a peculiar girl. You always were at water.
Don't think I didn't know you would have been a true whaler's
wife." Ruth, too tall for her mother's mirror, examined her
neck. What she'd taken for ordinary lines could have been
scars. But she thought they were merely wrinkles until now.

"No, not there. They were in front of your ears. Isn't it
funny? You were the one with the gill slits. Thomas was the
one who tried to stay underwater. It's always like that. You
never get what you want."

After her mother left, Ruth woke her son and returned to
their boat on the sea. It was true, she was a creature of the
ocean. She went out that night and stood on the deck shining
in the sea mist, listening to the beneath.

A few weeks later Ruth went into the forest to search for the
woman who had been the midwife. It was a difficult trail and
more than once she was lost. But she remembered the markers. All women were given the directions. She remembered
the driftwood planted along the way, a carved set of lines on
an old tree.

When she reached the old cottage, she found the woman
still alive. She was neat and clean in an old cotton dress, her
hair pulled straight back, plants drying on racks in the little
cottage.

"Yes, you were born with gill slits. It isn't rare, especially in these parts. Just that most of them pass away before the child is born."

There were many birds in the forest, ravens, songbirds calling from one tree. She found comfort in yellow slugs, the smell of the trees, and sounds of branches in the light wind. Ruth thought, I am happy here, almost as happy as at water. Happiness was not always a fleeting thing, but a state of mind, of being, after having lived, loved, even after being poor, alone, having survived. Even with the pain in her hands she had happiness.

The house was weathered and damp inside like the forest and smelled of the old trees. A large spider lived in the corner and spiders were worshiped. Water walkers. They brought light to the people on their backs from an island struck by lightning.

Ruth saw now that a man was there, sitting quietly, listening.

The woman washed her hands by habit, a constant thing.

"Oh yes, this is my friend Dick Russell. He works for the Forest Service. And this is Ruth, the basket weaver."

"And fisher," Ruth added. She reached out her hand and he shook it too hard. He was quiet, but he was taken with her and he had listened to the entire conversation.

The woman ignored them. "I always knew you'd come. Like a salmon. From the ocean to the forest so you could breathe pure forest air."

Ruth was lost when she left. Home seemed a different way. Finally, she realized she had taken the wrong path. Then, hearing a noise in the leaves, she turned. It was Dick Russell. He smiled and in his good-natured manner, said, "You are lost. This is the way to my world. Yours is over there."

MARCO: THE SON OF THOMAS

"Mother, are you awake?" Marco said one night. He was twelve.

He knew she was. She was silent, though, wanting him to sleep, to not have any conflict. There were shadows even in the darkness.

"Are you happy?

"Why do you ask?"

He was silent. She should have said yes. But it made her think of all the things that had gone awry. All the things she had lost and given up. And that would soon include the boy.

"Yes, son. I am. I find so much joy in hearing the whale songs. I find happiness in the small baskets and the boat going out into the water in the morning when the light is just perfect on the ocean."

But afterward, she thought about things she might want. A husband. Some help. A little spending money. Days in the town away from their village. Not to worry about her mother, Aurora, who lived on the hillside and was forgetting things.

She was worried about what she'd heard: There was a behind-the-scenes plot to kill a whale. The business leaders of the tribe had met with the Japanese businessmen and made a quiet deal to sell the whale meat to them. She wanted to protect the whales. She was already speaking out against the men.

Marco seemed to read her mind, but he said, "I'm happy, too."

One morning two old men paddled over to where Ruth lived and worked on the boat and Ruth greeted them. She already knew them. As was customary, she invited them aboard and cooked eggs, potatoes, and coffee. "There was a moon dog last night," one man said, pushing back his gray hair, his old skin taut across his bones. "A storm is coming." She thanked him for the information. "I better prepare," she said. For many things, she thought. "The boat is moored strongly, but I'll check everything."

She served the food and they spoke about small things and large. Then she said, "I know why you are here. I knew you would be here one day. But can't I keep him a little longer?"

"It's time," he said, looking at her, then at Marco, the small talk over.

Ruth looked down. She set his food before him and sat across from him.

She knew what was next. It wasn't like she was giving her son up. He would go live with the old people. She could visit at any time, but she would miss his breath, his conversation, touching his hair, brushing it into a braid, watching the whales with him.

Marco's school education was now over and his real one would begin. Now Ruth again cried and they smiled kindly at her and at Marco, but said, "Anu, we must take him now because the light passed through the stones just right and he is growing."

Marco felt his mother's hand, not wanting to let go.

All through school he knew he would leave, so he learned what he could, more than anyone else. Now it was time to learn other ways of knowing things.

Marco had learned how to think when he was still young. He had learned how to feel, how to understand a human. Listen, his mother would tell him. Listen to the world. Rocking at night on water, he listened to the sound of water against the boat, to the cry of a bird, the slap of a fish as it landed on calm ocean, the waves when it stormed somewhere out at sea. Listening, he would seem to understand the heart of the world. He was a wise boy. It was in his eyes when he was young. His mother saw it. His grandmother saw it. He laughed at things that adults find humorous when he was only six months old. He examined his mother's face with his hand and fingers and wondered at the scars beside her ears and later joked that she'd had a face-lift, but she just laughed and said they were a natural wrinkle she'd had all her life and it was just something she must have been born with.

He loved his mother and he treated her with kindness.

He was far from perfect, though. He had two flaws. He was judgmental of the others who didn't know what or who they were. And he was afraid of his own strength and power, so he seemed to lower himself and always gave in to others, never taking an initiative even when he saw an answer, even when they all saw his leadership abilities and powers. Yet when called on in school, he sometimes could not speak.

He was well acquainted with the ways of the other boys his age and even the young children were drinking beer and using drugs, whatever they could find, even hair spray. He saw them sitting in the doorways and behind the ramps. Or under the pier. They tried to hide their ways, staggering home, sometimes with paint on their faces. And they had knives. Sometimes they threw them in the ground to see how close they could come to someone's foot. The person with the foot on the ground was not allowed to move.

And he who lived with his mother on the old Trophy was to go another way. The stakes were high, though. He would not have an education. He would have another destiny in the world. He could not change anyone. Neither could his mother. But she tried. And that was what counted.

He remembered the night he got up in the darkness and walked to the chair beside her bed and moved the lamp. "I don't want to go away to live with the old people, but I know I am the one. I see it."

"I know," she said, taking his hand, already masculine, callused from helping her with their work.

The day he left, he remembered his grandmother telling about Lot's wife looking back, and though he knew his mother watched them leave so silently in the water, he waved once and then he didn't look back. He'd be looking back for years so it was a time to look forward. To what, he didn't know, but looking he saw the great ocean and it was hard work for the men who took him away—well, not really away—but *to*. And so he took over and helped paddle to a world he was from and was returning to and he was silent.

On the day he went to live with the elders in the white houses on the other side of the large bay, the people were so happy to have him there. They talked to him in A'atsika until he began to understand and speak back. He observed. He had freedom to walk, to swim, to watch the mornings. He could see some of the land from there and think, My mother is setting out for the fish now. She is making coffee. He watched for her boat, named after him.

He also thought, Somewhere there is theory, the big bang, the telescopes, space explorers, the attempted understanding of intelligence. Somewhere else there are people who study the Forbidden City. And here there is knowledge of the water, the land, plants, astronomy, another language. It is time now to learn new words, songs, and plants.

He searched stones, wandered, looked at the insects on the leaves. Moths with large eyes, birds, the cormorant, all lived there. He examined the faces of the people, their voices, practiced the songs. Moon. Rain. They loved his physical presence. He was air and light. Their world was a tight knot that his job was to unravel. There were no rules but he followed them anyway. There was heated water for him in the winter when the old women filled a tub for him with heated containers of water. He was told about the treachery on the other side. His mother visited often and she didn't have to tell him the news. He had grown sensitive. Each time she saw him, she also told him a make-believe story. One time it was how Marco Polo sailed the seas. The seven seas.

He was happy with the elders and the water was slightly warmer and Marco swam daily. Sometimes too far, Ruth thought when she and Hoist visited. Nevertheless, this was the beginning of Marco's conflict, the one he would have to face one day. He was recognized. The elders held him in a special place, this quiet boy who held himself straight and looked at the world with a clear, calm eye. He had the prayers and songs. Others, on the other side of water, knew it, too. Because of this, much responsibility would fall on him. At times it worried him.

"Mother," he said, "what will I become when I'm so different?"

She smiled at him. " I don't know, son. I guess you'll have to get a job in a paper mill, such an impossible feat, I'd assume."

RUTH

Ruth placed the dishes on the shelf, lined the cups on the rubber mat so they would not slide off in powerful waves. She was strong, or so people thought. When she stretched her arms, they were lean, dark, and muscular, the veins standing out. Inside the muscle, inside the flesh, inside the long body and even the skin beginning to age, the older life was beginning in its way toward a new form and inside all of that she still felt grief, even anger, but she would not let her people slide down to the bottom and she could see the people falling, sliding. Her hands hurt from holding on, as if to a rope that would keep the slide from happening.

The people her own age had not ever recovered from the war. The older people are still in the pain of history. Some say it is over, the A'atsika way. It isn't, Ruth wanted to tell the world that she hangs by her strength. Alone. Don't be fooled. This is just America happening to us again. She would like to keep them from ruining themselves altogether. All together. That is what a tribe is. There was an old person watching her. She felt it. That person had wisdom and pride and the beauty that came with their history, and that person or spirit or ancestor loved Ruth.

Ruth. She was beautiful, with hair graying, with intention,

the woman of water, of whales. Ruth watched the whales and never ended her wonder at them. Her love for them was ceaseless. When she saw them rise and return to the sea, when she saw them breathe spray, she was aware that there was at least one god.

"Why don't you go out more?" her mother always wanted to know. But she *was* out, just in another way. Out in the world. Out in the spray of ocean, the garden of heaven. Perhaps she was timid, but she preferred the world this way. There were times when the light of the moon had gone out and she felt a great loneliness. It wasn't for herself. It was for what had happened in the grasses of their land, their waters, not just the massacre there, the slavery, but the killing of the ocean.

She also thought of her son when she was lonely.

Peeling potatoes, she looked at the beautiful brown peels. Eyes, they call them. They are what she would plant behind her mother's house. Something grows from eyes, taking root as if a potato sends to earth what it can see, and yet the seeing part is what they say is poisonous about the potato. That first sprout is what can grow, planted, moving upward, seeing in the light.

At the edge of America was her boat, the *Marco Polo*. The man himself traveled a spice route, a silk route. People were always searching for something. Not just riches.

A pelican sat there, waiting for her to put out food, also at the end of America.

DARK RIVER: 1988

Whaen men decide in their secretly dark or hungry hearts
to work their own will, there is little that can stop them. They
have inner weather, sometimes unpredictable.

No matters remain secret for long at Dark River. At one
of the tribal council's "secret" meetings, an old rose-scented
woman named Wilma, her hair as unruly as Witka's, and
Wilma's heavy granddaughter Delphine, who had a knack for
gardening, walked with Ruth Small Just through the door of
the room that smelled of coffee and stale tobacco. The room
held only five men and a number of disordered empty folding chairs. Five men sat around a wooden table that had been
carved over the years with initials, fish, and women's naked
bodies. The women intruded.

"To the women who entered the room of a private meeting,"
said Dwight, heavy now and gray. "According to Robert's Rules
of Order, you are out of order."

Wilma laughed at him. "Who is this Robert?"

Dwight was now the tribal chairman, his hair cut perfectly
for the job, short and brushed back. He has fallen through a
hole in the world, Ruth thought, looking at him.

"This is not order." Wilma stood before them and swept her

hand around their table. "There are other kinds of order than Robert's."

"It's a private meeting." Dwight was abrupt.

One of the men must have told about them coming here. Dwight looked around at them, his gaze traveling from face to face, wondering which was the traitor. "We're a tribe. We don't have private meetings and you've been having too many of them here of late." Wilma took a seat in the room before the men, her bag in her hand. "You see these chairs. They are not empty. Your ancestors sit there. They are listening to you." She sat down, bag on lap. "Nothing you do is secret. We have heard about your plan to kill a whale."

The men looked at each other, uncomfortable.

"The decision has been made." Dwight said, facing his elder, but feeling as if he still had a boy living inside him, remembering her from old, her hands up as she sang, mumbling prayers in the old tongue. He was a new and different kind of warrior, he told himself, and not easily understood by the old ones. Times change.

"Unmake it," she said.

Milton, slower than the others, because of what his mother drank when she was pregnant, smiled with pride. "We're going to hunt a whale." He said it with awe and wonder. He was slow, they all knew, and not aware of the conflict that was taking place.

It was at this meeting that a reporter walked in. Ruth opened the door to her. The reporter was blond and Germanic and seemed to know Wilma, too.

Ruth, who along with the elders was against the whale hunt, remained standing at the door like a guard, then went inside and stood before the men. She, too, had become a different kind of warrior. "You want to bloody the water and our land when the time isn't right, when the elders across the bay haven't even been consulted and none of us have been asked."

"This is a tribe. It isn't a democracy." Dwight regretted his words as soon as he said them and saw the reporter take notes. She would begin to turn the world, or at least the country, against them. She took a picture of him.

"Get that woman out of here." Dwight pointed to the reporter. "And her." Meaning Ruth.

"Tribe. Right. That's what I mean," said Wilma, crossing her arms like a closed door. "One people. One decision. Take photos, Ursula." The photos were of men hiding their faces, turning their backs, looking away, Dwight looking angry.

The next day it was all in the news, including the *San Francisco Times*. The photographs were telling in themselves. When more reporters arrived a day later, notebooks and pens in hand, recorders turned on, the A'atsika men had already talked among themselves and were armed with new words. They argued treaty rights, and their return to tradition. Some of these reporters, especially the white men, thought the tribal hunters were men of mystery and spirit, foreign enough to their own America to be right. Yes, to return to their ways would be the right thing. After all America had done to them, they should be given that. When the animal rights activists arrived, the A'atsika men had to decide if they should have them removed by the police or if that would only look worse for their cause. The news had leaked out that they were planning to sell whale meat to Japan.

Dwight had many strong arguments for the kill. He and Dimitri Smith in his gray shirt and work pants, his brown leather shoes cracked from the salt water, did not have the image of businessmen. They had been through a war together, Dwight told the reporters. Nevertheless, Dwight harbored within himself a great and monetary and maybe even a violent need and so he had helped convince most of the men that they wanted to kill a whale in order to fill their hearts and souls with the wealth of something they wrongly believed had been lost and wanted back. Tradition, they called it.

"Whale-hunting," Dimitri said, his shirttail out, "will bring us back to ourselves." A part of him truly believed this. As close as he was to Dwight, he did not yet understand the negotiations to sell the meat to another country, or that it would stop an international moratorium on whale-killing, that it would open a whale market so Norway could sell their vats of stored oil, and that money had been been paid to the council for this. It was an intrigue too large even for Dwight to figure out, too complex. All he saw was the money on the table for meat in another country. "It's our traditional food. We need it. We are starved for it."

Ruth stood at full height in front of one of the male reporters. "I want you to know and write that their plans are not even near the original meaning of a whale hunt, that they've made a deal to sell the meat and that their meetings took place in seclusion and were secret. This is not the voice of our community. They do not represent us or our elders." She said, also, "And I want you to write that there aren't many whales remaining. I fish out there. I watch them." It was her joy to watch them spray and surface, roll and descend, come eye to eye with her. She recognized some who lived there permanently, in the safety of their bays. She had names for them. Black Mouth. Rock Beak.

"Their numbers are coming back," Dwight said to a reporter. "When one is killed, its spirit is born again into another whale. This is our belief. It is our way." He was bringing in the old beliefs, trying to sound like a traditionalist. In truth, Dwight wanted desperately to believe the old ways, to be a part of them, but he had become a soldier and a businessman and he had not retained the old way of being in the world.

"Then how do you account for the lower numbers?" Ruth tilted her long neck. Anyway, beliefs were only beliefs, not necessarily truth or fact or knowledge.

"The counting is off. Our count is higher than that of the scientists."

"Deathless," said Ruth. "Is that what you are saying?" To the reporter: "They are saying the world is deathless. But we have seen it differently in our lives. There are fewer whales. I fish out there. I know the whales. And the old people are against this. Only these few men stand to gain."

A great argument ensued. Nevertheless, the men on the council decided and the whale kill was to commence that fall when the whales passed through the waters by Dark River on their annual migration.

Three days later in San Francisco, Thomas Just saw the newspaper article at the office of the cable company where he worked: "Whale Hunt to Return for the A'atsika People." That night he took the paper home to his room and read how his people wanted to return to tradition. All night he was sleepless. We are going to return, he thought. We are going to be a people again. He was suddenly full of need and pride. He sat up smoking all night. Occasionally the sight of Ruth on their wedding day passed by his inner sight. Or their orange crate. Or his own grandfather. By morning he had convinced himself that, being the grandson of Witka, it was his duty to go home. By tradition he had to hunt. He had to be one who returned. He tried not to think of Ruth and the child he'd been told by Dwight was not his own. He was busy thinking, I am the grandson of the greatest whaler. Perhaps Thomas thought that he, too, could communicate with the whales.

It was time to go home, as if killing the whale, as if being like Witka, would excuse his lies and actions, as if he could, in one act, save himself from one history and return to another, slide into it with the ease he'd been lacking.

"All along we knew this day would come," said the old people who lived in the white houses, many of the front panels of their homes still whalebone, in a land with markers of bone, for they truly were still whale people. "They haven't praised the whales since they were children, if then. They haven't cleansed themselves. Some of them have been to war and not yet purified themselves. They have not fasted. They have not scrubbed themselves with cedar. They have not put themselves in the right mind. Nothing good will come of this. No one has spoken to the whales since Witka. Not even us. And we remember. Most of us remember those days."

"Marco will head the boat," said one old man. "He will be the captain. He is the only one who knows."

"Yes, I know." Ruth felt more sorrow, this time not for just the whales, who truly were still smaller in number. She watched them pass. But she and her son would, by tradition alone, be on different sides. He was the one to head the crew, to decide if a whale would be killed. Marco of the old ones had to abide by tradition. She looked at him, how he'd grown, and wished he were a child she could carry away in her arms. He knew it, too. He watched his mother's face and saw her feelings. He was a man now, tall, with black hair, with a face surprisingly like his father's. He was calm and sure in his movements. Marco would have to go on the hunt. Ruth knew that. He sat with old Hoist, scratching the aged dog's belly.

The old people who lived in the white houses sat down on the stones carved by the old ones with spirals.

Someone brought Ruth a cup of the strong coffee the old people preferred, Starbucks. They always asked, "Are you going to the city? Don't forget the French Roast," and Ruth laughed as she crossed the water. "Or the Yukon." Who would have thought the day would come when they would ask for Starbucks? She put her hand over her coffee cup. "No, no more coffee," she said to the woman who wore her hair in braids above her head.

After this, in her mind, day and night, Ruth tried to speak with the whales and send them away. Nights from her boat, she had been singing songs, pieces of the songs she remembered and songs she made up to fill in for what was missing.

. . .

It was thirteen years after his anticipated arrival that Thomas came home. He carried a suitcase someone had left behind where he'd first worked as a doorman in the city, he always the quiet, invisible man at work, the missing, himself the deathless. He returned to the A'atsika village not thinking, I am a body of lies, but thinking now, I am a part of tradition, grandson of Witka the whaler. He heard the familiar sound of ravens and crows. He carried in his pocket a stone whale, which he touched. It had been through the war with him for a reason, he thought, and the two of them survived. He stepped down from the bus onto damp, giving earth, land he had always known. No one was there to meet him but the familiar wind. Neverthless, it touched him with invisible hands as he thought about his grandfather who could go underneath the water, hold his breath and communicate with whales.

He walked on the half sidewalk, grown over with grass and plants, walked past the man who still made chairs from driftwood all these years later. The sample chairs sat close to the road, visible to tourists driving by. The chair-maker's hair was now long and gray. He nodded, but didn't recognize Thomas, who had grown stocky and older, even with thinner hair.

Thomas went past the grocery and fish bait store that overcharged for food. Cans and boxes of macaroni decorated the dirty window. He passed the tiny Catholic shop with its books of saints and cards, paintings and prayers of Saint Anthony, the beloved saint of lost things, and the prayers of safe return bought by the wives of deep sea fishermen and tacked to the walls.

"Why do you keep that Catholic stuff?" he once asked his mother.

"You never know." She, daughter-in-law of Witka, was going to cover all her bases. She even kept a small Buddha in the corner.

Despite the fact that his hair had grayed and was short, his

neck redder and thicker, his eyes fitting for a man who had
learned the art of war and then the practice of invisibility, word
was out quickly. Thomas Just was back.

He stopped first at the restaurant and said nothing to Linda
except, "Coffee, please."

"Well, if it isn't you," she said, looking at the face she and
the rest had never forgotten. "I'll be damned." Unlike everyone else, she would never like him, honor him, worship him,
because she'd seen Ruth lose weight and grieve when he didn't
return, and when Marco had gone to live with the old people
over at the white houses, and she always believed he could
have stayed home and that he could have returned home. She
felt things in her bones, as she put it, and she'd felt him and it
wasn't good.

"What'll you have, Thomas Just?"

He didn't eat. He only drank coffee until he had summoned
whatever it was a man of once courage needed to go to his
father's. They had never gotten along. His father's reputation
had even become worse as he'd gotten older.

He found the older man asleep and confused. He stood by
the door. He picked up his father's shaving mirror and looked
briefly at himself. Jesus, he didn't even recognize what he saw.
There were new lines, whiskers.

A moment of sun came through a crack in the curtains.
Thomas shone a mirror around the room. It reflected on wood,
knives, bottles, old yellowed newspapers, maybe even pain in
the wooden faces his father had half carved, and a sense of
time passing. Until the light came to rest on his father, the
woodcarver's, eyes, the face of the mask-maker.

"Who's that with the mirror?" He shaded his eyes, trying to
see. He looked old to Thomas, his eyes bloodshot, his long hair
tangled as he lifted his head.

Thomas didn't answer.

When the man opened his tired eyes, he saw Thomas. He
squinted through the light. "Are you a ghost? Thomas?"

"Both."

"Well, whatever you are, that goddamned light hurts my eyes."

Floyd the father of Thomas lifted back his old quilt and got up, fully clothed. Then he went to Thomas. "My son." He clasped the deathless body. "At last."

Thomas didn't clasp him in return.

His father wasn't the handsome man he had once been, though there was still a hint of the lady-killer.

"Hey, old man, how you doing?"

"Good, good now, my son."

He made instant coffee. While Thomas drank it, he said, "I need to wash up."

Thomas saw him hide something in a drawer. It was early autumn and the crickets around the house were loud.

"Where have you been all this time?" The older man sensed his son's hostility. Well, why not? He had dated other women even when his wife was ill, before she died. He'd remarried right away. A younger woman. It didn't last, and maybe Thomas knew he'd attacked Ruth that night he was drunk.

Thomas didn't answer.

"Anyway, I'm glad you are back," said the carver. "And I'm proud. It's a good time for us. We are going to come back. Have you heard? As a people, I mean." Floyd may have been a man who mistreated women, who hated and drank, but he had loved and known his own father, Witka. As he looked Thomas over, he wondered what Witka would think of his son. He wasn't certain.

He did know that Witka would approve of Marco, his grandson. He said so. "Your son. He is like my father. Wait and see. I can't wait for you to meet him."

Thomas didn't seem interested in Marco, either. He put down his bag. He used the mirror to shave.

"The big meeting's tonight. Are you going? Floyd was quiet

a moment. "Or is that what you are doing here? That's why you came home, isn't it?" the old man asked, realizing Thomas hadn't come home for the love of humans, for a woman, a boy, or for him. He who had not been here for his loved ones was now here for the whale. He looked at his son and, awake now, even though he'd flaunted his son's medals in a box, he saw all the way through him as if he were glass.

"I see you, son," he said. "I see right through you. And we are wretched men. Both of us. More than you even know."

As the sun traveled west, they left for the meeting together. People saw the wretched men and talked. "It's true. TJ is home."

Thomas listened to the sound of waves. All the while he thought, I am a hero to them, an island, but my father knows the truth, that I am wretched.

By the time they arrived, everyone was excited that the grandson of Witka had returned.

Ruth was already in the community center talking with some women and laughing with her head back, her legs slightly apart, when he walked in and first saw her and how well she seemed to have survived. They were laughing at her spotted oceangoing dog, still chasing its tail like a puppy, when she saw Thomas. The room was silent except for the dog. "Here, Hoist," she almost whispered, as if he might be hurt by this man. Then even the dog was still and beside her. Ruth's expression changed. She softened. Without even willing it, after all the years, she walked toward him, almost floating. He looked away, trying not to see her face, she who was his history, who was moving toward him until she was in front of him, looking at his face, his hair, putting her hand on his arm, him feeling he didn't want it there, and yet he did. He didn't want her there, but felt also the love in the touch and he wanted to cry. Again

Ruth felt herself sinking, as so many years before, and there was a pain in her heart that almost made her double over and fall to the floor.

She stood back, quietly. "Your son, Marco," turning her head in the young man's direction. "He's over there. That's him." Thomas glanced at him, the young man who looked so like him. He turned away. A deep silence fell over the room. They were watched. "Why?" Ruth asked, feeling his disdain. "Thomas. He's your son, by god. Go talk to him, at least."

But he was no longer Thomas. She was speaking to someone else, a stranger. A man with secrets, one whose life was unknown or injured, and who'd forgotten his world before. She saw this and she saw that he was as his father had just said, a wretched man.

She walked away, knowing everyone heard and watched, and she stood with a group of women. Linda put her hand on Ruth's arm.

She was an anchor but at least now she knew it had an end, a stopping place. It hit bottom. She could fall no deeper.

It wasn't the reunion she had ever dreamed. His love for her had ended.

She still carried his dog tag. She remembered how the two of them had once tried to walk across the river on stones and fallen in, laughing and choking on the running water, grabbing one another.

When Marco heard that the man standing there was his father, he turned to him and saw a wretched man. He kept his silence. He kept his distance, a wise young man already, waiting, observing with his natural dignity.

"Thomas, old buddy!" said Dwight. He cast a look at Marco, who was silent, solemn, a man now himself. Dwight felt things he didn't usually feel, the wish to take his words back, his lies, to tell Thomas that Marco really *was* his son, not as he had said years ago, that he'd seen Ruth with his father, but how hard to

keep covering up all his many lies, especially as they continued
over the years.

Everyone went to Thomas, except Ruth, her friends, and
Marco, who stood with a young woman.

When Marco saw his father look past him, he knew the man,
Thomas, was not his father except by blood. He, the boy who
was clear-eyed and calm, nevertheless felt as if parts of him
fell away, like from a statue with one arm, one leg, gone from
wars or excavations or thefts. There was no bond, no spider
silk of attachment. Thomas wasn't curious about his son, his
wife. Marco watched the man that was his father. He looked
at the eyelashes, such a small detail, straight and dark, showing something of character Marco couldn't quite figure. He
looked at the way Thomas tried to buddy up to the other men.
How they clapped him on the back, glad to see their old friend.
He thought, I know why he came back right now. He came
back because of the whale. He came back to help them kill
the whale. Marco didn't think that maybe his father thought
he might return to tradition and find himself. He didn't know
that the man had spent years with his shirts over the back of
the chair in a room that was not far from a freeway, thinking
of how he could face himself, let alone the people at home who
believed things about him that were lies.

Marco thought, My father's heart comes down a pathway like
a stone. He stands in the room of men I will have to be with,
men who have done dishonest things, and Thomas, my father,
doesn't know it. Perhaps he doesn't care. He is thinking of himself. He doesn't even acknowledge my mother, his wife.

All these years he had been told stories about his father,
the war hero, the man of his mother's childhood, the man she
waited for. He remembered the day sitting in the airport when
he didn't appear.

* * *

When the hunt was first proposed, the old people in the white houses said it was not the right time to hunt; the people were not prepared. Marco dreaded the hunt. It was a lie, Ruth had said. A scheme. Marco agreed with his mother's protest, but if the hunt was going to happen, his being there was the only thing he could do, no matter how knotted his heart.

One day when he was visiting his mother, as he sat at her little table, Ruth looked at him with her dark eyes, her wet hair wrapped in a towel, and she said, "You'll understand the right thing to do. Don't worry. It will be fine."

He was serious and intelligent. He had grown. His shoulders were wide and strong, tanned under his straight hair, so like hers. His arms like hers, too, only stronger. The old men had taught him to paddle their old cedar canoes. He was powerful from paddling ocean current and waves, and from swimming and diving, a secret he kept from his mother. He moved with a kind of refinement.

She sat across from him. "You'll know." Because the old men in the white houses had taught him the proper behavior and the prayers. "You are the one who has been given the songs."

Oh whale, take pity on us. We are broken. We are weak. We are small. We are hungry mere humans.

He was the one who would hold the old harpoon, although it was only a token position, since the whale, if the hunt took place, would be killed with a missile harpoon and machine guns and Marco would only sing, guide the way, and offer words. He felt torn in half, feeling love for whales. He once swam with two of the whales. They watched him with their ancient eyes and he felt his own small being as a human.

Marco, with his thin mustache, was by rights the chosen, but there were those who thought it unfair, even though he had the strongest of bodies, the quietest of eyes, and clarity of mind.

Thomas listened when the elders said Marco was the one who had been prepared. This began in him a growing respect for the boy.

Others thought it wasn't right that a young man would be chosen over warriors to hold the honored place. "Hell," said Dwight. "Some of us have seen war. We know what we're doing. He's just a kid." The older men had life experience.

"Yeah," said Dimitri, "but remember. He's just the one carrying the old harpoon. He's like the queen, a figurehead. He won't be doing anything else."

Marco, unfortunately, knew only a part of what led up to the decision to hunt, the politics, the dealings, but he had his conflicts: He had the depths of tradition, but he was also a man, and as far as young men go, they want to be with their peers. They want others to be like themselves. It is why they are the "meat," as his father, Thomas, had once said, why they are sent to fight the wars of other men. Marco could fish and mend nets, as Ruth had taught him. He could speak the language and he understood and knew the whales that passed by. He could sing, pray, swim, canoe, fish, bring in wood, survive alone if he had to, but he couldn't stitch together the truths of divided worlds, double people, let alone the factions and jealousies within his own tribe, especially when the jealousy was directed at him. Nor did Thomas know the doubleness that existed here, in his own place. He knew only his own.

Ruth tried to forget that Thomas had returned. She told herself Thomas had become another man. But she looked for him around every corner, through every window and door, her eyes constantly searching. Still, she kept to her stand against whaling. Because of this and because she had inherited some of the old whaling implements, her mother's house, where she sometimes stayed, was searched and razed, torn apart by angry men. Aurora, distraught, sent for Ruth. When Ruth saw the damage, she fell into despair. Realizing she'd underestimated some of the men, their desperations, and even forgiving them, Ruth said, "They are not angry, Mother. They search for the past. They have lost it. They are needy." But they did not find the old whaling items they were looking for. The lid of an old ship's trunk was torn off its hinges, the ceiling at her mother's was taken apart and left in ruins. They took an old drum that had been given to her father by their cousins up north. It was painted with an octopus by the last few members of the Octopus Clan. Numerous things in Aurora's house were broken, including her figurines. "They broke them on purpose," said Aurora, who had been home at the time and afraid of the men even though she'd known nearly all of them since they were first born. She'd watched them grow up. She'd given them cookies. Later, even though she was crying, Ruth's mother said, as she ate the strawberry-rhubarb pie at Linda's restaurant, "It's okay. I'm trying to pare down anyway. I'm going Zen." Linda sat next to her and took the pins out of her dark hair.

Ruth laughed. "I'll stay around for a while and fix your ceiling while you meditate." She stayed at her mother's for two days until she'd managed repairs and Aurora was no longer afraid.

When Ruth returned to the boat where she lived, just as she feared, they had gone through her things, too. The whalebone mask was gone. The bank of her son was broken. Her nets were torn. Hoist sniffed the deck, smelling the feet of the men.

Ruth and her mother pretended nothing had happened. The two women, seemingly undaunted, kept their chins up and never mentioned the incident in public. Alone, both of them wept, and each day they discovered more missing, a ring, a wooden whale carved by Witka, the old master whaler, even Marco's fishing rods and reels, and their woven baskets. Ruth's nets and winches were ruined. She had repairs to make and her hands already hurt.

In addition there was Thomas.

"He hasn't said a word to me or Marco," Ruth told her mother, "I don't understand. His own son."

One morning she woke and found sweet Hoist bleeding on her boat. Hair matted with blood. She bent over him and ran her fingers through the fur, looking into the eyes as life stepped out of them. She prayed her little spotted dog, so rambunctious, hadn't suffered. Nothing equaled the killing of her dog and it only made her more adamant against the hurt. There was nothing else to lose.

She didn't have the heart to tell this to her mother, but Marco knew. He heard it from one of the older people. And he came to be with his mother when they wrapped Hoist in blankets and gave him to the sea.

Ruth knew that someone had come out and boarded the *Marco Polo* while she slept, so quiet she never heard them, nor had the dog barked. Perhaps it was someone familiar. The boat seemed dirty to her now. She scrubbed it down. She hoped her father was watching over it. For the first time she was lonely. She cried as she wiped oil soap and water across the surface of everything. Worrying about her safety, Marco came to stay for a while, but nothing could fill the emptiness.

At her home Aurora discovered the thieves had taken the old photos. "Those are the most precious," she told Ruth. They were photographs of the twenties, the old canoes, the people in their woven clothing and harpoons and spears, evergreen hats, shell necklaces. They were the flensers, whale-cutters, at work with their tools. Witka with his hair askew, and Aurora's father with him.

For Ruth this was a revelation. "I think they want to know. They want to remember. It's so the men can try to remember, try to do the whale hunt like they did in the old days." She knew this without doubt. They were lost and needy and inside them all was a drive from the past they carried like DNA, a drive to return. She also knew there was another facet to the story. They'd been offered money for the whales. For the meat and fat. And their attempts were all wrong. They hadn't even gone to the elders.

"Where's your dog?" Aurora looked at her daughter. "Oh no. Not that, too. Oh, we should have kept silent and left them to their plans."

Ruth continued her stand against them. She picketed meetings. She wrote letters. Even Thomas, she realized with her broken heart, only came home to strengthen his identity, to reach for something lost, to join the whaling crew. She stood against this man she had known all his life and always loved.

"What about this?" she said one night at a meeting. "The ones who saved them? What about our ancestors calling them spirit fish when the white men called them devils? What about the whalers who helped the ones that were stranded in the sudden ice farther north? They used everything in their power to save and free the whales." She looked around. "And who here has the kind of relationship to the whales that our ancestors had? Who among us knows the songs and the correct way to bring in the whale? Who will prepare by fasting? Who will sew its mouth shut so it doesn't sink to the bottom of the ocean? Which of you knows what our grandparents knew? We can't jump into this because someone has made an under-the-table offer of money. We know this." She looked at Dwight. Dimitri. "We've all heard about the offers. It's no secret. You've been offered large amounts but we have to do things right, and look at us. Just look at us."

They looked around at each other. The room was smoke-filled. They saw each other in Budweiser T-shirts, jeans, dirty running shoes on men who didn't run. There were Styrofoam cups on the tables. They sat on folding chairs. They heard the sound of the Coke machine when another can fell. A few handsome young men asserted their identity by having grown long hair. Thomas looked at the others, wondering about the money, surprised he'd heard no rumors.

The women who came with the men, some in T-shirts and jeans or hot-pink tops, looked at Ruth with hostility. She was against their men. Her own people.

There were a few older men with their lives written on their faces by the sea, thinking of the whales glimmering in sunlight, the young whales in kelp beds bending, blowing, riding with currents. They were thinking, This isn't how it used to be for us. It's not good. They thought Ruth was right, but if they stood up with her, they would lose. Health benefits. Housing. And she was an outcast in some circles, a puzzle in others, a hero among the few. She was a rare woman who was not afraid to use words.

Ruth understood the ocean like the other fishermen. She knew the unpredictable waters, the large waves, the near-collisions, how an earthquake far away could change the currents without warning. But she also knew people. Because she'd been shy as a girl, she learned to see to the core of them, the kindness of a gruff person, the hardness of a friendly one. She saw the vulnerabilities and the cruelties. It gave her a voice.

She said to the crowd, because by now there were people coming in from other towns, "Tell the sea what you are going to do. It is already listening to your words, deciding things in a new language. The whole world out there is waiting to escape your human grasping. The mind of water is listening, the mind of the water is thinking, is willing it another way. The thoughts of the world know. Truth is outside this room of bad choices."

At the end of all this they would still have wants and needs never fulfilled. Ruth understood that humans could be such empty vessels.

Marco, perhaps, was too young to know what was in the

cravings of the other men, too innocent. He'd lived always with those who loved him, protected him, even at the painted white town with the elders. The truth was, he also wanted to know something of his father. He told himself his father had shrapnel in his brain like Ruth told him and had forgotten them or that he'd been through something and lost the thing that made a man, his memory, his soul. Maybe, Marco thought, he could get past that place.

Marco and his father both also believed the rituals were still with them. They did not know the whole story. The selling of whale meat, the opening of the whale fat market of other nations and whaling in other countries.

Marco had a picture of his father, a man in the war, in the clothes of a soldier, the greens that didn't really match any jungle. He'd seen these men on television at his grandmother's. He had pictures of his father in his mind, pictures that didn't fit this man.

How Marco wished he could snap his father open and see what might fall out.

But if he did he would be surprised to find that the room would fill with visions of fire, and a woman blown to pieces, not just one woman, but many. A little girl would fall out of him, his daughter, Lin, in the other country. His remembered and cherished childhood with Ruth. The days they loved in the green house by the river.

The meeting began. It was exactly as Marco thought. The few women arguing. The men implacable, like walls, their faces growing red, unchanging in their opinions, wanting the women to just say, *Yes, sir*.

But Marco had been the child listening to the stories during long nights, the one who went to the stone petroglyphs hidden in the rock world, the one of the whale who gave birth to the humans, the beginning of the octopus and other creatures of the sea.

At the meeting, Marco sat at the table in the center. His arms were powerful and strong. He listened to the other men and had his own thoughts.

There was so much darkness in the room. Light was swallowed by the lies and thoughts and hopes of what used to be that would never return.

The men were unmoved. It was decided still that they would hunt.

Come near me. Hear me. I am asking for you, whale.

Hold tight, old Wilma thought. You are only mortals, not at all as constant as the sea, as day and night.

More than one of the elders dreamed that night. Their territory seemed small by day, but when they were quiet or slept it was large and vast. *Someone go tell the sea to keep its creatures away.* They said this to Ruth in their dreams. Somehow she heard, and she stood outside singing, her hair blown across her face.

That night on his mother's boat, Marco was awake listening to night birds, and remembering how when, as a boy, the people had come for him, and his mother had known they would.

By now the wind was howling outside, moving the dunes. A body of sand turned over.

HUNT

On the day of the whale hunt, the gray day, only three women had the courage to stand at the shore facing the ocean fog as it lifted. Far out was the roar of water, the sound of a storm beginning in the lead-colored sky. Their eyes closed, the women sent their hearts across the water, willing the whales not to come near land. Ruth was one of those women. Old Wilma was another. Delphine, the heavy, sweet-faced grand-daughter of Wilma, was the third. Wilma, whose face could sag with sorrow or crinkle with happiness, was the daughter of treaty-signers, the daughter of one of the last true whalers, one of Witka's crew. She had also been the keeper of the women's songs and washing houses. She alone knew how to play one of their musical instruments, a metal hand instrument always painted red and sounding like the songs of seabirds. In fact, it spoke their language. Her granddaughter aspired to be like her grandmother and watched her closely, always, and practiced the sounds of the birds without even using the instrument.

There were other women who didn't have the courage to join them at the beach, but their hearts were with them. "Join us," Wilma had begged. However, to appear at their shore would have meant going against their husbands, brothers, or sons. Time and history had reduced their world, maybe even the soul, as easily as a sand castle is washed into the sea. Maybe their absence was why the whale did not hear the few singing women who gazed out past black rocks at the horizon. The three on the beach did not judge the others, even Linda, who was too sensitive to stay in town that day. Linda closed the restaurant and went inland to stay with friends in order to avoid nightmares with blood and her own all-pervading sadness.

Ruth knew there would be consequences against her. Already the anger, the hatred, the fallout from her protest was as alive as if another creature had grown and pervaded the tribe, a monster as in the stories of the past, the cannibal that wanted to eat the people, and she felt that she alone stood in its path. Some saw her as their ruin. They blamed her for the news coverage, the loud protests of the activists, and even the storm that later arrived, as if she had more power than she herself had ever known.

The three women told the whales not to come. But the whales no longer heard their voices or thoughts. Perhaps because this hunt had become a spectacle and not a holy thing. Their voices were drowned out by the sound of speedboats and a helicopter, the pilot spotting the whales so the men wouldn't have to wait for them or search. This was not the way it had ever been done in the past. This was the first whale hunt since the 1920s. Everyone was there. Reporters, like the one Ruth had called. Newspeople and watchers from outside, from other tribes who swore later that they themselves would never whale, and the many protesters from San Francisco and thereabouts. It was a spectacle. Ruth thought no whale would be near all the commotion. Watching, she also thought how few knew or remembered how to paddle the canoes except Marco. Marco had explained and taught some of the others how to paddle, but still they were a sorry sight.

The women watched as the men moved the two canoes away from land in all the chaos. Long ago, the women used to hold up their skirts and go out into the cold water and ask the whales to offer themselves to the hungry people and to those women with breast milk, to feed their families, all of whom loved the whales with their great breaths rising out of water, their barnacled bodies, their ancient eyes.

Those men strong enough, including Thomas and Marco, pushed the canoes into the water and jumped in with the ones already inside, some of them not strong enough to row. There was chatter as they left, directions. There was food and drink and noise. Marco was surprised. He was given to prayer, as he had been taught.

From out on the water, from in a dark canoe, Marco, so vividly alive and aware, looked back and saw the women on shore, knowing his mother was there. He understood his mother's position every bit as much as she understood that he had a role to fulfill. The women looked beautiful standing together, he thought, like the figures of spirits the old ones carved. He smiled slightly at them as the waves moved him, but they, of course, could not see him.

The old people watched, also, from the white houses on the other side of the water. They could barely see the awkward men try to paddle amid the spectacle of speedboats alongside the two canoes.

"This is terrible. I hope I am not really seeing this," said a man named Feather who recalled the days when people called out lovingly, bringing the whale in, promising to care for it and treat it with respect, to inflict the least pain, and to use it all to save themselves from hunger.

The new hunters didn't remember that they should cover a whale with eagle feathers on land, how to make light with its oil, or how to make baskets with its baleen. Ruth's mother, as a girl, had done this. In the old days, Aurora had gone to the whaling captain, Witka, and asked for permission to cut off the baleen from the gums of the killed whale. He would pro-

nounce, "I give you, the weaver, permission to use the baleen,"
Then she soaked that amazing part of the whale mouth which
had strained plankton, algae blooms, and other green sea-rich
life from the full waters, the small of the ocean drop by drop
making the whale large. She remembered its purpose. Oh,
baleen, its wonders, its thin strands of beauty and strength.
They took it inland and at the edge of the lake she and the
other women cleaned it with rags, scraped it. They soaked it
until it was like fiber, soft and ready to weave the threadlike
strands into baskets.

In those days, too, anything unused would be reverently
sent back into the ocean, the men singing.

Now the men seemed to have lost their hearts and the
women who still had them were against the hunters and the
division was a desolate thing for a tribe, whose purpose was to
be One.

Thomas's mother had been named Martini, for the beauty of
the name. No one then had heard of the drink. The word had
just been said once. If Martini were alive, she would have been
foremost against the actions of her own son, and especially
against Dwight, a boy she'd never liked or trusted since he was
a child, always sneaky, always trouble, a thief and a bully, and
Dwight who had gone against Ruth, always, even as a child,
as if jealous.

No one now even remembers the taste of whale meat. That's what
Martini would have said if she were alive and standing strong
in her little frame with the three others on the shore.

The women waited all day, watching the sea, the helicopter,
catching glints of light. Then came a light wind and Wilma,
the oldest woman, her dress blowing, her skin lined deeply, sat
down on the wet sand. In her dark, bony, veined hand was a
white bald eagle feather given her as a girl by Thomas's grandfather, Witka, who had been her lover for a time. He'd had that
gift, attracting women. Back then, lovers were acceptable. She

cried about what they used to be as a people and what they had become in such a brief passage of history. She'd watched all this history unwind like a thread, leaving an empty spool.

A whale sprayed and breached in the distance. "Oh my. It's a whale. Do you see it? This is terrible. It's going toward the men."

"I know," said Ruth, closing her eyes as if to ward off the sight.

"I hope the old white house people can't see this."

"A storm is going to come," Wilma said, opening and closing her hands, holding her back. Her arthritis was acting up. Ruth sat down beside her and pushed back a strand of Wilma's hair. It was the dusk of her life and Ruth could see that. The wind, with its own mind, blew the gray hair back again into Wilma's face. Maybe the storm would disrupt the hunt.

It was so difficult to have to go against your own people who had already been wounded and persecuted and to want to see them thrive, to really *be*, like they once were, and to see how compassion had been taken away from their lives by their experience in the new and other world as if they'd been transported away from themselves. Now they were merely trying to fill themselves up but not with the heart, not the soul. They'd lost both those along the way, some of them. Yet Ruth and Wilma's hearts ached. Ruth was most keenly aware of suffering and thought of the whale, hoping the men would not be there, that the spray was far from them, heading farther west, faster.

Wilma's predictions based on her hands were always true. As the wind picked up, Ruth worried about the storm coming in, about Marco, even Thomas—yes, she admitted it—out there in wind and crashing waves. She was a fisherwoman. She knew what the ocean could do with a boat as large as her old Trophy, let alone a canoe. She'd heard the sound of a storm early that morning. And then, far out, even as the clouds moved in, she and the others saw the struggle begin. "Worse,"

Wilma said, "I feel it from the body of the ocean," which was now almost her body.

It was a sorrowful thing, to watch an old woman weep, giving up and letting her sweater, unbuttoned, be blown by the chilly incoming wind. Wilma placed her hands over her face, her body wracked with sobs. You'd think even the heart of the world, already broken, would ache just to see her. "They don't know what this means," she cried.

And so it began, and then it lasted too long, which was not a good sign. Even when it was over, they still sat there. Two young men behind them built a fire and downed cans of beer. Blue Ice. The women barely noticed them, except one wanted to talk. He told Ruth, "I was in Vietnam. Everywhere the women and children cried. That's all they did, all the time. They cried." He had said the same words to her so many times, every time she walked the beach.

It was early evening when the men came in with only one canoe, and with help from the Coast Guard, the other canoe in tow. Both vessels had many ropes uncoiled and were trying together to bring the whale up toward the dragging beach. It was not full-grown. By then some of the men in the canoe were not sober and they were laughing. Delphine turned away. "This is even worse than I thought it would be." Others came down to watch, a few cheering, and the three women viewed this scene with sorrow and even horror, the excited men in T-shirts and wet jeans breathing hard as they tried to drag the sand-covered, bloody, weed-covered whale up the ancient dragging beach, once smoothed solid with fat and blood. Whales had been brought into this place for over a thousand years. More, perhaps. But never like this. Now they had the help of white men. They had the help even of reporters who had arrived to reveal this action to the world. No matter their views on the event, the watchers saw the situation, and that the whale could not be brought in without them. There was nothing else to do. There had not been enough planning, and so together they all hefted ropes. Dwight wore his Rod and Gun Club jacket for the photographers. The whale was sideways, then righted, and then, as an afterthought, Thomas and someone else ran for a truck with a winch for towing.

Ruth felt that she could hate Thomas forever for not trying to stop them, for being part of it, until she saw him when he returned with the brown truck. He looked pale and serious. He alone looked as if he had done this with purpose, as if he were sorry now to be involved, and had truly believed that they were trying to do this in the right way. And so she had compassion for him, the father of her son, the man whose missing years were a secret to her. She saw in his face, in the way he held his body, like a bow without a string, that something terrible had happened to him in those years, that this was terrible, too, with unforeseen consequences, more than he even knew until he became a part of it. And she realized he hadn't known about the money the others had accepted until it was too late. She, who had fought them, did not tell him, and when she announced it at the meeting, he simply didn't, or couldn't, understand. In all the years he'd been gone, he had no idea what the other men had become. And she was their enemy.

The wind grew stronger.

Watching him and the others, seeing the blood of the whale, the sun a red line going over the horizon, Ruth searched for Marco. He wasn't present.

Ruth went down to the whale and the men. The whale, though large, was even younger than she'd thought. It was a mess of wounds. It had suffered, she could see that. "Where's Marco?" she asked Thomas. Her words were urgent, hair blowing about her face.

Thomas looked at her. He shook his head. He didn't know. Even though he and Marco had spoken in the canoe, he had no idea. He thought of Marco and the whale. In the canoe,

Marco had said, "I hear it beneath us." It was a low rumbling sound. It was the same sound Witka had spoken of. Then it came to greet them; it breathed out in a strong spray. It looked at them. It moved the water. It was friendly and it was too young to be killed. Marco said, "This is the wrong whale to kill." But there was yelling in the background. Thomas heard his son and he was of two minds. He looked at the whale. The waves were changing, the wind blowing the spray of the whale toward him, a mist. He heard the other men, their excitement, their preparations to shoot it, even if it was friendly. The canoe was precarious. And then he, Thomas, shot it with them. Maybe he was even the first to fire. Hell, he couldn't remember now, except at the same time wondering, *Why?* Why am I doing this? He would later wonder, At which second could I have stopped myself? But then it was the familiar feel of the weapon, the sounds. It was because he had the rifle, a gun. It was the feel of it, of war. It was habit. Somewhere, in the old or new of his memory, he heard other shots. In spite of its size, it fought back, as befits the whale's reputation as Devil Fish and sea demon. He shot again, almost falling into the water, as Marco looked at him with surprise, Marco wondering why his father had shot the whale, and Thomas, too, wondering why he had fired, why the weapon in his hands had the life it had, or the death, but this all happened as if it had its own will. And he saw Marco's face when he shot. This time to put it out of pain as much as to stop the fight. "I'm sorry," he said to the young man, and just at that moment the whale whipped about and broke the canoe. Thomas and Marco and the others were cast into the bloody water. The Coast Guard helped them out of water. Those in the other canoe pulled in two men, almost upsetting their own balance. There was confusion and spraying blood coming from the blowhole, all of the men covered in it, the sea red.

Someone from the Coast Guard boat yelled, "We got them all. Everyone accounted for."

Still, Thomas searched the scene. His warrior intuition told him something wasn't quite right. His jungle law, something that told him when there was danger, when an enemy was near, or death in his proximity.

The storm came in and many of the young men left as soon as the whale was dragged to land. Thomas thought Marco was among them, and he was angry they had gone indoors to watch a football game. A ball game, no less, leaving the whale on the beach, a large mass of blood and fat and skin needing to be cut away from the enormous bones, the spilling innards shining and the flies coming from nowhere, even in the night and autumn wind. This was what Ruth had protested.

"Hey!" someone called out. "We need some help over here."

And then Ruth came again to ask about Marco. She asked, standing there in the whipping wind.

Thomas didn't know. He was thinking the blood was too familiar. The sound of helicopters, as well. It all made him nervous.

"Where's Marco?" she repeated, a frenzy in her, her eyes, yet she sounded quiet in spite of the certain knowledge that something was not right.

"He went in already," Thomas said, almost brutal. "Like the rest of them." He was angry, but he thought his son was probably angrier. Worse, his son had seen him. Really seen him. And he had been brutal to the whale and he wondered what it was in him, in other humans, and he was wishing he could change time, go back hours, even years, and change events. He wished he would have stood by Marco and said, *No, it is a friendly whale.*

Never kill a timid whale. He had been told this by the old people.

Ruth's eyes scanned every face in all the fast motion. Searching. "Thomas, you don't know him. You don't, but he wouldn't have gone in. He wouldn't do that." She started to tell him, *He's lived over with the white house people*, but instead she entered the house of her own fears, the son she searched for, feeling, knowing she would not find him, she would never see him again, his dark soft eyes, and her face already began to line with another grief.

As for Thomas, he himself wanted to leave as soon as the whale was dragged from the water and the men cut it, laughing, talking about its sex organs, calling it names, all the love for the animal missing, and he thought, Jesus. They are like the men at war. What his grandfather would have thought if he had seen it! Thomas was ashamed of them. Now he hated his own men. His love for them had led him to crimes, including this one. He never wanted to talk to any of them after this, some of them drinking in the boat that day, smoking marijuana, one had put beer in the blowhole of the whale with irreverence and stupidity and Thomas had made him stop. "You fucking idiot!" he yelled through the noise.

"You're the fucking idiot. Where you been all these years, man? Huh? You want to explain that one, hero?"

They didn't apologize to the spirit of the whale, nor did they sing to it or pray as they said they were going to do. He alone prayed and he did it silently because he thought, really believed, the men would laugh if they heard him. He realized they didn't even believe in the lives of their ancestors, that it was as if those old ones, the ones whose presence he often felt, were only stories to them. Maybe they'd lost all feeling because they'd had to in order to survive in a place where kids shot guns, killed dogs, and died of alcohol poisoning, but he'd hoped this would be something different than just a killing, that it would mean something, that it would *do* something for them.

Now Thomas knew only that he'd stay there all night if that's what was required to do this job right.

In silence, he apologized to the whale. He was sorry they

had caused it so much suffering and pain. He wanted to make amends for those who hadn't prayed or sacrificed, not knowing his son had done both. Not only that, but Thomas thought they'd need a dozer to help them with such a mass of innards and bone.

As Ruth searched for Marco, Thomas continued to cut into the whale. The helpers, the flensers from the north, patiently, even in the wind, taught him to cut, taught him to lay out the meat in eight-pound slabs on a kind of paper, and when they had enough, some drove it away to be frozen in lockers in town. The fat and oil had an odor to it that made him sick.

Ruth went from house to house asking, "Have you seen Marco?" But she already knew. As a mother, she felt it. His absence was everywhere. Wet from the rain, she began to run, her hair in her face. She went to Dwight's. The Breaker, she called him. She took hold of his shirt as if she could shake him, and she did, with her great fisherwoman's strength. She hit him in the chest over and over, crying now. "This was all your doing," she said, her knees starting to buckle until his wife, casting a look of pure disgust at her own man, said to him, "You could at least go out and help the other men." His wife, Candy, took Ruth into the kitchen and cried with her at the table about the s.o.b., the wife all the time hating Dwight, too, as she would forever after. She had believed in him. They all had. They didn't know him. Now she saw him and it made him all the more hostile. But still the younger men had all looked up to the man who sat on the brown plaid couch in his Rod and Gun Club jacket and said to Ruth, "Hey, it's cool. Just chill out. He'll turn up."

Ruth blamed him for this. And she blamed Thomas for returning. Thomas had come for the whale. Only for the whale. It was his way of returning to himself. He was not returning for her and their son. She didn't know that now he was sorry. That now, without showing it, he knew he, too, had lost.

Ruth returned to where the whale was a mass of red and

fat and bone. "Marco's nowhere." The rain was now falling on the whale, the men working. Water was rising up the beach from the storm.

Ruth said with finality, "Marco is gone. He is not missing. He is dead."

Later that night, Aurora, with hope, called everyone she knew. It was useless, but she asked if they'd seen her grandson.

Marco had the coveted role. He was the traditionalist they all wanted to be, and they all could have been if they'd just done it. Tradition had been awaiting their return.

Word spread that Marco was gone. Later, the women came to Aurora's house to be with Ruth and her mother. They assumed he had drowned in the bloody thrashing of the whale.

Once again, Ruth fell to the same linoleum floor as when the man named Death came to the house with regrets to inform. This time she was not even crying, just silent, a stone that passed down and down through forever. Aurora, after some time, asked for help. She went outside to get the men. Thomas came to help. He and Milton, the slow-wit, lifted and carried Ruth to her girlhood bed, her hand over her mouth, her eyes staring through the ceiling now as if looking for the spirit of Marco, who was following the path of souls along the Milky Way.

Thomas, gentle with her, pulled back the covers, removed her shoes, and placed the blankets over her familiar body in the room he remembered from years before, even childhood. He would have been a liar if he'd said he had no feelings left for Ruth, but then, who was he to want her, to want anything beautiful and right? And yet, he was not without compassion.

Ruth's mother tried to comfort her. "Marco could be somewhere and we just don't know yet."

"You know it's not that way." Ruth said the words with tightness. Bitterness was her voice.

Milton, still there, said, "I saw it. I saw them fight."

"What fight?" She tried to keep her voice calm. Milton could be scared into silence.

"Someone hit him. They wore a big ring. I saw it. He went under. They held him down."

Ruth would question Milton later. So would the police when they got wind of it. She would ask, "Was there a tattoo? What kind of ring? Could you tell whose fist? Did they hit his head? Did they hold him under water until he died?"

"Yeah, he hit his head."

But some said Marco had been hit by the tail of the whale or was in the broken canoe, and that in the chaos, no one noticed and each group had thought this promising young man, a new traditional, was in the other boat.

Thomas was silent, thinking of Marco.

"I saw Ruth with your father," Dwight had told him when Thomas didn't want to go out with them to visit the other women. In the other country. Over there. When the mail plane arrived near the jungle, the men he saw from home had teased him cruelly. "Your brother or your son?"

"Ruth wouldn't do that."

"What do *you* know? How many men do you know are still married, man? Look around. *Dear John* . . .

But after he returned he went to the tribal records and looked at Marco's birth certificate and he knew without a doubt that he was the father. He could have gone to them then, Ruth and Marco, but he didn't. He had guilt now, another reason to hate himself. And he had already ignored them—now what would he say or do? It wasn't pride so much as passivity. And what difference would it make now?

For a moment in the canoe, it *did* make a difference. For a moment, they talked. Marco, his son. *My son*, he said to himself. He thought in another wave of guilt that it was his fault Marco was gone and that even the men he'd killed in the war had to kill, were in that other world, the one Marco now entered, and they were all carried in that same wave of *his* fault. It was a tsunami of memories that could not be held back, faces, ghosts, loves. Night after night he lay sleepless in his father's house and they all came to him as if they were truly there, in flesh.

On the boat that day of his death Marco had asked him, "Are you afraid?"

"No," Thomas lied, because he was always afraid and he didn't even know of what. Fear was his constant, his daily habit formed years ago. By noise, bombs, the smell of chemicals in the air.

Then, in the boat, Marco said to his father, "Do you hear it? Do you feel it?" He meant the whale. Thomas realized that the boy was a true whaler. Marco felt its presence first, heard the deep rumbling sound of the whale. Thomas said, "No, son. I wish I did," because he'd lost all his capacity to feel. Did he even feel the soul of water?

But Marco said, "I do," and breathed and was silent as he looked around at the light on the waters, the *firmament*, which was the very word for it, the presence around them. "It's young. It's not the right one to hunt. It is friendly. It just wants to see us. We are its relatives." He said it out loud. The others heard. He'd said it to turn the men away from this whale. And then Marco had to watch without judging the men and what they were doing. Marco, who had been a true man, a strong Indian, alive. Yes, he'd also thought he could impress his father and that his father might begin to care about him. They'd all thought they could prove themselves as they set out in the two canoes.

After the thrashing and yelling and blood, after they'd hauled the whale in, Thomas thought Marco had gone in with the other young men to watch the ball game. He had been angry with him. His judgment was too severe; the fierce judgment of those who also judge themselves. Not knowing where Marco had gone, now this came back to him.

Thomas tucked in his shirt as he left. It was going to be the fourth time he would cry. How many things can a man hate himself for?

He, Thomas Just, was the man who killed the whale.

That night the breakers rose up and took the whale away. In the morning, to the dismay of the people, it was gone. In the water only the dozer and the winch remained.

DARK HOUSES

It was the custom, when a person died, to keep the houses dark and when the sun went down, to live in darkness and silence, and so it looked like a ghost town. In the old days, darkness meant not to burn the lamps that used whale fat. Later, kerosene. Now the electricity was kept off to show regard for those who lost their loved ones, and the people fasted for three days. On the fourth they came together to sing songs that were so slow and deep and mournful a passerby would cry just to hear them.

Often there was no body because many died at sea. It was the custom once, if it was a land death, to take the body on a slab of wood to one of the islands out in the ocean, the island of ancestors, and to place it in the trees. Next to the body were the person's favorite items, a special necklace or drinking cup, sometimes a picture or carving. There was a special clan of people and these were the only ones who could go to that island which looked so green from the mainland. They were called the Moon Woman Clan. The moon was related to the wolf and to the women, so most often it was the old women who took the loved human out there, rowing through whatever the ocean offered that day, setting out with the tide in the early morning, returning with it late.

But this custom ceased during the influenza epidemic when so many died that there was no room on the island for the bodies. Then there was the massacre by the Americans seeking gold in the hills and even the babies and elders were bayoneted and shot. There were too few old women left to row and the Americans had burned the canoes so no one could escape. Still, some had lived, had gone into the forest and pretended to be trees and thus became invisible, so there are people remaining today.

Even if the custom of burial in the trees still existed, Marco would not have gone to the island where the eagles and sacred condors once visited to make their meals. He would have been buried near the cemetery marked by whalebones. As it is today. But with no body, now there was just the rule of darkness and silence, the people wrapped in blankets, together, later singing the slow, deep songs.

To the griever there is darkness anyway. Nights are lengthened, time is endless. Even in daylight darkness is a room of corners and shadows, things are not there. After the fourth-day sing, awkward, kind neighbors bring food to be eaten. Those who loved Ruth—so many—touched her hand, her shoulder, held her lightly, but no one could read the world inside other human bones. They could touch the skin and not feel the grief and pain it held only a skin's-width away.

"You haven't been sleeping. I can tell."

Ruth was pale. Her mother wanted her to eat. Ruth's hands wanted only to touch Marco's hair, his cheek. She wanted to go backward in time and watch him sleep, count every eyelash, and then to tell him, *No, you can't go. It is all wrong.*

No one but Vince, the old weathered fisherman, saw her walking the pier at night. He thought she was a sleepwalker. It would not have been strange. But Ruth was looking for the remains of her son, Marco Polo Just, the one now traveling worlds she would never know, just as she'd always hoped, although she wanted it to be land he traveled, not the spirit world, not water.

She looked for the white shoes he had worn that day instead of his moccasins because the rubber was more secure against the sides of the canoe. She never dreamed how tender the vision of a Nike might become.

Vince, the old, weathered man whose body was created of coffee and cigarettes, wondered if he should tell Aurora, at least, that Ruth was walking in her sleep near water and it might be a dangerous thing.

Because she was so lost, it was a good thing when Ruth looked up one day and saw that the white houses on the other shore had disappeared. "My God," she said, coming back to her life for a while. "Look!"

Aurora could not see the houses, either. But she had a new worry now, knowing Ruth would go there. "This isn't a good time to be on the water," she told Ruth. "It's so rough." It was the season of quick changes in the ocean. "I don't think you should go just yet." Aurora fiddled with her spoon at the table, warning her strong-willed daughter.

"But they might need help. I have to check it out, at least." It took her worries off Marco and herself.

"Call someone else. Old Vince could go there."

Ruth feared that a sudden wave, like the swell that surged high enough to carry the whale back into its world, had taken away the old people and their homes. It had been an unusual wave, too high, too close. Who was to say there wouldn't be more? Ruth took off her robe, dressed, and went to prepare the dinghy to travel to the shore of the elders, the old houses where the People Who Remember lived.

It was a poor decision in the continuing stormy weather, but she was overcome by the thought that the elders were in need.

As it turned out, there was a high wind. Soon the water itself seemed to cry out. She "felt bottom," as they say about water in ocean storms before the big wave comes.

Then she was carried. By waves so large that Ruth had to make a choice. She could try to return to land, with no guarantee of reaching it, she could fight the water to continue on, maybe running out of gas, or she could wait for the tide to change. She decided that last was the wisest choice, to move *with* the water and not against it. And so she sat in the waves, covered with her wet cape and warm enough with the life jacket, letting herself go out farther into the ocean until water changed its will. Otherwise, just as in her life, it would take everything she had just to remain in one place.

It was good she had the time to think. She went over Milton's statement. She believed him. He was not cunning enough to lie. Marco, the child once held in her arms beside her in bed, had been murdered, and she tried to think of why. And who she could go to. The tribal police would not investigate Dwight or the others. Those outside the tribe would not believe her or, if they did, would not give it much thought. Besides, after killing the whale, no one wanted anything to do with them. They were ostracized, disliked right now by most of America.

Thomas knew Milton told the truth, but he'd said nothing. Ruth knew Thomas well enough to know he still had some feelings, even if dwindling, toward the men he had known all his life, those like Dwight, a few years older, who had always fished with him, had gone with him to hunt in the great forests, to drum and sing at the ocean, yet Dwight had always fallen short of Thomas and his resentment wasn't always held at bay.

Ruth was tired of her own people, tired of struggling with fishing nets and her boat, tired of Thomas, tired even of grief. She couldn't yet think that there are always times of respite, a saving grace. For now it seemed she had nothing left. She waited out the waves, wishing Hoist the dog were with her.

She looked at the water and the lead color of sky. She had strong arms and she knew the ocean. She thought of the stories of deep sea fishermen, with the sudden winds, flying manta rays, the octopus like the one Witka met, or the octopus who came out of the ocean on the day after Thomas was born and how everyone thought Thomas would be special because of this event. But he was only a man, after all, and a broken one at that.

What Ruth didn't know was that on land Thomas was making his own plans. He'd used the brown truck, gone to the lumberyard, and bought wood and posts and cement and was creating a realm for his own sorrow. He was remembering the past. He was moving into Witka's old house up on the black rock. He was building yet another wall.

Ruth thought of the history of their breaking, her tribe, even the tsunami of 1967 and its huge wave of water that hit the town, just missing her mother's house, falling short only a few feet. It was still remembered and talked about with an awe of nature's amazing destruction. That day the Japanese and Indian women were at work cleaning and cutting fish in the fish factory, a large dark brown building, a roof of rusty corrugated steel, when the water hit. Two women had survived and remembered it and told of the crash of the wave that hit the building like a train, water entering, the tables floating. One reached for her glasses and that reach almost cost her life. "Still," the woman said, "I could see them there, swirling just before me before I escaped." Miraculously she floated out on a wave of water that came suddenly and from nowhere. "I saw the other women. Their clothes were like wings. Their legs and arms like angels flying. Then they were gone."

After a time, the tide changed. But Ruth knew already what tomorrow would bring, the breakers bouncing back against the storm waves from far out at sea. For every action there is a reaction. It's true especially in the ocean. And so tomorrow, from what she knew of the ocean, there would be large, rough breakers. The word meant waves, but the thinker in her knew it also meant people, those who unmake other people's lives. Dwight was a breaker. He'd broken her son. He'd broken the lives of women. He'd broken Thomas in some way even Thomas didn't know.

But the breaking went back further, to the Spanish, the Russians, the British, the teachers and American missionaries, the epidemics in 1910 that killed more than three fourths of the tribe, the enormous whaling boats that nearly brought the whales to extinction. A breaker was not just a wall of crashing water, even though people had spoken of the tsunami and collapsing earth walls.

She even thought of the breaking when she had looked so often at the photographs of Witka and her grandfather and Dimitri Smith in ill-fitting suits, sitting in front of the white church. Yes, they had easily changed from Catholics to Shakers because the Shakers' beliefs were more like their own, and there was healing and a belief in the significance of dreams, although none of them believed in celibacy.

Finally, in the rich smell of the sea, she reached the shore of white houses. Now she saw that the houses were still there. They had been blackened and were nearly invisible against the hillside. They were the color of the rocks behind them, rubbed with black charcoal to reveal their grief. Ruth, soaked to the skin, walked up the beach and two old women greeted her. They'd been watching her out there. "We were worried. We saw you go up and down and then out too far."

"*I'ist ka a*," she said to the women. It meant many things: hello, how are things, are you well, I greet your heart. In this case, *I greet your broken heart*.

The charcoal-rubbed houses had black openings and windows and it was a bleak scene. The people were mourning. They, too, had loved the boy who lived with them for so many years. He had been the future. Unlike the fast that had been observed on the other side of the great bay, they had been eating. They ate smoked fish to keep up their strength and their dugout canoes had been pulled far onto the sand, where they looked like dead fish turned on their side.

"It's over," an old man said, his clothes hanging as if on sticks. "But you, you are a strong woman. You fought, you love your people, and we thank you." He patted her shoulder. "They say when a real whaler dies at sea he will become a great whale. Maybe Marco will travel on. Maybe he will return one day and feed his people." He tried to sound hopeful, but Ruth saw that he was bent more than before. "When they are ready."

Ruth touched his face and felt the unshaved roughness. "I was worried about you. I couldn't see your houses from the other side."

"We're okay over here. But night is coming on." Ruth could smell it, the fresh scent of darkness. "You must stay," he said, breathing the same deepening air, the wind that had no name in English.

She merely nodded her agreement.

Inside a blackened house, a woman, Hali, made a bed for Ruth. She set about the task in a full skirt, her long hair down her back. Tule grass with soft-woven blankets over it. And Ruth, without even eating, fell asleep and cried all night without knowing it, tears falling from her eyes, running down her temples into her hair and the blankets.

"Look," Hali said to the others. "She mourns in her sleep."

The next morning, with damp hair, Ruth drank strong coffee. And then the old man gave her Marco's things in a bag, some clothing, a canoe Marco had carved, stones he had gathered that were alive from the mountains. Ruth said, "Thank you." She hugged each person lightly before she left. Some cried and patted her on the heart.

"Be careful on these waters," said the woman with hair that looked like string.

"You know," said the old man, Feather, who knew Marco's skills well, "I can hardly think it was an accident. Marco knew the ocean. He was strong. He could swim forever."

"I know." Ruth looked into the water again, as if for her son.

"Mark my words. There's going to be a drought. A wrong thing was done. Maybe more than one wrong thing. There will be a drought," the old man warned Ruth. "Get ready for it. *N'a sina.*"

PART TWO

PART TWO

HE BUILDS THE FENCE

As predicted, the drought begins, but at first no one notices. Everyone is busy with their lives. Ruth has nets to set. People go to work and home, and Thomas has moved into Witka's old gray house with the woodstove and the shelves with yellowed, patterned paper remaining from the 1930s and the kerosene lamp, the old Frigidaire. He had forgotten there was electricity and if he felt like it he could put in a light. He thinks how they used whale fat to see in the dark. The people say the whale always brings light. It enlightens. The whale is illumination. They have always meant this in the many meanings of the word.

He is in the home with the little fireplace and hearth, the light of the ocean, two trees outside permanently bent by ocean winds, leaning. He sits beneath the roof he'd built himself, years before, for his grandfather Witka. Wooden steps climb up and down the rock and a railing he'd also built when his grandfather had become frail.

Then there is the path to the sea and tide pools he once loved with their rich, changing contents, orange starfish, anemones waiting to return, and out there are the stumps of an ancient forest beneath water which had been revealed only once. They were covered again with sand and water, but he would never forget the two-thousand-year old trees that appeared for a short time, never again to be visible in this ocean, not in his lifetime, he thinks. Yet, they were not as old as his people who have been in Dark River since the beginning, in one form or another.

He recalls the whale. It was beautiful in its way, gray barnacles on it, sea lice, as if it supported an entire planet. He remembers how it breathed and he didn't pray except for under his breath, and Marco, too, both of them so secret in their prayers. The others had been drinking and it made Thomas despise them, his own people. Then, how the spume of blood came high up to the sky, a fountain of death covering them. The killers didn't love that whale or sing or care for it the way it was supposed to have been done. He wishes he had not been a part of it.

Like Witka, Marco had felt the presence of the whale. Except for his tidy, pulled-back hair, Marco had been like old Witka, down to the thin mustache he couldn't have known about. The whale came right to them, to look at Marco, who said, *No not this whale*. There was an argument and a struggle, but no one noticed. The action was so sudden. Only Milton sat and watched it, his mouth open through the yelling and noise.

Marco's decision should have held, Thomas knew that. He remembers Marco's look of surprise and something else on his young face when he looked at his father who had fired. He had stared at him. Seeing him. Without respect but with something like understanding and love, nevertheless.

Thomas fired. Once again in my life, I fired, he thought, against my will. It was not by design but by habit, fear, adrenaline. Maybe even memory.

He only barely knows how Ruth must feel, losing the son she'd watched from his beginnings. He feels only a fraction of her pain.

The wretched man no longer wants to see the face of water

looking at him. And so he decides to build a fence, the wood already purchased, the fence already planned.

He builds it taller than himself so he can't see the eyes of the ocean watching him. He doesn't want to look at the creator of life, the first element. He doesn't want to think of countries on the other side of the Pacific, the great swaying body of water named for peace.

He holds the hammer at its end the way his father taught him. Children come to watch, even as another storm approaches. He ignores them when they ask, "Hey, mister, why are you building a fence so tall?" They don't even know him.

He doesn't want to see. Or be seen. He can't say that. He wants to disappear. He can't say that, either. So he says nothing and soon they leave.

It is as if the fence he builds will be a wall between him and the faces of ghosts, the past, even his son. Marco. He wants a wall.

His back hurts. He digs in the few places where he can find earth, not rock. He digs the postholes with a digger and no gloves. His hands have blisters. The wood has splintered, but the brand name is still intact, new as if it were just attached. His hands would hurt if he thought about it. Instead he thinks about the cement. Three bags. Four. Damn, he didn't buy enough and he doesn't want to have to get a ride back to town for anything. So the north corner doesn't stretch quite far enough.

When the work is done, he puts the tools away and goes inside and sits in the corner like a spider and remembers and thinks and Thomas has a full mind. He thinks of the daughter, Lin, he left behind. Digging reminds him of the land mines he had protested. It was a civilian area. It was where their allies walked. "It's not a war zone," he'd told the men. "You can't do that here."

Thomas forgot there were no longer any rules.

"There ain't no such thing as a civilian," said one soldier. No such thing as a place where no one was shot. "Everyone here is a VC or pig or enemy of some kind. Remember this. There's no room for peace on any inch of this goddamned land if you want to stay alive."

They kept digging, rigging the mines. The redheaded man said, "Just watch your own step," as if threatening.

He remembers the soldier who said that, just a kid, really; he still had freckles. He remembers the way they eyed Thomas with suspicion for his concerns and he knew they would kill him if he didn't keep silent. He still sees their faces, dirty, angry. After a while, they showed no fear. It had been trained and wrung out of them like water, or blood out of cloth.

He refused to dig and they all watched that, too, especially the red-haired one. But it was war. It was fast. They soon forgot. Everyone but him. He tried to remember where the mines were so he could go back later and at least build a fence around them, because he didn't know how to decommission them. He didn't even remember if that was the right word. No children running toward water were going to be threatened. No water buffalo blown apart in the air. No young lovers roaming or old women going down to wash clothes, or wives going to the floating market where everything from ducks to lotus flowers were sold. No legs lost. Because even in war there were still lovers and there were still clothes to be cleaned in the water. And the people there reminded him of his own people just wanting to live and work.

And now he *has* built a fence, a wall, in the hot sun, on the other side of the world, the side which will have no rain with the coming drought.

He considers the wall he has built. Is it a haven? No. Is it protection from the wind? No. He hates himself too much to seek protection. It is to keep dreams from crossing the ocean and coming to him. But nothing ever comes in from the water that isn't polished away by the sea.

. . .

One morning Thomas gets up to answer the door. It's Ruth. "You need me," she says in as formal a manner as she can muster.

He laughs. "I don't need anybody."

"Let me in," she says, walking past him. She opens the old curtains. She looks out the window to see the world, but there is only the wall.

At first he's ashamed of his place. Books on the floor, a dirty towel on the doorknob. Food on the dirty counter. He moves aside because she is pushy. She passes him again and sets some food on the counter with tiles no longer grouted, having never been rightly finished. It is a kettle of stew.

"I won't eat it."

He swears to her again that he won't.

"I'll leave it just in case," she says, trying not to look at his place, not to smell it.

"You are losing weight."

She knows he doesn't care.

"Do you need coffee?" She knows how he loves it. She has a thermos and places it beside the stew.

Behind her the waves are coming back in, but he doesn't have to see them now that the wall is up. Still, there are the tide pools, he remembers again, the places he and Ruth used to look at with awe, happily, places of great mystery and discovery for them. He closes his eyes. He doesn't want to remember her or anyone.

She pulls one old curtain aside. "Come here and look, Thomas. Look out this window. Over here. Your fence hasn't entirely worked. It hasn't kept everything out. They've come up to rest in the shade. Those are your kin."

He looks at her to see if she is kidding with him. He gets up to see. And then he sees a seal napping beside his door, waiting for its black-eyed mother. Two others on the other side of the house, their dark soft eyes, and the whiskers. One yawns. He has provided exactly the shade they need.

He looks at the seal, his cousin. Ruth is serious about the

kinship. He's forgotten all the old stories, although they will soon return to him, the octopus, the whale mother. And now he remembers the story of the woman who married the seal and her family rejected her when they found out that the man with beautiful eyes was a seal with winged, webbed feet. The seal is one of his clan ancestors.

"Marco was born with webbed feet, you know." She is just talking, but she is also still grieving.

He looks at her without commenting. He knows she was born with gills. All the stories live in our bodies, he thinks. Every last one.

Ruth says to him, the boy she grew up with, "Why didn't you build yourself a corner instead of a wall? You've lost all the beauty now. Even if the rain does come, you won't be able to watch it fly toward us from over the water."

She hasn't lost any of her own beauty in spite of her grief. She still has her nearly black eyes in a face golden and fine.

As it happens, he does have a corner in Witka's little place where he remains trapped with his own memories, where he sits and recalls. Like the water, he reflects. Unlike water, there is no light, no sign of clouds or blue sky.

Ruth asks, "Do you need anything?"

"No." He needs more than he knows, but she has left him a thermos of juice and a bag of cookies. Pecan Sandies. She remembers his favorites all these years later.

The next thing he sees is Ruth leaving. She stands in the air and light and holds out her arms and holds her face into the sea breeze and rare sun, eyes closed. The wind blows back her hair, her shirt against her. He remembers her younger, but the years have fit her well. She, like Thomas, looks too thin.

She should scream at him, he thinks. She should hit him.

She is kind because he is a lost soul. Now he will live, if you could call it that, behind a wall, in the gray house of his grandfather Witka, the old man who sat in this very place and watched for whales and smiled at dolphins and sometimes frowned on his own people for their behaviors.

Ruth doesn't know that Thomas, crying, saw the seething of the sea, the pain and death of the whale, that the loss of Marco was the final thing for him as well as for her, the breaking thing. She doesn't think that she opened his windows only to have him shut them again as he went into the darkness like the octopus coming from water into the cave when he was born. And Thomas doesn't know how she weeps for hours alone, how when she fishes and empties the nets or repairs them or turns the winch on the Marco Polo, she wishes that she, too, could turn her back on water, close herself in, except at night when it is peaceful and the sea shines in the moonlight, compelling. Then the world is new and she watches the water.

A month to the day after Thomas built the fence, a memory comes to him, but it comes in flesh and bone and blood, in the shape of two humans, a mother and father, still grieving their own son. So many years later, they arrive, the parents of one of the boys in his platoon, his special operations group, come to find him in Witka's gray house on the sea. They are Murphy's parents, visiting him. Murph, who had died on their search-and-destroy mission. Murph, the one with red hair. They drove by the tribal office to ask for the whereabouts of Thomas Just. Ruth's mother was there that day asking why her health benefits were no longer available. "They broke into my house. Now they are cutting off my health insurance." She was being persecuted, she said, because her daughter had protested the whale hunt. Without thinking, hardly looking them over, she told the woman where they could find Thomas. She still looked gray.

"It's true." The heavy woman behind her desk at the tribal office didn't bother to get up from her chair. "Your benefits are gone. But you'll have to take it up with the council, not me."

"Nothing any of you do surprises me anymore." This place,

she thinks, I need to leave it, but it's all she's ever known and
she almost falls as she leaves. Ruth will have to make a scene.
She'll do it, too, thinks Aurora.

Murph's parents drove a Toyota Corolla and they had something of a look of hope in their eyes. They knew Thomas had
survived. They'd had news some years ago from the Pentagon
that this man who had been missing in action was found, but
they had no address for him. Nor could they get his address
through Social Security. They went over their boy's letters,
finally, and found out Thomas was from a reservation on the
coast. They just thought they'd go there and try their luck at
finding him.

The parents, the Murphys, are an elderly couple, the woman
quite frail, with short hair and narrow shoulders, overly thin
in her dark green slacks and flowered blouse, her back curved
with time. She loves Thomas Just only because he'd known
her son, so her eyes are warm when she knocks on the door
and tells Thomas who they are.

"Come in." Thomas holds the door open. He has little to say.
His hair has grown. He pushes it out of his eyes.

"Well, we've lucked out finding you. We're so glad to see
you." She looks at him a moment. "It's like seeing a part of
our son."

"Sit down." Thomas clears the papers and a shirt from the
cushioned chair and pulls up a kitchen chair, brushing off the
crumbs. He moves them close together, near his own chair.

The father still holds his hat in his hand, against his body,
then sits down and places it on his lap. The mother looks out
sadly at the distant sun descending behind the top of the wall.

The man was himself a veteran of an earlier war and with a
slight southern accent he tells Thomas how he had been with
the men who had liberated the Jews from one of the camps. He
would never forget seeing those living skeletons, seeing them
like that. He still talks about it. Thomas can tell he'd once had
a straight, taut body, that old man, and he was proud of his life

in the war. He had saved people. It was only time and the loss of his son that had made him stoop and age. His was a life lived that had worn him out, but at least he hadn't been diminished by his own deeds.

With Thomas, his own actions had reduced him, his memories ever inescapable. And now Murphy's parents. What could be worse, he thinks. A small smile on the mother's face. Of course Thomas remembers their son. He sees him at night when he should be sleeping, the water buffalo Murphy carved his name on. It was the beginning of the war for him, Thomas, newly arrived, chilled in spite of the heat. Murphy was the beginning, whooping, shooting at everything, everyone.

"What did you build the fence for?" asks the mother. "You ruined your view. It's so pretty here."

He doesn't tell her he can't look at the ocean or across it. He doesn't say anything. He just tries to smile. Then he asks, "Can I get you some coffee?"

The father, a small man with thin gray hair and jeans perfectly creased, says, "I think I understand," placing his hand on his wife's knee, silencing her. It must remind him of the war, the man thinks. "I couldn't face the Atlantic after World War Two. We even had to move to the Midwest."

Thomas is quiet for a long while. He sees Murph, the violent one, the worst of the batch, but they want to know about their son. Then he says, "He always talked about you." Tears brim even though he is lying; he can't help it. "He said he'd be happy just to sleep in his own bed and know you were nearby. He wrote you letters, but there was no one to give them to. He had them in his pocket. They disintegrated. In the jungle weather it all comes apart. Especially in the monsoon season. They were ruined before we could get back to have them sent." He gazes off toward the ocean, seeing only his fence, not yet gray with age and sea wind, seeing roads running like rivers during the fierce rains. He tells them, "He died quick, you know. You should know that he didn't suffer."

That much is true.

They are all quiet a long, uncomfortable time. Then the mother begins crying.

"Say," says the mister, "that's quite an old refrigerator. You don't see many of those."

"No, sir, you don't. It's from the thirties," says Thomas. Remembering to offer them something. "Would you like some water or something?" Remembering the strangeness of the word *sir*. Thankful for a moment for Ruth who left behind the food and juice. "It's fresh berry juice. Made from hereabouts." And he puts some of the cookies on a plate and offers them to his guests.

Out of courtesy, the mother takes a cookie and sips the juice. "It's good. Thank you, son." She wipes her eyes with a hankie. It is scented. She fusses with her hair. None of them know what to say any longer.

They seem to be disappointed. Finding him didn't have the effect on them that they'd expected. They must have thought he would look like their son, that he would be their son, that he would take his place somehow. But they are just three strangers in a little room with a dusty woodstove, three people making small talk until finally the father says, "Well, thank you for visiting with us, son, but we have to be going now. We're going to go see my nephew in Oregon."

Thomas tries to smile, but he cannot bring himself to do anything except stand and go with them to the door.

The man looks down to the water.

"Your steps down there look like a real workout."

"Yeah. I guess they are."

At the door, before they walk away, Mr. Murphy stands and salutes.

Thomas doesn't want to, but finally he salutes back, awkwardly.

He doesn't say how Murph wanted to torture everyone and pee on them. He thinks how he was turned inside out and the only feeling their redheaded boy had was adrenaline, hate, fear, and insane laughter.

He stands and watches them leave.

• • •

Thomas sits in the darkest corner of his place on the small bed and he bends over, his face clenched like his fists. He has learned not to feel and now he is forgetting that skill of unfeeling needed by the best of warriors and doctors and priests, those who bear sad news and carry the weight of death.

Milton, the one they call the idiot, says he saw someone hold Marco down in the water, onto the back of the whale, as it rolled in agony. Milton is not smart enough to lie. Over and over again, Milton has said this, but he was the one whose parents drank more than the rest so he had been born with strange eyes and hands with palms and no lines, and he limped, and no one put stock in what he said. But Ruth does and now Thomas ponders this, that someone injured his son. His son.

That night when he falls asleep he is nineteen. He is nineteen, and they are sure to die. They are dug in and there is firing around them. Fire falls from the sky. He says to Murphy, "Wouldn't you just love a Big Mac right now?"

"It's the planes trying to block the North," someone says.

"Our own planes?"

They laugh as if hamburgers and fries had never really existed. They laugh even if they may be surrounded by people with guns, people smarter than them. They can't stop laughing. Even when the fire comes, he is stifling himself laughing. He puts his head down and smells the molds of the earth.

"Fighting for world peace," Murphy used to say. "Yeah, and so here we are with bulletproof jackets." A lie.

"Yeah, and not even a flak jacket. I lost it somewhere, and it's damn cold at night. They could at least give us a jacket when we have 'em shot and burned off our backs. So this being down here on the ground is the infantry airborne!"

"Yeah," someone says. "Bulletproof jackets. Like those shirts, what do you call them, Tommy? You know, you Indians wore them? They were bulletproof."

Thomas's jaw tightens. "How would I know? I never heard of it." But he had heard of the ghost dance. His grandmother had been a ghost dancer before the massacres, but she said they'd known, they all had, that they weren't invulnerable humans. "That was just some bullshit the white men made up," she said. He and his cousins laughed to hear an old lady talk like that. Their grandmother in her navy blue dress and church hat and the ghost dance dress she kept. It had raven feathers off the arms like wings, and a single eagle feather in the center.

"Get down, you idiot!"

He escaped being shot one time they were ambushed; he sank as far down into the mud as he could, so deep the earth looked flat. He was walked on. He heard *their* voices above him. He held his breath a long time after they were gone, waiting.

I am earth, he thinks now. That's why I lived. I became the earth. This became his way of surviving.

As earth he noticed the plants. Even the roots were being destroyed. He thought nothing would grow back on that end of the world. What would his grandfather have thought? Even with war around him, it broke his heart.

He never challenged or fought their own military action like some did. He was a follower of orders at first. He understood, name, rank, serial number.

Now he was a container of history, pain, convictions, beliefs, memory, and courage. All those were in him. Now was a carrier, of weapons. M16's (twenty-three pounds), grenades, grenade launchers. Above were the C-130 transport planes. Out there were the once-green mountains.

He remembers Murphy. He can still see his eyes.

There was one boy who lived through their last ordeal together, the saved all-American towheaded blond boy. Thomas has pushed him away. He'd been pushed to safety and he fell to the ground, but he watched, wide-eyed. Afterward Thomas never forgot him. He disappeared. Maybe he ran. Maybe he told their story. Most likely he died; there were fires even at the river and daytime was like night because of the smoke. Thomas was the lone survivor.

He thinks of his daughter, Lin.

The lone survivor sees his daughter running toward him when they find him. He remembers. For him, it all became one thing, the many pasts, the present, all one memory; a kite in the sky attached to a string, his daughter Lin running, he and Ruth once running together with a kite across a field near the river, an eagle with its wings spread, a fish in its talons. There were the sheer curtains blowing in a breeze, blowing inward as in the summer at their little newlywed house, their green fruit box house by the river. Everything falling, wind in a plastic bag floating down. Fishing weights in water. Bombs. Ruth with skinny legs holding up her skirt filled with fresh-picked apples and then letting them drop, watching them fall on the very bed where he now lay, at Witka's where they hoped they'd live together one day, the house willed to them.

Remembering, in Spanish, means to pass something through the heart again, and now all the years are going through his heart again as he tries to turn away from the ocean. But he hears it and he knows it is out there. Some sleepless nights he goes out. But this night in his sleep he says, "Oh, look at all those beautiful life rafts."

THE RAIN PRIEST

In Dark River where the A'atsika live, no one seems to remember or notice when the clouds first abandoned the sky or when the coastal rains ended, but what the old man predicted after the killing of the whale is coming true. Without observation the ocean tides slowed and then the winds of the world decided not to blow, even the gentle ocean breezes that move the curtains of summer windows, breezes that blow the long hair of women and ring bells that were once on ships. This is not noticed at first.

At first, with the long days of sunlight, there are picnics on the warm, bright beach. Women and children walk in the ocean and it feels nearly warm against their legs, so rare a feel, so luxurious that there are no complaints.

But suddenly it is realized that the moon no longer pulls water back and forth with its love and will. The tide goes out and seems to stay out longer.

One morning Aurora says to Ruth, who stops by on her way to town for supplies, "It's still out. It's not right. It just doesn't seem right. Look." She pulls back the curtain. "I just did the laundry a while ago." Her clothes hang on the line, limp and already dry. "It's like the silence after a death out there."

"There *was* a death," Ruth reminds her mother. Everything *is* still. "There were two of them."

"You know what I mean. It's eerie."

Ruth tries not to think of Marco. Instead, she remembers the old man from the white houses who said there would be a drought. He is a prophet and she did mark his words, as he asked, writing them in her diary. Now she looks around. With the stark clear light, the flaws on all the houses have become revealed. A cracked window suddenly cries out for repair. Worn paint is revealed as it now peels. A house has settled with age and seems to be sinking. There is dust on siding, warped wood under the trailers. Although these things had once seemed dim or normal, now they stand out in clear detail calling for attention. And the plants Aurora has tended so carefully she now waters and still they wilt.

Ruth knows there will be a drought, perhaps a long one. The old man said to be ready. She fills drums with water and stores them on the boat and at her mother's home. She buys dry ice for the fish. She buys towelettes that are premoistened for washing. Aurora watches her daughter shop. "Aren't you being a little premature about all this?" she wants to know.

"It was predicted," Ruth says. "He said to be ready, and I will." She is already tired from the heavy lifting she did on the boat earlier, before she walked from the marina up the hill to her mother's house that day.

"The water is too warm," Dimitri tells Ruth when she is out walking on the marina. She still has luck because she is salmon fishing. Other fishermen return with small lots of fish. Worse, some have empty nets, winches unused, troll lines reeled in. Their boats are clean, rubber aprons unused and hanging on hooks. Everything is clean. But soon it will be time to go out for the fish coming down from the north.

Only those who go very far out to deep sea return with

their ever-thinning takes of silver and yellow fish, but there are fewer of the bluefin tuna than in the past, not enough for the businesses they have built over generations. Old Vince, who has been around a long time, swears, "Someone put a curse on us. I can't imagine why. But it's a curse all right. I know one when I feel one."

"Of course we know why." Ruth reminds him.

Over the last years, the elders had gauged and counted and made certain the waters weren't overfished. Now the fish have abandoned them, taking along all they have to depend on to survive. The *Times* sends two newsmen out to look over the situation and they conclude that the conditions are unusual but it is the drought and a dreadful dry heat in their area that has caused a change in the temperature of water. As for the receding waters, they report it as a cyclical event, though everyone at Dark River carries a long memory and knows this is not true.

At night, the drummers and singers sitting near fires on the beach have silences they don't remember between their songs. No ocean. They listen and hear an emptiness painful to the ears. For the first time, they hear their own heartbeats, the blood pulsing. It scares them not to be hearing the ocean louder than themselves.

For a while Ruth is still able to long-line and fish at the river, still having some amount of luck. Her concerns are less than the others who depend on larger hauls, who have new rigs. Hers, she inherited. She only needs gas, things for maintenance, whatever will support her and help her mother. She has no large bills. But soon, she too catches nothing. The beach begins to widen as the ocean takes itself into the distance, going away from them, turning its back on them. Seabirds arrive in flocks and clouds. They eat the exposed fish. They stand in the wet sand and feast. More arrive and there is much noise, the beating of wings like thunder. The pale ghost crabs try to bury themselves, but everything is vulnerable.

The old woman Wilma says, "I know what it is. It's a crack in the ocean floor. We are going to have a tsunami like we had before. The hell with what the reporters think. The water is gathering out there. Then it's going to turn back and come in."

There are people who still remember the tsunami, or lost loved ones in it, and so, many of the tribe decide to pack up what they can and leave. Even if there isn't a wave of water, it doesn't feel right there. They leave for towns inland, moving in with relatives, taking belongings whose worth surprises them. They take a satin pillow with SWEETHEART embroidered on it sent during World War II, a pillow they once thought silly. Or they take a whalebone carving. Who would have thought the faded rug someone's mother made of old clothing would turn out to be the most valuable thing in the house, better than the recliner, or that the small bearskin passed down from a grandfather would be preferred over a large television? Indian still, they take carved wooden masks, some made by the father of Thomas. Or whale vertebrae, old photographs, even a terrible painting by their young daughter. They take their kittens with them, and flea-bitten dogs. Dimitri's new young wife takes her goat, and the goose sits in the backseat of the car, looking about, as usual. For a day or two in the terrible new smell of the place of the receding sea, the drying seaweed, there is a caravan of leavers, some honking at others as if the reserve is a large city.

As for Ruth, it seems to her that the wide sea is holding its breath, waiting for something, calling for something, but she believes it is not going to cover them. Besides, Aurora will not leave her home. "Ever," the older woman says, hands on hips.

Soon even the river from inland slows to a stream, then to little more than a trickle. There is still enough groundwater for cooking and washing, for flushing toilets. Then, hardly enough water for people to cry, and at a time when weeping might help.

Afraid, no longer enjoying the weather, those who remain
no longer let their children go to the long, wide, far-reaching
shore in case the ocean tide really is holding still out there as
the leavers said and might change its decision to stay away
and return with full force, unwinding in one great curl, then
another, swallowing them in dark green waves. But it is a very
rocky place, the exposed land, and there are stories out there
and the children yearn to search for treasures they know are
there, metal from ships, Japanese glass, hunting harpoons
of the old ones. There are also the European treasures, most
longed for, from storm-wrecked ships. Who knows, maybe
even the eyeballs of halibut, lenses they could look through
and see a different world, large and curved?

With everything suspended, they are given time to think,
as if thought and the ocean are both great existences, vast and
able to change in a single stir of wind, a single moonlit night, a
turn of mind with memory or hope.

They think about the whale and what they've done, who
they have become in time, each person examining their own
world. They do not feel the spirits that once lived in the fogs
and clouds around them. The alive world is unfelt. They feel
abandoned.

Nor do they know, as the stench of rotting seaweed stings
their noses, about the flooding on small islands on the other
side of the ocean, as if the earth has tilted somehow, been
thrown off course.

Who would have thought this drought might continue past
any remembered by the people before written history? It may
last longer than the one that followed the signing of the treaty
by the wrong people, those who were not the true leaders.

It had happened before, in smaller ways, for briefer times, as
when the tree stumps from ancient trees that grew before the
birth of Christ were revealed. Everyone had walked across the
remains of the sea to touch the stumps with hands that needed

a feel of the ancient, as if humans need to remember they are not solitary in time.

It happened most brilliantly in a coastal region of Asia when a sharp range of crystal mountains that lived beneath water, and were thought to be merely a myth, suddenly rose and shone like the mountains and caves of their ancient stories, as old as Confucius. The mountains everyone had believed in and dreamed about for years were suddenly revealed as prisms, reflecting a blinding light, making the heat in that place all the much worse. Sailors that arrived examined their maps. They thought at first they had lost their way and were in a place not of crystal mountains but of glaciers of ice. Then they tried to chip the clear mountains away to sell, the crystals even more valuable than fish. Then the water returned and everyone, except the fishermen, was grateful.

In Dark River, the boats, skiffs, and other water travelers dry-docked back along the marina look dark and skeletal. Nevertheless there is a quiet power in it all.

With everything in silent repose, the situation calls for action, but no one knows what. Prayer hasn't worked. Old songs haven't worked. Everyone has dressed up and gone to the church and some have even fallen into spells and spoken in other languages, and so one day Ruth, who stands in good relations with the old ones, walks out where the water had been, eyeing things, the barren distances that were ocean, and, up close, she spots a shining brooch that had come from a woman who must have been leaning over the side of her husband's old whaling ship. It might have been diamonds, but she thought it would curse her to touch it. She is watched from windows when she walks, as if she might never return, or the wave would come rushing in and drown her. What a shame that would be, with her long dark hair hanging down her back, her lovely form.

But then, her home is out there, between the black promontories. It is remote, but the boat never looks abandoned like the others, or uninhabited. Her clothes hang in the still air, airing out, if you could call it that, because she doesn't want to waste any of her spare water on washing them. The boat, on land now, is silent as if awaiting her return.

But Ruth, walking, does not go to the *Marco Polo*. She is thinking, as Thomas had done, thinking of the old stories and how so many are still alive and true. She'd heard there was once a man called the Rain Priest who could take away curses or change the waters and call down the rains. He could call water to come. It was his gift. He was called when the signing of the treaty caused the old drought.

This was, according to the old stories of Thinking Woman, A'atsika ancient law before god had arrived with the missionaries, before they'd ever heard of Moses parting the waters. The Rain Priest was their Moses. He had saved them once and Ruth thinks this may be their only help. She is uncertain, but she thinks time is an element, like air and water and stone. It could be sailed on or dropped into or broken open. Sometimes it is entered like a dark cave and no one returns from it. They pass on to other places. So why shouldn't time still be this way? Why should stories and truth have existed only in the past? Why shouldn't the Rain Priest of "long ago" not be able to climb out of that crack of time from the past and crawl into today? Perhaps he could call the water back to them. Or maybe he had sons or grandsons and he taught them how to break a drought.

The past is its own territory, after its broken laws, its walked-over truths. Ruth knows this. And once people forget that territory of "the way it used to be," the doorway back is hard to find. But it is still there, she knows it. Maybe it can be found.

She wants to take this up with the elders. Perhaps they know a ceremony. All this is what Ruth thinks as she walks over the sand to the still-black houses where the old people live. It is no longer a shore because the ocean has gone away from their place, too, leaving large dark rocks, sand, and debris. The sand seems infinite. The birds are gone now. Silent races have lived on this salty ground, whitening in dry places as the once-rare sun now pours down on it. The water in the distance looks like a mirage, a heat wave with gray wavering lines above it in the air.

Ruth picks her way past the beached trees, enormous ones, her sweater catching on them, as if they are grabbing her to ask for help. She walks with her eyes always scanning the black volcanic rock, the sand, and realizes she is looking for some-thing of her drowned son Marco, a piece of shirt, a bone, as if she could find a particle and use it to revive the whole young man back into being, the way the tree roots want to become trees again.

When Ruth arrives at the dark houses, no one comes to meet her. Maybe they know why she has come. The absence of peo-ple makes the houses look like old carvings with open mouths. She is afraid of two things: that no one is there, that the people have disappeared as was said happened once in the past when the ancestors sought places with water, or that they knew she had arrived to ask for the impossible and perhaps they'd gone into hiding up into the black rocks.

But then an old woman in a dark dress, her hair loose, comes out of a house and says, *"Anina, it'sak amin,"* looking at Ruth, the mournful, lovely woman who had let her son come to them to learn how to carve, to make fishhooks out of bone, to dig out a canoe, to speak his own language. The old woman tries not to cry. She pushes back her hair, which itself is still down with mourning and is gray twine undone. She looks at the face of the generous mother of Marco Polo, the man who travels the world somewhere beneath water now. Into Ruth's dark eyes she looks, seeing there Ruth's father, and she looks at Ruth's graying hair. She thinks, Ah, the bones of Ruth's face are as beautiful as the carving of the women gods, and she thinks, Perhaps one day this woman will come here to live. She is becoming one of us, always she has been becoming one of us, but she ignores what she wants Ruth's destiny to be and says, "We still have water to drink. Do you?" and she takes Ruth inside and pours a large bowl of it for the younger woman.

Ruth drinks so fast some spills down her chin, but it feels good. "No. We don't have much water. The river is just a trickle. There isn't much underground. The drought has gone far inland. It is dry and brown there, too. *Anamsi'ika'a ja nin.* All the people are becoming afraid."

They sit on carved stones. It is cool in the old dwellings, no matter the heat outside. Dried fish are passed around on dishes, cool bowls of water to drink, and they have Girl Scout cookies from the mainland. Chocolate Mint and the new peanut butter ones. Ruth smiles and then laughs out loud. "The girls have their best customers over here. Where do you store these things?"

"You forget, we have a cool spring. We have to lock them up so the animals don't get them. Every single creature loves these."

They talk about the weather and the water. They talk about the people. They talk about Marco. "He was the best. We miss him, too."

After conversation and time pass, Ruth says, "I came for a reason."

They look at her and wait. She is shy about her idea, but she tells them. "I have an idea. I was thinking to send word to the people in the north, up to the man who is friend of sharks, octopus, and whales." She'd heard of him, even if it was from long ago. She wants to know if they could find that man, the Rain Priest, or his relatives, and ask for his help. "I don't know if he still exists, but why not try? If he was there before, he might still be. Maybe he's awfully old, but not being fully human, he could be there. Or maybe he's had a son or daughter. I hope you won't laugh at me. It's all I can think. Maybe I'm foolish to think this."

But they don't laugh. He might have been one of the immortals, they aren't sure.

The people believe, some of them, that the immortals still exist.

"Maybe he would come to us."

There is a long silence. "Yes, I've heard of him," says the woman whose braids are wrapped around and around her head like one of their old baskets made of whale baleen. "He came before. But that was back when they signed the treaty. Even though they had no choice that time, he came to us when the water left. It was not like losing our Marco and the little whale they killed. That man, he was the one who brought the water back to us then."

"It seems like only yesterday, but that was long ago," says one of the men. "The oceans were so full in those days. That was when you could have walked into the ocean on the back of fish, they were so plentiful." He looks out, biting into a cookie. "There were so many. But why would the Rain Priest come to us now even if we could bring him up from beneath a whale-bone grave somewhere from the north, or if we called him down from a cloud in the sky? Look at what our people have been and done since then."

This is considered. The braided woman says to this man with the pipe, cookie, and worn suspenders, "The people are still here and they are visible and thirsty and humble now. They have been through pain. Now their hearts and souls are revealed. In the hard light everything is seen. I can even see the other side from here." She looked across to where the others lived. "Even their skin is parched over there, they are so thirsty. Maybe they are ready to be Real People again."

"What if they aren't?" someone else says, sitting on a pallet in a corner.

This, too, is considered, because then it may not work.

The man looks at Ruth. "Because it is you who ask, we'll see what can be done." This man is called Feather, a name his wife called him because he seemed to float everywhere. She even noticed that he floated above the water when he was out fishing and didn't know he was being watched.

He goes outside to look at the dried-up place and at the sky, and he walks about. Returning a long time later, he tells Ruth, "I think it's possible. But it will take some work. What do you have to offer?"

"What do you mean?"

"A sacrifice."

"Haven't I already made one?"

"Bitterness won't work in that world."

Ruth is embarrassed. She *is* turning bitter, is becoming like Thomas, which is what she fears.

Money or gemstones are not good enough, even though an octopus might have taken them, being a lover of coins and shining things. A healer, too, if it would pay for gasoline to a ceremony. This Rain Priest, once they could find him up north, if they found him, would want something more. Rain is almost too much to ask for. Asking for the water to come back to the river is even more. It means changes not just here, but also inland. And to ask to be given an ocean is like asking to change the earth's tilt on its axis or to ask for the moon to move away from its course.

"It will require a great deal. Yes, it will take a large sacrifice."

Since it is Ruth who asks, the sacrifice will be hers. She thinks about the Zodiac she has bought to replace the old dinghy. She bought it with some of her salmon money. She offers that. "That would be good," says old Feather, following her thinking. He knows about the new Zodiac. He'd seen it a few times out there before the drought, orange and moving quickly, better than the cheap and beaten-up dinghy of her father's, and it was light so it lifted easily onto her fishing boat with ropes so she could haul it. He is thinking, rubbing his chin whiskers. "But it's not enough. For all that, he might want more. I think he'd want your fishing boat."

She doesn't act surprised, even though something in her stomach lurches. She considers it. Maybe drought isn't so bad. This crosses Ruth's mind. Maybe there will be a tidal wave, as some have said. Maybe it is just part of the natural rhythms of the earth and sea, part of the weather cycle, as the newsmen say. She's already lost so much. Her son. Isn't that enough? She even feels angry. She's worked so hard for what she has. Harder than the others. Alone, too. And then the men, angry at her protest, stole beloved items from her boat. But then she exhales and seems to crumple a bit. "Yes. Okay, if that is what it's going to take."

"That's so much," the old woman says, leaning toward the man quietly. "Where will she live? What will she do?"

"I'll figure something out. There's my mother's place. I can live there. She needs help anyway."

"That's not all," he says, businesslike now. "We also have to pay all the people who will pass word along the way to him, and those who will beseech him."

"What will they require?" Ruth is resigned by now.

"What about Witka's old house? The Rain Priest would like that, I'll bet. If you took down the fence maybe he'd even stay there."

"No. Thomas lives there now. He would have to give that up, and I'm the one bargaining here. Besides, he could never do it." It was his grandfather's. Ruth knows Thomas better than anyone else does. They understand this. The two of them grew up together almost as one person.

The old man knows it might take even more. But what no one knows is that right now Thomas is sitting in the dark little house on the black rocks considering his own sacrifice. He has broken into his father's proud glass case, taken his medals out, and put them in a leather bag. He, too, is thinking. Many weeks of drought slid by and the smell of rotting things permeated Witka's house. At that house with the fence before it, Thomas himself feels responsible for the drought. He knows what is happening, that the ocean is mourning after so much had been taken from it, after Marco and the death of the whale. It is mourning for everything, the death of reefs with the lives he'd watched at night, the dead zones. The water had receded from him and his fence. He doesn't even hear it at night. Now all he has to listen to are his thoughts.

As the clouds have deserted them, his own fog, too, has lifted, and now he looks into the chambers of himself.

He regrets leaving his daughter, Lin. He still sees her bony knees and skinny legs as she ran toward the helicopter toward him, crying. He had never returned for her. He could have told the truth and taken her, but he hadn't thought of it. He was thinking of her mother, his wife, Ma. She had chased Lin and been blown up by a mine. And all he could think of was his own grief about leaving. He is still in grief. He could have said, *She's my daughter*, and taken her. He thinks about what he had left her to, if she was alive, the life he could have given her.

He remembers flying over the brilliant green of a beautiful land. He looked down, thinking, I am going to help our country, my people, *their* country, *their* people. He is still in battle. Now he calls out in Witka's home, all the names he can remember, the men he'd seen die, the woman he loved. He cries out for Song, the old man of the village, and for Lin, and he calls out for Ruth. Then for Marco. Saying his name over and over. He cries out for all that is no more, and it is so much. He'd spent all these years living in a fog. Now it is moving away. Instead of the fog of self-hatred, he also sees that he had compassion. He had been wrong, and he was not wrong. I killed, he thinks, but I saved. I ended up loving and then hating myself for it. It was a world of doubleness. There are no clear lines between evil and good. He is both. This is the slow dawn of his knowing.

And so he makes decisions. A sacrifice is in order and he knows it. Truth-telling is part of the price, if he can do it. He leaves the little house during daylight while Ruth is gone to the elders, and he hitches a ride with a passing truck into town in order to make arrangements.

At the old white house dwellings it is decided. Ruth stays for the night and the next morning she walks back to her boat in the heat, with remorse and doubt, feeling she'd committed to giving too much, wondering if she believes in things that don't exist. This is the wrong mind, she knows, but she has been the one always willing to give, always searching for help. She remembers when she was a girl and she was told by her grandmother that she would have to give her dance clothes away to another girl at one of the ceremonies, even the red blanket with the black raven sewn on its back in tiny, nearly invisible stitches. It had been given to her by her cousin in the north and it was not their traditional clothing, anyway. "But this is our way," said her grandmother, a woman learned about the past, and one given to wearing ribbons woven into her braids. Each time Ruth saw the girl, the happy recipient of the blanket, she had to push down her feelings of envy and loss until one day she saw her and thought how lovely the girl looked, how happy she was to have the dance clothes she wouldn't have had if not for Ruth.

Now she would have to come up with smoked salmon, blankets, woven baskets, and money. Goods for the journey of words northward. Something for each person who will speak and pass along word of their need. This year there were no berries to dry and offer. She'd already been robbed of most of her earthly goods by the men and boys who hated her protest against them, and now she might not even have fish to sell.

She forgets how practiced she is in new beginnings.

Ruth stops at the *Marco Polo* long enough to get some things and then walks to town and, saying nothing about what has just happened, she takes her mother to Linda's for pie, made this year of canned ingredients.

"It's just not the same." Aurora puts down her fork.

"Yeah. Nothing is," Linda says, looking out at the black rocks, dismal. The pencil in her jeans pocket breaks when she sits down. "Damn, I keep doing that! Do you know how many pencils I go through in a day?"

In the forest, two young men each carry a gallon of gasoline. Michael David, age thirty, and his younger friend, General. They have been paid to start a fire. They would not be caught. It is guaranteed. They had Ruth's wallet and they would leave it behind. She'd already been caught starting fires by Dick Russell, and the Department of Forestry. The women make small burns in order to grow their grasses for weaving. They know she'd be the prime suspect. And there is going to be a new hunt as soon as possible. These boys want to be part of it. Michael David and his friend have brought the two gallons of gasoline to pour over stacks of dried pine needles and down a line of forest. It has been so dry it won't take long at all for the fire to take, and it doesn't. As soon as the smell begins, as soon as the fire is lit, the crackling sound becomes loud and the smoke begins to rise.

At first Michael calls out as if winning a war. He is jubilant and cries out, then the flame turns toward him and he begins coughing but still laughing until General realizes the wind has shifted. "We gotta get out of here!" he yells, coughing, his own eyes burning and tearing. The great flames begin to catch and rise up tree trunks, then tree to tree, and it is mesmerizing to look at, but frightening, too, as if they are being bombed. There are loud sounds of cracking and popping, explosions as the fire travels not away from them but toward them.

Michael backs away first, then he begins running. General is hit by a flame and screams as his shirt catches fire. He runs and takes it off at the same time, screaming. He is badly burned and all General can do is get in the car, crying, "Oh man, oh man. Look at me. Oh shit!" And the smell, like meat cooking.

"We'll fix it," says Michael. "We'll go home and fix it."

"No, man, you gotta take me to the hospital."

"Then they'd know it was us."

"Forget it." He is crying. "I gotta go to the hospital." Then he falls silent, eyes wide open.

Michael drops the wallet on the road where it won't burn.

As he drives, Michael concocts a lie. They were on their way to go fishing when they saw the fire. They tried to put it out. General took off his shirt to smother it.

Meantime, smoke is seen as far away as Kimbal and the fire trucks pass them on the highway, loud sirens screaming, and later there will be the copters and planes and one fireman takes a look at the boys' car and tries to get their license plate, but it is hard to do, as quickly as both vehicles are driving. ARL3 is all he got. But the car, anyway, belongs to a man named Dwight, they discover, who will have an alibi because he is in Watertown visiting his sister.

At Linda's café, half the town hears the sound of loud trucks full of water. They mistakenly think they are the trucks bringing them the water they've been loading into five-gallon drums to take home. But the trucks pass by. They don't hear the sirens.

In the distance there is still smoke. In the little dried-up town on the reservation they think at first it is a rain cloud. Soon the world is red with the fire bursting from the trees, crowning, spreading, a horrible rose-colored light. "What more could happen?" says Aurora. But at least no wind is blowing in the deathlike stillness. Still, they watch the news until late that night.

Dick Russell is the Forest Service employee who first sees the fire. He is the sole worker for the area near the reservation.

He has also been a fire jumper, but the chemicals had given all the men on his crew Hodgkin's disease and cancer. He is one of the few survivors of his team and now he just likes to work the forest.

He is a mixed-blood from a tribe farther north where he knew an old woman who was able to stop fires. He had forgotten about her, but now she comes to mind and he calls home and has them fly her in. He picks her up at the airport and drives the distance to Dark River. She arrives in town and eats a hamburger and then he takes her to the fire and she says, after she looks over the situation, slowly, "Okay now, you go away," and he does as he is told, though he is afraid to leave her alone. But all the while he waits, he remembers the Hawaiian queen who stopped the volcano. First, they had to take her to Hilo and put her up in the most expensive hotel, then feed her the finest of meals. Then she instructed the needy people to bring her bed and some other furniture along, including her special pillow, filled with the softest bird down. Well fed, happy, not in a hurry, she had them place her bed in the path of the volcano and sure enough the lava ended right where she slept.

And so this old woman from the north, not having such a bed, lays her large body down on the ground in the direction fire is traveling and she begins singing and talking to the fire and the fire dies out just before reaching her withered old body, so like an ancient tree itself. But no one knows anything about how the fire ended, just that it must have run its course. Dick Russell and the woman celebrate that evening with halibut chips in the local tavern and she is nearly toothless, too, but still wants corn on the cob. Then she wants to see her relatives at the old white houses and, because of the drought, Randall drives his dune buggy across the bay to the old people, who laugh when they see the Fire Extinguisher, as they call her.

"So, it was you. We were getting so worried."

· · ·

The sheriff found what the boys left behind, Ruth's wallet, proof of her tribal identification, driver's license, some cash, insurance card, boat license, and other information.

A few weeks later a rainbow curves overhead. The people who have remained go out to look at it. Clouds float over, but they are thin and high, with no rain.

"Aye," says Wilma. "It must be raining high up. It's a shame it passed us over. Oh, we need it. Come down, cloud. Come to us. Our plants are dried yellow. Our houses are ugly and dusty. Our fish are gone. Our cousins and friends have gone away."

That afternoon a stranger comes to town. He rents a room at the Midtown Motel, where the yellowed ceiling had already started to leak even before he arrived. "You gotta see this," Al, the owner of the motel, said to his wife Thelma the previous Thursday. He had examined the ceiling, the roof, and the plumbing. There wasn't any possible place to leak. "Damn. It's supernatural," he said to her.

When the strange man comes to town, he requests that room.

"It has a leak," Al tells him.

"It's okay. That room has memories for me."

Al rents it to him. Who else would take it, anyway? "But still, why would he want to be in there?" he asks Thelma. He takes the man buckets to catch the water. Maybe the drought had affected the guy. Maybe he wants to be near any water. Then, too, Thelma says, "Maybe it's a miracle. The Catholics would know, wouldn't they? Maybe he's a priest."

The new man is somewhat handsome and beautifully dark with unusual eyes. He wears nice jeans and a long ponytail. Someone has ironed and creased his pants so it is assumed that he has a woman at home, probably a wife or girlfriend. On the other hand, Linda says, "Maybe he has money and sends them out to the laundry." Anyway, the girls and women keep watch

on him, his nice thin legs, his quiet manner, his hands fine
enough to be an artist's hands. At first even the older women
eye him, but not for long, and after a while, when the young
women smile at him, their mothers and aunts poke them with
their elbows. They've had time and experience enough to
assess him better than the young girls. There aren't words for
it yet, what is strange about him. "Something about this man
is not quite right."

Except for his exceptional legs and good looks, he seems
ordinary enough to most. He eats at Linda's restaurant and
leaves better tips than the other men, making them feel cheap.
She gives him special service and wants to run her hands down
his hair, his back. He says "Good morning," in a cheerful, man-
nerly voice and the other men look up from their coffee cups
and conversations about what they used to catch besides the
clap. Unlike the other visitors and strangers to town, he doesn't
complain about the lack of water. Unlike the tourists, he doesn't
pass through quickly because the ocean is so far away. He is
friendly, but still is shy and withdrawn. No matter who tries,
they can't get to know him.

He isn't a fisherman, that much is certain. He seems to find
a beauty in the desolation because he is often seen out in the
moonlight standing where the water once was, looking into
the moonlit distances, looking all around as if he could even
see where Ruth had been caulking and painting the boat in
case the Rain Priest, when he arrives, needs the boat in better
repair. Of course, she is the only one who knows about her visit
to the once-white dwelling places.

He walks and he collects shining things from the land that
was once ocean and from the streets.

After a while, the Christian converts feel afraid of him, and
there are many. Except Wilma says to them, "Think of all the
strange things in Christianity. What about the fishermen following Jesus Christ? Just how likely do you think that would
be? Look at old Vince. Think about it, will you? Would he lay
down his nets and follow a man that looked like Jesus?"

They picture Vince, a cigarette in his teeth, talking and pulling in his nets all at the same time, cursing, and how he sometimes stepped on live fish but never fell the way they wished
he would. Yeah, what were the chances that could happen?
Would he lay down his nets? They were comforted even if
what Wilma said didn't fit the context at all.

Then one night in Linda's café, the stranger with unusual
eyes stands up, and in front of Aurora, Linda, Dwight, and the
others he has avoided, simply and for no reason anyone could
understand, he announces, "Everything here is out of balance.
I have to leave for a while." He leaves too much money on the
table and walks straight-backed out the door, with everyone
watching, thinking he *is* a crazy transient after all.

"The hell," says one of the men.

Linda, towel in hand, goes over to the window and watches
him walk away. Others join her. "No. He's right," she says.
"It's not just the drought. It's something else. Something here
caused it." She feels it, too, the lack of balance. She doesn't
mention the whale hunt. It's been the largest silence of all.

Vince, the best fisherman in the café, has ignored all the gossip about the man. He is smoking, his face pale, "You know, it's
true. Things aren't right." He blows out the smoke. "I just had a
weird experience. My boat was just jammed up on a stone. The
wood was going to crack if it stayed there because it's so dry.
You know how I used to work for the mines. I know how to
take out a rock. Damned if I didn't have to cut open that stone,
and damned if I didn't find fifty-three toads in there. Plus one
I killed by accident. Toads. There weren't no holes in it, either,
for a toad to get in. They hopped away toward the river."

"Vince, don't creep out my customers." Linda poured him
more coffee. "Besides, the river's a long way off."

"It is. I know it. They're probably still out there hopping and
you don't believe me."

Ruth is up early in the morning, outside, breathing. The early
morning songs of seabirds are gone, but the rose of light still

comes to the land far away, as if starting at the bottom, coming from the earth. Then it rises.

The pilings of the pier look like black bones. Everything is skeletal. The large pile of stone, it looks like, made of cans from the factory, shines at the top, silver in the light. The rest has sediment and years of earth have turned it to rock. There are boat houses on sand. It should be salmon season, she thinks, hoping they will return one day and are not all dead.

Ruth is surprised when the police and the man she recognizes from the Forest Service come to question her at her mother's house.

"Come in," she says. Thinking at first that they are there about the whale or her son.

Then one says, "How long have you been starting fires?"

She laughs.

"How long have you been lighting fires?" the man repeats. He has a mustache. She looks at his eyes. He is serious.

"We light one every year for our basket grasses. They need fire to grow. Why?"

Then she realizes the men are trying to get her for starting the fire. She thinks, perhaps there is no end to the anger, the hatred, for telling the truth about the whale, for calling the paper, for talking and protesting. "We didn't light one this year because of the drought."

Dick Russell says nothing to the sheriff because the feds are going to be called in and he wants to know what's going on here. He wants the feds. Later he'll bring out his evidence.

Aurora has been listening. "She hasn't been out there. I can vouch for her. I'm her alibi."

"You're her mother." The sheriff is cold. He looks Ruth up and down. For signs, for feet with ash.

Russell knows Ruth didn't do it because he knows the forest and the land. It was burned in a place where those grasses wouldn't grow, so after the sheriff leaves, he orders an inves-

tigation of his own. And later the old people will tell the Fire
Extinguisher that Ruth had been with them, sleeping on the
little pile of blankets they had made for her.

Dick Russell, the one who listens to the questioning, looks at
the few baskets they have left. He studies them. "Do you mind
if I take one of these? I'll bring it back."

"Do I have any choice?" Aurora is worried. It's an older basket. It has memories and she hears songs in it.

The phone rings. It's about the injured boy.

"It's for you." Ruth hands it to the Russell.

Dick Russell already knows about the boy with the burns.
He'd already received a call. But he'd known it wasn't Ruth
even before he heard about General. The plants she wanted
didn't grow there. The young men hadn't figured on that.
Then Dwight had said he'd driven past on his way out of town
and seen her going into the forest. Russell knows the timing
is wrong. Dwight must have lied about being at his sister's in
town.

And General is in the hospital, the burn in the shape of his
shirt, a flammable fabric, but General doesn't feel lucky and
later Michael David would tell on him, each of them putting
all the blame on the other. A few days later, Michael went to
Dwight to get paid. Cash, so they couldn't trace it. But he was
followed by the police.

As it turned out, Ruth had been over at the place of the
once-white houses, Fire Extinguisher tells Russell when he
goes to pick her up with his dune buggy a few days later.

But then General, in so much pain, confessed and Michael
was picked up, though he wouldn't turn in Dwight. Michael
couldn't have been smart enough or honest enough because he
hardly knew right from wrong. His mother had been a heavy
drinker and Michael smelled like alcohol at his birth; the whole
town knew it. He wasn't held in jail for very long; instead, he

was sent to stay with his grandmother. Threatened by Dwight if he told, he kept silent about the money. He also believed he would be a great whaler soon, and he told that to the police in order to impress them. But not long after that the grandmother called the police and said her grandson just bought a new boom box and running shoes, and she didn't know where he got the money.

So the police began to ask him more questions.

Thomas, too, had seen fires, smelled smoke in the war, and the odor made him remember, all these years later, being pushed out of the copter by the sad man who sent most of them down to hell and to their sure deaths. He had heard about Ruth; Aurora had gone to his house to cry that she was afraid her daughter would be arrested. "Ruth's too smart to start a fire during the drought." He calmed her with his words.

Everyone knew Ruth worshiped the forest and she had cried as she watched the smoke rising over it and the way the air above the heat moved as if a mirage of water.

Dick Russell knocks on the door of Aurora's house.

Ruth has been crying. It's unusual for her. But lately she's restless. She paces at times. She cleans her face before she goes to the door. He notices anyway.

"Do you ever eat?" he asks.

She thinks he is implying that she is too thin.

"Well, how about dinner tonight? I'll pick you up at seven." He smiles. Randall is younger than Ruth. He is a mixed-blood and clean-cut. He wears his hair short and his clothes are fresh. In his mind, she is not a suspect.

She looks at him. She hasn't thought of him as a friend. "Okay, sure." She's uncomfortable with the idea, but she needs an ally. "I'll see you then."

Like Ruth, he knows the horsetail and how it is used for arthritis, the oldest of plants on earth. Silica its makeup.

Russell has gone along with the sheriff. He's Indian. He wants to know about Marco. He wants to know about the whale. Even though he is already in trouble for raising problems and his job is on the line for getting involved in Indian affairs. There's enough evidence, says his boss, who believes himself the salt of the earth, but they still believe Ruth is a perpetrator of some sort. That's what they call it. Not a culprit. A perp.

Ruth no longer sleeps, but she does go out with the Forest Service man. At dinner there is too much silence.

Before he left, the new man in town told Al, "Hold my room. I'm paid. I'll be back soon." So Al and his wife keep the room with the leaky ceiling open for him, although Al calls in a few friends to come over and look at the water in the ceiling and the water dripping into the large bucket. "Look, it's a one-floor building. A flat place with asphalt out in front," he says. But they also notice the pieces of polished glass and bits of shell on the dresser, the creased jeans on the hanger. One Catholic thinks they should call in the archbishop from over in Arcata. Al says, "No way. I'm having a hard enough time just keeping the floor dry, even with the buckets there. All I need is a bunch of miracle-seekers from Rome. I been putting the water on the plants outside." The plants, nevertheless, are still wilted in the unusual sunlight. "Besides, he's paid up."

A week later, when it smells of rain, Vince swears it is the toads. "And I was the one that let them out of there." But at the same time the strange man returns, looking different. When he stops by the office, Al notices the man's face is calmer. He feels good just to stand near. But the stranger, Al said to people later, didn't go right to his room. He walked out onto the beach and continued to walk. He walked west like a mirage, looking in the heat wave as if he wore a blanket of wavering clouds, then he was only a shimmering shape of a man and it seemed he went north and then disappeared.

• • •

Ruth, the lightest of sleepers, is asleep when the man climbs
quietly into the boat and even more quietly into the top bunk
above her. Ruth sleeps through all this, but she is awakened
later by the first sound of dropping rain. Slowly at first, the
water tapping like at the Western Union when she was a girl,
then the sound of all the raindrops seeming to run together.
It smells of rain, too, the way it smells inland. She goes outside. It is the best thing she's ever smelled, the sweetness of it.
She stands, wet, and breathes it in, the water pouring straight
down on her, making everything look blue. Soaking wet, she
breathes it in. Then she returns and puts a towel over her head.
Going back to her bunk, she sees the man in the bunk above
hers.

She already has her knife in hand when he props himself up
on his elbow and smiles at her, to show he is harmless. "You
snore," he says.

She knows who he is. And here is the rain. Heart sinking,
she says, "So, you! It's your boat now, isn't it? You are the
one."

"Yes." He feels bad for her, she can tell. "It was you who
made part of the sacrifice. It was you who asked."

She walks back out and stands in the rain, as if it might not
last, her face to the sky, her lonely face that looks like that of
her father, the original owner of the *Marco Polo*, then she looks
back at the bringer of rain.

She sees that he is an inward kind of man. When she talks to
him, she gets the feeling he might cry easily. His must be a very
hard life. She thinks he would like to be ordinary. He would
like to work at a gas station or garage or even a 7-Eleven, or
as a greeter at the new Wal-Mart near the city. And he is a
kind man. He has a calm face. His countenance is special. A
normal life has not been chosen for him. Like the rain, he has
his job to do. Just as prayers are sometimes only one-sided, so
is he. Just as light enters the sky and falls to the earth, this is

his life. As water falls from the heaviness of pregnant clouds. She suddenly feels as much compassion for him as he did for her. He thanks her for it, as if reading her thoughts. "Yes, it is my work."

She opens her suitcase and begins packing what she has left, not much, not forgetting anything that reminds her of her son Marco.

"I'd make coffee," he says. "But you'd better be going before it is too wet."

She smiles, declining his offer. Somehow it seems ludicrous to think of him making coffee and she even laughs, despite the fact that he is, after all, a holy man.

It doesn't take her long to be ready. "Goodbye. Thank you." She is looking at the sky, the fast movement of clouds.

He doesn't shake hands when she leaves. He merely says, "It's restored."

It is raining hard when she walks down between the black rocks to her mother's house, carrying the case, changing hands often because it is so heavy, and the wetter the sand becomes, the more difficult it is to walk, and it is not a short distance. She thinks that now she has nothing except what she carries, and while she is afraid, there is a kind of freedom in it, too, a sense of relief strange to her, of having nothing, of the rain meaning something. Everything of the past is still there. Time is an unstable element, but it doesn't matter; the birds are returning.

The rain has started inland, too, without her knowing it. The man's words come to Ruth: *Part of the sacrifice*. What else was given, she wonders. What was the other part?

She walks up the steps and knocks once on the door before opening it. "Hi," she says.

"Oh my." Aurora hands her a paper towel. She wipes the water off her daughter's face and looks at all her angles and bones. Then Ruth puts down the suitcase, which is ruined, and removes her shoes.

"Mom, I don't have the boat." She will have to explain it all, her visit to the once-white houses, her sacrifice to the drought, the loss of her father's boat.

"Shh." Aurora waves her hand, sitting on her usual place on the couch, and listens to the news. "I'm watching the flood. It's better than watching the fire or hearing about the drought. Look." The news is full of talk and pictures, water running down the streets, water back in creeks.

Dry grasses will magically turn green again. The farm animals will find relief. Drop by drop, the world will live.

But it rains without stopping. The veterans say it reminds them of the war and monsoons. Some of them go into their houses, now leaking, now wet around the edges, and they don't want to come out. There is rain upon rain. It even rains on days when there is not a single cloud in the sky. The ponds fill and the people finally conclude it had been him, the man who disappeared the same time as Ruth's boat, stole the old thing, but who knows, maybe he wasn't a thief or a womanizer, but instead maybe a rainmaker; surely he'd been a strange one and Ruth hasn't even reported the theft to the police and that in itself is strange, now, isn't it? She'd never part with the *Marco Polo* willingly. It was her life. It was her father's life.

As the ponds fill, frogs come up from the ground as if from graves and reappear, their sounds at night comforting the people, making it easier to sleep. Then the turtles climb out with their sharp, determined claws and are seen sitting on logs and beneath leaves.

Vince maintains loudly that "his" toads are the cause of the rain. "I never *did* see anything like it. And *now* look. You see what I mean?"

. . .

Soon the water begins moving down the river again and it looks as if the plants might even turn green, that they will bloom again one day soon.

The strange man in creased pants brought with him blessings. They realize something extraordinary has happened. Al at his motel wants to keep the room free of customers. His wife convinces him they can't lose any business.

When the ocean begins to return, it isn't the feared and sudden wave that loosens itself from its long waiting on other lands to take away houses and children like some believed. It is a steady movement, approaching the shore. Everyone watches it come toward them.

From the black rock, Thomas observes its return. Like the sky, he cries. He has given his word. He has made a deal with the rain and he is going to stick to it. He is going to travel to Washington to tell the truth to the army, and then to Saigon, now called Ho Chi Minh City, to see if he can find his daughter. His tickets are in his pocket already. He believes his sacrifice, his looking at the truth of his life and no longer hiding, brought the rain and, in all truth, it did help. It was a part of something given. No one else knows this, not Ruth, not anyone. As always, everything has its part, but the Rain Priest had purposely avoided Thomas and the house where Witka, a man he'd known, once lived. In fact, he remembered Thomas from when he was an infant held up in his mother's arms at the entrance to the cave and he will see him again one day, he is certain. And then, Thomas doesn't know about Ruth's part in the deal and the loss of her fishing boat. Ruth doesn't yet know about the mysterious money deposited into her savings account for her years of struggle raising a son by herself.

Now the people who had feared the tsunami return with their loaded-down cars, a mattress on top, a truck filled with plaid chairs and table legs. Before long the porpoises skip across the water like runners, and at the marina the boats begin to lift as if levitating.

At the restaurant, Vince orders a cinnamon roll. "Do you think those toads were ever tadpoles or do you think they were just always full-grown like that?" He lights a cigarette and watches the water. He puts his hand over his coffee cup when Linda comes by with refills. "I've got to cut down. The drought gave me high blood pressure."

Nobody knows why the stranger had come there, but the downpour he created made the men stay inside and think, and then the plants began to blossom, so after they had first wished him away, they then saw he brought with him blessings. You couldn't count on first impressions.

The rain continues. Not long ago there had been a new hill of earth deposited by dump trucks in a single night. It had been shaped by busy machines and explained away as the place of new buildings being planned by the tribal council. It washed down and exposed the body of a whale they'd lied about some time ago, saying it had washed up and that it hadn't been killed. It had come to shore dead, they said, maybe hungry, a sign of overpopulation. But the people, once thinking it had drifted back to the sea and been eaten by sharks and swordfish, now go out to look at it with their umbrellas. Even Thomas comes out of his house and goes down to the place. He finds that the whale is riddled with bullets. Revelations. Near it is a crumpled empty pack of Marlboros and an empty bottle of whiskey. Thomas is not even wearing his rain clothes. He stands in the mud examining it and shaking his head, then casts a glance toward the House of Dwight, as they call it, and those additions to the homes of the other men on the council, his cronies who voted to pay themselves, and now it is all clear to him. Thomas goes over to Dwight's and says, "You have never been honest."

"What are you talking about, Bud?" Dwight is tucking in his shirt, as if preparing for a fight, his chest a bit larger.

"What have you done?"

"Shit, Thomas, you know what life's like here."

"Yes, and I want to know what you have done and why."

Once the truth begins, it continues like the rain, one revelation after the other.

The women look at their men who have lied and taken from the others. Some of them are their brothers, their husbands, their fathers. Then they understand why the rain and ocean left them, why the fish had gone away, the sun ruined their homes and gardens. And they have questions. How had Dwight suddenly come up with money for a new Jeep and to work on his new home, even though he said he was doing it for a trade? "Yeah. Especially when so many of us are not living well at all," says one old woman who, like most, was just scraping by.

Then, too, there was the long-ago past. The rain revealed even this. Not far from here another hill fell, mud sliding down into water in a great heave, and the old place was exposed, a harpoon of older times, rock carvings made with love and the human desire for survival. It is the truth that the rain revealed recent human wrongs, but now a history also opened up again. In this place, the mud fallen away revealed the buildings of shell they'd heard about, the seashell buildings that were written about in the old records, the ones they'd believed washed away—if they had existed at all—into the ocean some time in the distant past. They are buildings of art, homes the people of old once lived in. They shine and gleam, even without the sun. The rain washed away the earth and cleaned the dwellings and they shone with all the colors of the nautilus shells that rose up to the surface of the black sea at night from the bottom. These are a part of the beautiful shining worlds, the homes of their ancestors of long, long ago. The rain, through flooding, has returned the past to the people.

• • •

There is still much talk about the stranger. He must have been a rain-dancer and no one knew. Someone says they thought he had an eye in his heart because he made them feel, and one of the things they feel especially when they see the shell houses uncovered by the fallen hillside is that the past is still with them. They feel beauty again.

"I just wish we could have sent him to the Sonora," says Aurora. But after the hillside collapsed and Dwight's house fell to pieces on wet earth, she feels a secret glee.

Besides, the Rain Priest reminded her somehow of the octopus that walked out of water that time, she tells her daughter. "I couldn't identify it at first, the feeling I had, but then I did. He had a feel to him. You should have seen it, but you were an infant yourself," she says. "There was nothing like it. Could you clean my glasses, dear?"

AFTER THE RAIN

Aweek or two later, when Vince comes in to the café, he is still wearing his fishing clothes. Many faces turn toward his dirty gold-colored overalls and his worn woolen shirt.

"Gee, Vince, you're smelling up the place," Linda says, pouring him coffee, all of them accustomed to the smell of fishing boats. "And now you're using too much sugar in your coffee."

He pays no attention. "Ruth, I'll be damned, but I found your old Trophy. Way out there. Way out." Vince chewed a toothpick and squinted, but there was a small wave of happiness across his face, being able to tell Ruth this, for not only had her boat been stolen, it was about damned time something good happened for her.

"No way, Vince." Ruth is afraid to even hope. She thought the *Marco Polo* would be far north by now. "Where is it?"

"I'll take you there. It's about seventy-eight degrees northwest and I've got it plotted. Pretty far out, though."

He's already up and so is Ruth.

"But there's one thing," he says as they leave the café. "I saw an octopus climbing down out of it as I approached. I said to myself how strange it was, because it was so large and everyone knows how they hate boats, and yet I swear it looked straight at me like it wanted to be seen."

155

"Kind of like the toads," Linda says, overhearing as the two leave.

He talks all the way to the marina. "It was the eeriest thing." And then there is the noise of the boat starting and they head out, cutting straight through the water. Ruth stands in the spray, looking for sea life. She knows the sea. She thinks of it as time and right now it all seems timeless, as if she can pass through years to the past. As she reaches her father's old boat, so cared-for, she feels as if no time has ever passed, that she has moved backward.

It looks clean, tidier than Ruth ever left it. She walks through it, feeling strange to be in it again. *Ghostly* is the word that comes to her, but only because it is such a strange sight out there, alone on the water, no other ships or boat, no rocks jutting out of water, just the blue and white *Marco Polo* with everything in its place, except Ruth.

Vince sits on a chair as she examines it. Then he decides to look for tentacle tracks. "They've got to be here." He tries the engine with her. "She starts, all right, but I better follow you back, just in case. Strange that someone would just take her and then leave her out here. What do you think they wanted with it?"

Sacrifice, Ruth wants to say, but doesn't. She does want to stay and touch every last thing, to understand the octopus, all eight legs of it climbing away from the boat left behind by the peculiar, handsome Rain Priest who did, for a time, own the boat. But she must return and go back to her life and get the *Marco Polo* ready for salmon season. Before long she'll have it tuned up and full of gas and ready to go out. Still, she looks around lovingly and touches things, the coffeepot, so clean, the bed, so unused. And then, that night, just as she goes to bed once again in her own place, she sees it on her own pillow. The pearl sitting in the middle of it. The pearl that had belonged to the mother of Thomas, the one that had once been left in the cave, according to everyone who told the story.

• • •

Ruth tries never to think of Thomas. But still she does. She takes him food, coffee. She checks on him. One day, taking coffee and a kettle of chicken soup, she thinks she will soon say, *This ocean is the place of life, damn it!* Turn around! And she will start to tear down the wall, using a crowbar, the claw end of a hammer, breaking the wood, pulling out nails. On this day there will be smooth water, a light breeze. After she does all this she will sit down, calm, on the ground, and he will come out and take her in his arms and rock her and tell her that he always carried her picture and someone will drive by with the car radio playing "Ain't Nobody's Business But My Own."

But of course she will never do that.

One day, visiting, she sees he is different. He is clean and awake. He is packing. He has changed his mind about going to DC to see the Wall with his former buddies. He couldn't say why.

"Thank you for the soup," he tells her, but that's all he says.

She wants to ask him, *Where are you going?* but something about the way he speaks, she understands something. He has made a decision. She is silent.

HE GOES BENEATH

Someday we'll hide in the ocean. We'll swim out and hold our breaths like old Witka and disappear. This was what he said with his friends when they were boys. *We'll never come back. We'll become whales like the story says.*

Thomas goes to the sea only at night, the same time Ruth walks there. He goes down to the pier or the docks, carrying a wool army blanket. He turns his back and drops himself into the water of the Pacific, of Peace. The Great Being. Awkward at first he holds to the dark pilings and looks around him to be certain no one watches, but Ruth had caught sight of him one night, so now she follows just out of sight and afraid. At first he stays beneath the water briefly, then surfaces, gasping for air. She is more intimate with water. She knows how much goes on beneath its surface. There are currents and undertows, the unseen. There are tides within, beneath, that would take him far out to sea. If he would let them. She knows this.

In water is the snow of creatures, plankton that glows in the dark. It is blue-dark, green-dark in the swells of waves. Underneath the cold, dark, enchanted world the sea is full with life barely seen. It bears a different weight, a different gravity. Sometimes the beam of his waterproof light is refracted from beneath the water. She knows he is seeing the white suns of fish, the anemones.

There are creatures that thrive on darkness. He has become one of these. Some create their own light, like the ray and the shrimp and the plants at certain seasons. The light-makers. Thomas has not become one of these. For the most part his light intrudes, he invades. She wants to tell him that the creatures of the night do not want his light, but this is all the life he has right now, his going beneath. She doesn't want him to know she follows his descents and passages. For now, as he is awakening, he is a creature of night water.

Ruth knows he is practicing, like Witka and the other old whalers. As if he is trying against time to have the world back the way it used to be. He doesn't know some changes can never be reversed.

There are also the nights both of them remember facing the ocean, walking, looking at the tide pools. And with his memory he still sees black snails, kelp and its golden bulbs awaiting its return to the sea. Even on cold days he used to walk the beach out to Old Spirit Rock with Ruth. It was in the days before girls wore pants, so her legs were always cold and wet.

Old Spirit Rock was formed by a war between wind and land. It was a place the old people wouldn't go. At the very top, wind has shaped a hole into the rock and sometimes, when wind blows from the right direction, it is heard singing like a flute, sometimes a howl like the cannibal who wanted to swallow their people.

Some nights he holds himself to the wood, shining his light, looking, as if he would see Marco. Instead, on a ledge, is an orange starfish, the kind he loved as a child when he and Ruth were explorers together in the magic of the world, wandering the lines between land and water at the west end of a continent.

At first he stays down briefly, then longer every night, holding his breath until his veins might burst. He, Thomas, sees and touches the barnacles in the disintegrating wood pilings and posts, creatures closing and opening, like him. Many lives hanging, holding. He is where small fish take refuge in between the pillars, where the gobies live. Then, again he rises to the surface, gasping for air, cold after these moments gone from this world.

Ruth knows his alphabet, his syntax, his silent language. She feels him. His very skin cries out. When in the day it seems he does nothing, she knows something is taking place, even if it is invisible. Nothing is ever static. If he were a spiritual man he would one day emerge from his dark house like a prophet or saint, enlightened and shining. But for now, the closest he comes to this emergence is from the water and though his heart carries such a great weight you'd think it would pull him down. For him it is the only time he feels unburdened.

While at first Thomas wishes he could remain forever, that he could drown, instead he begins to see the beauty of the water, the thickness of life.

Some nights, he enters this world only for a minute at a time, then longer, and there is happiness for that time, or peace, at least. He descends the way a chambered nautilus does in daylight only not so deep and far.

Ruth counts the seconds. Not much later, a minute, then even longer. It ran in his family, she thinks, even her Marco.

If it rains and Ruth is cold out there in the rain, she leans against the rail and pulls her coat tight. On a clear night, she looks not just at him but at the moon path and the shine of natural light, a manta ray in the distance or floating blooms of plankton. Some nights, when she catches sight of something shining, she feels happy and smiles.

Maybe she loves him still. You'd think so since she watches over him so carefully. They say love is the closest thing to hate.

That saying was created by someone who knew little of the many layers of emotions, she thinks.

He is the reason why there are nights now she is on land instead of asleep in her fishing boat where she is accustomed to waking and beginning her day early in the morning, before dawn, setting out to fish.

"You need your sleep," her mother says. "It's dangerous work you do. You can't afford to follow him around at night or take him food. You are paying for that food. You are getting dark circles."

"He's still my husband."

"Some husband." Silence.

Yet they both remember how Ruth's father, their spiritual leader, had made their marriage whole. Ruth with shell earrings down to her chest. They were at the sea. Ruth had woven her own hat of fine grasses. Her father, with the same finely chiseled bones as Ruth, wore a scarf around his head. A dog peed nearby and Ruth laughed. She couldn't help herself. Her father said with a smile, "This should never be too solemn an occasion. The coming together of two people is to rejoice."

That night Thomas had looked at Ruth with love, her graceful form and happy eyes. Ruth looked at his beautiful—how else to describe it?—blue-black hair and wide face. The feast was salmon cooked in wide leaves that had no name in English. Everyone was there.

And then he came home one day and he had joined the army.

"We are warriors," he said.

"But you need to be here with your people. You have a wife," her father said. He was dismayed at the decision of Thomas.

Maybe it didn't count anymore, tribal worlds, marriages.

Now, instead, he has a Medal of Honor, a Silver Star, his Purple Hearts, all on ribbons, something for bravery under fire, bronze, stripes and things she doesn't understand, and they

were sent to his father when his dog tags were found, also a
folded flag. They were all kept inside his father's glass case.
She didn't know what any of them meant, just that they were
honors and his father carried them around and never missed
a chance to show them off to anyone nearby, no matter how
often. His father, with large carver's hands and a rough face
that was a book of his history. An ugly-hearted man who created beauty. He'd carved the faces of Ruth and her father into
near eternity and then sold them at a gallery. He didn't seem
to grieve the son he lost. He was proud of his son's medals. He
went drunk to the ceremony for his son's memorial.

But she watches Thomas, her hands in her jeans pockets, alert,
in case he falls into trouble. She is bound to him for life in
ways neither of them understands. She is a strong swimmer,
prepared to dive down and save him. He could hold his breath
longer than her, but he was a weak swimmer then and now
he has aged.

How strange, that he goes into the water nights—he who
was born on the day the octopus walked out of the sea and into
a cave on land. And peculiar, too, that at his age he is trying to
do what his grandfather had done, like all the tribe's men had
once done as boys, seeing how long he could hold his breath
underwater—diving after treasures on the bottom, old spoons
found from whaling vessels, coins, once a pair of glasses that
belonged to a Brit from a whaling ship. Ruth knows the stories
of disasters on ships that entered these unpredictable waters or
found themselves butted up against the rocks in a storm. Then
there were the Americans who shot at the rocks that looked
like sea lions, only to have their bullets return, sinking them.

But it is not strange at all. This man underwater among
urchins and jellyfish, in kelp forests bending, is seeking to
return to before the history of the white man's whaling ship. It
is instinct. He wants to go back, to understand the old ways, if
not to live them. If they are ever to be whole again, his people,

her people, he will do it right. For whatever reason he has taken this on.

Ruth recalls when the whales migrated by in the past when she and Thomas were children. Great numbers of them, spouting water, rainbows in the mist of their breath. On the northward journey would be the infants, small, dark, shining. Everyone watched their passage, the tails up from water, the spray, the descent.

Her mother had seen the last one killed in the traditional way, that day Witka came out of the water dripping seaweed. They found a harpoon made of stone in that gray whale and it had been there for at least a hundred years. Everyone was surprised. Then there was an absence of whales, as they avoided the place for a while after that.

Thomas has locked himself away, a bent man. Witka's place is now the right place for him.

By the time he surfaces the last time, he is blue with cold, thousands of particles around him, in his light, each one something alive, phosphorescent. He pulls himself up, an awkward heave, difficult to lift his own weight. Ruth looks back and she sees him wrap the blanket around himself. He has never seen Ruth watching. Even if there is dew, he never sees her footsteps; he doesn't look that closely at the world any longer.

He loves the blue-dark, but he doesn't see it as his ancestors did. He no longer sees the jellyfish as the ocean pulse or heartbeat. Instead, one night, he sees them as parachutes floating men down from a plane or copter, revealing some poor man's whereabouts before he even had a chance to land alive. A sky full of them. It was beautiful when he first saw it until he realized anyone could see them. Then there were the quick rescues, surprise attacks, men climbing ladders in the sky the way he'd heard angels did.

OUT THERE

Thomas hears the ocean and he remembers the river. During the dry season it was a lazy river on its journey to what he thought was the Delta. Even during the day now at Witka's, Thomas hears the ocean "out there." Out there. The words remind him of what the old man said, the man who seemed to be the chief of the village or shantytown where Thomas stayed and remained.

There was a coastal city upriver somewhere. Some of the goods came from there, others from water by sampans and brown boats. But they lived on flatter land, with rice paddies fed by the water. He had a map. He looked at it, trying to figure out where he was. He'd studied the legend. *Legend*. It was a good word for kilometers and miles, things covering space. As if the world was merely a story, and it was, one story laid down over another. As it was in his older country, too.

It was so many years ago now, but he envisioned the women he once saw on a rarely traveled yellow dirt road. They were drying rice on the road and at first he saw them with some fear. They gazed at him, also, like small forest deer, watching a man standing with a rifle. The rice covered half of the road. It was the only flat, dry place where the newly born sun would dry their crop. A child on a bicycle traveled by, eating fruit, bumping along the edge of the road to avoid the grain. The women watched him, one bold enough to have her hands on her hips. The boy nodded, smiling. He tossed down the fruit seed. His bicycle wavered into the ditch. Thomas wanted to plant the seed. It was hope. It was a future. He wanted a future to grow in this place made so nearly desolate by bombs, craters and burned woods.

Thomas had no idea how he'd come across the women drying rice on the road. Or, later, how he'd fallen asleep, too asleep, there in a makeshift village, one of many.

But there he cried without crying, just salt water running down his face. He was too hardened to cry, or at least he thought that way. Nevertheless the ocean of the body flowed. Then an old woman in a neck scarf sang to him. When he looked at her she smiled and he saw compassion in her eyes, in her wrinkles and dark teeth, and he thought of what she'd seen all her life. Damn, but he could feel it coming from her and that's what made the rivers flow, and yet she had it in her to smile and gaze, compassion like one of the Buddha shrines they'd seen along the way, and he began to sob.

There were bodies burning. He could smell them. A woman woke him. He was sweating. "Drink," she said. It was some kind of rice water. No, it wasn't burning bodies. It was a fire burning and something was being cooked. He didn't want to eat. He turned his head away.

He was not injured, but he seemed to be. He slept as if he couldn't wake. Or wouldn't, but finally the woman woke him and she looked familiar. She used a sea sponge on his face. "There," she said, and went back to weaving a mat. Next time she put a rag on his head and left it. It was wet and cool. Ice. He thought of Ruth at home, weaving. He thought about Ruth's long black hair, falling over her shoulder, him pushing it back. He remembers pushing it away from her face even when she was a girl and they'd been out running on the beach. He must be an old man now, he thought, because that was a century ago.

When he woke the second time there were some boys in the room, running about with sticks and yelling.

"What?" he said, as if they were speaking.

They were trying to chase a cobra. The boys were sweating. "They come by boat." They came close to the snake, then backed off.

"On the boats?"

"Done move. Done get up."

No. They come on the boats. Then they come here. He listened. They spoke in a dialect he didn't recognize. It was not distinctly northern, not southern, and he was good at languages.

It was a beautiful creature, the cobra, when he saw it. The high wide neck like a pair of wings.

This had once been a country of snakes. Who knew now? The poor people were gleaning rice fields that shone like mirrors of the sun with water, and cobras lifted their puffed heads looking for rabbits or rats and shelter. They were hungry, too.

He wants to remember what happened to the cobra. Rabbit, he remembers.

Someone shot a rabbit when they were struggling through the jungle. How long ago? It was softly furred, with dark eyes, and running to hide. He cried. He who never cried. And then as they traveled through the next village they tried to destroy the rice before the NVA approached. After trying to burn it, and failing, because it wouldn't burn, they contaminated it with chemicals. He wondered, now, if anyone had ever grown hungry enough to eat it. He was upset by all of this. In his world, his old world, these things were not done, but now he knew worlds overlapped, many of them, as if they were transparent pages in a book. One world held fog, and whales were swim-

ming across it, as was a tribe, a nation, his own. Then spread
across it were boys without wisdom, layered over the once-
beautiful world with fire and chemicals.

His men killed the termite mounds which he thought most
beautiful, like the land itself, and the termites would immedi-
ately begin to save the young and rebuild. In the same way the
people tried to put their lives back together again and again,
moving to a new place, going to the water if bombs were near,
leaving if bombs were at the water, knowing there were land
mines, trying to divine where they were, sometimes succeed-
ing. And he protested the destruction.

But, then, he was with a people. He was again part of a people. Thomas never asked how these people survived. Or even
where they came from. Above where they lived were the
remnants of an old building, a once-beautiful house of concrete, painted yellow and blue. The walls were down, rubble
all around. There had been an exquisite painting on one inner
wall, a painting with hills of green and trees. The place had
been fenced in once, but the fence was gone now. And down
below it, their little village was a makeshift place, put together
with debris from the war-broken world. There were washed-
up things from the river and they were sometimes used to build
or patch up other things. Below them, the houses were built
on stilts, but he didn't think the river could rise that high. The
old man with blue cloth around his head, tied in a knot at the
side, said to him, "We are not Vietnamese. We are people from
the mountains." From the highlands, he thought, the "Armpit."
Or was it the place where everyone killed everyone, even their
own soldiers if they moved wrong or scared a man by surprise,
or if they hated him. And he wondered if they hated him. He
thought they were misplaced and he was lost, or had been, in
Muong country. But these were people of the earth and they'd
survived. Like him. A tribe, or what remained of one. Now
there were silent, empty villages in the mountains. The Tigers

had been there. It's what they called themselves, the airborne men who instead of being in the air swept across the land, destroying everything they came upon because it was a war.

The old man with the blue cloth said, "You look the same, like us. Ugly."

Thomas laughed.

The old man's face was red with lines and scars. He kept a cloth for wiping the sweat off his forehead. It was blue in color, lovely against his forehead and then against dark hands and blue veins. Every night the old woman washed it along with one of the two scarves she always wore around her neck, even in the heat, in the wooden tub. "We had to come here," the man said. "We learned to make friends. Some of us went to Saigon. Now we feed the enemies even when we know who they are, but we have never smiled behind their backs. Up there . . ." He pointed to a village Thomas couldn't see, its distance impossible to gage. "Up there, they hate us. They say, take sides or you lose your heart." He laughed. "They mean in two ways."

The old woman gave Thomas a cup of strong sweet coffee. "We used to have more beers."

Thomas laughed, but weakly. He realized it was an underground restaurant they'd been trying to run. Noodles and beer. He looked around. There were signs in several languages. Outside were places to sit, a few chairs and two tables, a single, broken umbrella. It was a half-bent store where they also sold Tide, Crest, Marlboros, and other American products bought by those who had once worked in the PX, the army store, including a young woman named Ma. He'd seen her before somewhere. Those who did come by to eat noodles or drink beer saw what a shambles their lives had become, felt sorry for them, and left extra money for their purchases.

Thomas didn't ask where the beer came from. It was American. Coors. Bud. Or the cigarettes. Where these things might

have been scared him. But he did lift his head one day and say
to one of the kids, "Where the hell do you get the ice?"

"Out there."

Later he saw that they went to the river to get it. It was
delivered by a brown boat with a sail the color of a tobacco leaf.
The beer, too. He watched the young boys walking down with
skinny legs and returning later, carrying things back, him all
the time thinking where they went was unsafe, that there were
sure to be mines, and thinking also, how could he trust them,
even though they were the people he'd saved, but he did, he
trusted them, the ones who reminded him of his own world.

"Still," said the man, sitting, putting his straw hat beside
guava fruits and flies, "it's been a sad place and life's been hard
for us. Out there."

Thomas lived day by day, one after the other, aware that he
was missing. There were mists from the water and it was cold
at night, but the daytime sun was sometimes fierce except
during monsoon season when blue-black clouds and thunder-
storms moved across the world, casting shadows and shafts of
darkness. It was like his dreams without the sound of roaring
jets and fire, just black smoke.

A guava tree was near the bridge that had been bombed
and no longer crossed the river, and next to the village was a
bamboo stand, a forest of them, green with light. They bent in
the strong winds, but even then he heard the frogs and sometimes he saw ghosts in there, but he never mentioned them
because everyone there saw ghosts. The land was peopled by
them. These were silent ghosts, merely standing. One wiped
his forehead as if he were tired, weary, as if a ghost could not
ever lie down and die.

When the river flooded, it shone with light and he thought of
home. The houses on stilts were up to their thighs in water.

The river at night shone with the lights on it. If the flood was unusually high, people left their doors by rafts, some painted in beautiful colors, blues and pinks with designs on them and words written for safety. When he looked, he wished for the spray of whales. "Where I lived we had whales," he told the man.

"How terrible. I've heard of them."

He saw the river at night with all the lights on it. People passing.

The river flowed by. So did time.

It would have been impossible to name the place, if it had a name. Most places didn't, being new settlements. Besides, all the names ran together. He'd been in too many places. The airborne dropped men here and there. The maps changed with every bomb and battle and raid. Forests were gone. Towns were lost, corpses taken away, towns were renamed and the names would stick.

When he tried to decipher his vicinity, the closest he could come finally was that he was in the South, somewhere on a river that ran into the Delta of the halved country. Much of it had been occupied by troops, infiltrated, destroyed, and deserted. When his major had looked at the maps and charts and said they weren't that far south, Thomas finally went by feeling, like you could when the enemy was near. After a while, you could feel their presence, the silence of them. Something spooky, and it was nearby and you didn't want to breathe.

He had been afraid. Some soldier, he thought. On the ground, using a flashlight allowed him to see, but it also allowed him to be seen so he became still and waited, trying not to move, to breathe, to itch. He wanted to die at first and get it over with. To just be gone, to shoot himself. But then why not wait and take someone with him? Maybe someone evil or trying to kill a child or a friend. The smell of this war was not right. He remembers it still, of human flesh, chemical, smoke, cordite,

napalm, fear. Cordite and rich, oily orange. It remained in his
nostrils for years in San Francisco.

At first they never saw the consequences of their actions
except fire, streaks of light, holes in the ground like craters of
the moon. Then they were on the ground and after a while
they even stopped complaining about it because there was
so much fatigue Thomas could barely drag himself until he
heard a sound in the leaves. Then the energy came, adrenaline. His heart beat faster. Over time he'd seen the advantages
the enemy had over them: They didn't need gear, they didn't
need anything but what they could glean from the dead and
fallen, the trees, the strips of bamboo, even a tossed-away can.
With those things they devised weapons and traps and they
fought the war. They, who had won every war with almost
nothing but cunning and the knowledge of their own land,
the Chinese boats they tempted up a river at high tide only
to leave them stuck on posts in the water, to sink when the
tide went out. They had beat the French, also, with patience
and fortitude, pulling and pushing their weapons up hills that
the French believed impossible to climb. Thomas tried to think
like Them. Finally Thomas needed, like Them, to be light in
order to survive. He put a knife in his pocket, one in another
pocket, his rifle ready. Two grenades. He kept a tin of food
and other items in his pockets. By leaving other things behind
he walked easily, he could have hidden away in the forest or
jungle, soundless, from where they walked. But the Sergeant
above him said, "Carry it or we'll shoot you now before you
die later on your own." They were wrong. On the ground, in
the sky, anything would kill you. It didn't matter what you
wore. The water was the enemy. The trees were Cong. The
earth was a bomb. The rain was dangerous. And you had to
be prepared to kill anything faster than it killed you. So he
picked it all up and then left a little along the way when no one
watched him. It was a trail here and there that could have led
straight to them, but he'd already thought of that and tossed

items to the sides. He knew the enemy always watched. They were there when his men walked by. He saw a face appear now and then from the leaves, then disappear. It was eerie. It was crazy as hell, he thought. Really, it *was* hell. Then he'd heard an owl in a tree and it reminded him that somewhere there was a normal world. If anyone shot it he would kill them. He also thought maybe later people would fish from the bomb craters. Or swim in them. In places that now looked like the moon. Maybe things would become almost normal again one day, except for the bodies, the graves, the grief, the calculations and manipulations that had to be made for survival.

One day he stopped still. He was going through the still-remaining jungle without his things and he came to a tree with glasses, cups of china on its branches. Someone lived there, but where would they get the cups and blue bottles? They even had a teapot. It was their kitchen hidden in the jungle where it was easy to disappear and hide a foot away from everything and anyone. He could not wait around to see who lived there, if they were dangerous, if he should shoot them. He was touched by this and his heart hurt, but he disappeared quickly by ducking down and getting away as fast and silent as he could. He became a snake in his movement, a lizard with his eyes, seeing, seeing. He thought like a lynx. He was covered at times in mud and he thought it was good, it kept him unseen, the insects away, and he wandered into mists not knowing what would be there, just feeling with a part of himself he'd never known as he entered darkness. His body had eyes. His back had eyes. His fingers had eyes. But so did the trees, the leaves, the moss and stone.

Because he was a lynx and snake, the other men began to tease him and call him a "brave." The sergeant gave up on him and called him the walking dead. He was already decorated and promoted, though god knows he didn't care. He'd won a medal for saving a man. Now he tried to sleep in trees and pretty soon they thought maybe it was smart, not carrying all that shit. But he also knew when to dig in. Maybe they joked, but they knew in truth he could feel what was there. He could feel what was around and so everyone followed him and if he stopped, they took cover.

His thirst was constant even though he breathed water. It was hard to see through the smoke of things burning, but there were the skeletons of trees, of homes once with large doors and gardens, of people now in huts somewhere, or dead.

They made fun of the dead, sitting them up with a canteen and cigarette in mouth, spreading their legs, and he, Thomas, felt nervous about it. Men at home didn't touch the dead. It wasn't permitted. He felt singled out because they knew he didn't like it, because they had instincts there they hadn't felt before and they could read a man's mind and face. He looked at the plants. Even the roots destroyed. The trees turned over. He thought nothing would grow back in that world. It went against every-thing that was in him. Thomas, the grandson of Witka, who respected life, grieved.

His own comrades were leery of him.

"You're a sorry excuse for a man," said someone. And every-one looked at each other and laughed.

Anyone could see the Americans coming, hear them, even smell them, but they had force on their side, and machines. Fire. Bombs. But not the intelligence of living on that land. If they jumped out of a chopper in daylight, they were targets. If they jumped at night, they had dye so they could be seen by each other, but then they could be seen by anyone else "out there," and out there was everything, everywhere, the sur-rounding heat of noon sun, the dark silences of night.

They traveled in the copters and they set down in many places. He ran into Dwight in Da Nang and Dwight said, casu-ally, almost his first words a lie, "Your father's sleeping with Ruth, you know." And then he said, "Hey. Have you heard this isn't a war? That's what the president says. Did you know Lenny, my cousin, is here now doing body bags? Counting 'em."

Thomas thought of how his father had always wanted Ruth and all around him the men were losing their wives and lovers, getting letters of betrayal and loss.

Dwight had always been jealous of Thomas, a small part hating him, his buddy, his friend. Thomas never knew it. "Okay, well, see you, bud," Dwight said, throwing boxes and bags of food into a plane. "Don't come back in a bag." Thomas waved down at him as they left, feeling pain, grief, doubt, his body wracked not by the war this time, not by what he saw daily, but by what he imagined from Dwight's words. They grew like a strangling jungle plant from a seed.

Then he didn't know if Dwight was still alive. Dwight had CARPET BOMB written on his helmet. Thomas's father always had his way with women. Thomas had trusted Ruth. Now he doubted her. But no, she wouldn't do that. But then, other men's women were betraying them every day. Dwight's words lived. Words have their way of living on long after the breath, long after a history, long after.

At first when Thomas arrived he prayed to the creator with tobacco. Then he believed only evil existed. The Firmament according to Thomas's new understanding of the world: And god created good and evil. God created jungle law. In the darkness of the void, god created water and it fell from the sky and he created evil and he created fire and it fell from the sky and the earth was full of fire and black mists mingling with black smoke and jungles of beauty and forests in which a man could be trapped. He said, Let there be and it was. Let there be man and there was the enemy standing right before you. Let there be light and it fell from the sky with great beauty and with the power to kill. Let there be daylight and there was morning with bodies all across earth in positions unimaginable. Let there be mountains and let there be weapons that devastate them. Let there be animals that roam earth and the men will kill them. And god created the North Vietnamese and the South Vietnamese, the Americans, and eventually he would create the Khmer Rouge, and the capacity for men to torture others and to laugh about it.

He had been watching keenly the split in the human heart, including his own. He took to the airfield and with orders to report to one of the worst places in the world. When they arrived he found himself seeing a river of blood and he was sick with it and the smell of gas, napalm with its ceaseless burning. God created it and what kind of a creature was this god, and he was afraid at first, then he hated, and then he was no longer Thomas. Monster. That's what he was with brother M16 and AK and grenades. What a family he and his weapons were together. There was always a tumble of events and he was too tired to remember them except for the flies which god also created.

And Major God said, "Here, give the guys these green hornets." Amphetamines to keep them going. The arc lights so beautiful, one guy said, "Wow. Would you look at that one?" Then there were the heavy clouds of smoke. "It's us. Goddamn. And they are firing on us! Where'd they come from?"

"And I thought I saw Them coming up from the ground. I don't believe it."

Then there was the new boy on the block. Michael the new kid lost his glove and had tender hands and so that hand was sore. They had to wade through water. No one had counted on that. This made their fine boots crack, their feet, too, and they hurt all the time and you'd never really get used to it, but they did. "Shit, man, this hurts like a son of a bitch."

"Yeah, that's to remind you you're still alive." Another joke they had, America's least wanted. "And we're the airborne, too."

Then there was the downpour of the monsoon and flooded trails they slipped from. There was the heaviness of clothing that was wet and the smell of sweat and fungus and infections of men injured and growing more infected. And someone, some fucker, stole morphine from the medical supplies and Thomas pointed his gun and said who did it but no one confessed and what could he do? Maybe the thief needed it more. He made one man search the others. Hey, we don't have to take orders from you. You're just a grunt like everyone. But they did because he looked, really looked, like he would shoot them, but it was nowhere. There were only rations, toilet paper, crackers and tins. They hadn't been to camp in so long they thought they were deserted. No music. No cards. No cooked food or cold beer. No mail planes any longer.

Then it was nearly over, they were at the end of it all, of what was supposed to be a short-stand recon mission. They were sent there suddenly and never told why. The map. He took it with him. They were in the copters. Dropping down. It looked like they were leaving their bounds, he thought. He yelled something about it to the pilot. "We're lost or something. Look." Showing the map. The pilot said, "Shut up. Go back and sit down, soldier."

They went now against their will, in silence, the men believing they were in the wrong place. No, feeling it. But Murph was crazy and he said, "It doesn't matter. I don't discriminate. I'm going to take out every living thing wherever we are. This is search-and-destroy. They told me."

Helicopter had been a good man, but now Thomas was aware of everything all at once and he felt awake like he saw it, really saw it. Only the new boy Mike was still sane, but he was green and new, and he looked afraid and eager both at the same time. Jesus, why'd they send him with them? What were his chances?

Then they were in the wrong place. There were no men there, just women and children and elders, and no place around there for men to hide except a bamboo stand and down a ways under the bridge. Just rice paddies. "Where are the men?" Thomas asked the people who were there. The others looked around. Their plans of action were never perfect, but this was too far less than perfect. There were no Cong there, not that he could see or feel, and not even any weapons that they could count, and everyone was scared and crying. It was the wrong place. Thomas felt it all along. They'd fixed it as an enemy camp and instead they found scared faces and no northern dialects. He knew the dialects. Now they were gods if they wanted to be. They were deciding gods over all the inno-cent people, the mothers covering their children, the crying, the ones staring down, waiting for what came next. His men were the ones who decided life or death.

"Oh yeah!" said Murph. "Look at that girl." He walked toward a young girl.

Someone else began to light a fire to the "hootch," which was really a temporary building the people had made of found items.

"Stop!" Thomas yelled. "There's no one here."

"Hey, you know you can't even trust a baby."

Everything happened too quickly and then when he fired that day, no one fired back. They just looked at him. He can still see the surprised look in their eyes, Murphy after the girl. He was surprised, too. He didn't think he could do something that fast, that unable to be changed, restored. Or did he just think they were surprised because it had all happened and there was no decision to it? Everything there always happened too quick or too slow. There was no normal time in war. And having that finger on a rifle or an automatic—it was all too easy. Then he recalled the dirty faces of the men, the helmet under which he sweated. Sweat. They could smell each other, the fear on each other. He hadn't believed you could smell fear. You could smell it, a stench strong as anything else created by bodies.

Thomas pushed Mike to safety, Mike, the fucking new guy,

they called him, who watched everything wide-eyed and in shock, but he hadn't even worn a helmet, just an olive drab scarf of torn cloth like he'd seen some bad war movie and Thomas saw his head hit something. Afterward Thomas never forgot him. Mike disappeared. Thomas saw only the afterimage of his blue eyes, light blue, frightened. Maybe he ran. Probably he died out there because there was fire all down the hill, even the water of the rice paddies seemed to be on fire and the river was burning.

Then the Americans dropped down and searched for them. They found the bodies, what was left of them, and found Monster's dog tags with all the rest and found a deserted, burned village.

At Witka's, Thomas covers his face with his hands. Then he goes out to the water and drops himself in. Dwight sees him when he's on the way home.

"Hey, you're all wet."

"I went for a dip."

"Don't kid me. You fell in. So, are you gonna go to DC and see the Wall? You should come. Where are you staying? Your dad doesn't answer the door, so we haven't been able to find you."

"I'll catch up with you later." He wondered what they knew. Damn the travel agent.

Back at home in the dark, he remembers leaving this place he'd been from since all his ancestors had carried him through their cells, then flying over, seeing water and the reflection of the sky in water, then clouds and waking to green, green land. Brilliant green, colors he had never seen before. He looked down from where he was flying at the clouds piled up high.

Once in his life there was rice. Now there are black stones in the water, whales. But something was starting to grow again as if it hadn't heard the story of what the world was aboveground.

The whale hunt set off his memories. He needs to speak them over and over again and he realizes he is telling Witka. Witka's spirit in his house, the spirit of the old man who still lives there:

"Lots of them were like that," Thomas says. "Sometimes the men just fired, heard a sound, saw anything move, and fired. Like what happened to us."

He tells about the way they had no shelter and ate rotten food. "I felt only fear, and I wished I had the courage to shoot myself so I did not have to witness it, and I would have, too, except I knew someone else would do it for me."

He'd felt terror, then the need for survival, then nothing, then hatred.

He omits a part of it at first. But Witka knows. And Thomas knows that Witka knows. To be a hero you always have to betray something or someone. Witka forgives him but Thomas doesn't feel forgiven yet.

"Don't get me wrong," he says. "There were good men, good men." He read about the attempts to rescue American POWs and MIAs. He'd been one. "Some real good men." But mostly now he hates everybody, as if the whole world were to blame for the rain and the flooding, the weight of his army clothes with rain and mud and his own thirst and sweat constant, always dripping and it was all in the line of duty, the way the world goes, really goes, leaves, and it was all only money in some people's pockets. How small men are to try to prove they are warriors, better warriors, better hunters. He says these things out loud.

"You know what the worst day is?" he says. "The worst day is the one before you go home because you think you have come this close, so near, and then you won't make it."

The A'atsika people hear speaking coming from the house. They avoid the place. Maybe it is haunted, the place where Thomas lives. The house talks at night and there are no lights.

It remains empty, they think, so why did he build a fence? But in daylight it is silent. Dead silent. The seals love the shade of the fence. They sleep there. He wants them to leave, but they are there like guardians, his relatives who watch over Thomas. Thomas who is a container of history, pain, convictions, beliefs, memory, sins, and courage.

So when he was found, so many years later, Thomas was the lone survivor according to the historical record, if there was a living record. Otherwise, Thomas was dead because he threw his dog tags down on the ground. Yeah, he thinks, I am alive and I am dead. He is history the way Dwight is civilization. But in war your life is at its height, watching for danger, wondering if you can make it to the next place, believing you can't. Sometimes not giving a shit. Sometimes too afraid. The mind wasn't built for this. Nor was the spirit. And always you know someone is watching you and they are thinking the same as you: Someone is out there. Something is there, and there is a boundary between self and self that is crossed only in a world like this. These are shadow-covered realms. A person watches himself when he is not himself.

Strangely, the thing he'd done that was dishonorable was the only, the most honorable thing he'd done the whole time.

He says, "I have a daughter there. I didn't want to leave her."

Now he is thinking about Lin and her mother, Ma. About when Lin was a baby. He sees Ma bending over her, her hair falling down over her face.

He is thinking about Lin when she is out there somewhere thinking about him.

LIGHT-YEARS

Years pass. Lin thinks she is maybe twenty-two now, or older. No one alive knows Lin's age, but her hands are still the hands of a girl, her face bright and delicate.

She pushes her black hair behind one ear. Where she sits it is quiet, a park where old people sit in daylight. From only a street away, she hears activity and noise, buying and selling, motorbikes and hawkers. A world is going on, lives being lived. She watches bats cross the body of the distant moon, and thinks she is as far away from her own blood as the moon is from earth. The bench where she sits is rock, old enough to be green in color, as in the cemetery. It was not destroyed by the war. There is a sweet smell. The road that is near her, behind the ginko trees planted by the Chinese, is the one that brought her from far away. It is larger now and traveled by automobiles, bikes, and without a sign of the people who once marched, ran, or died there. It is as if she'd traveled light-years and arrived now at a place where time and space intertwine. And in the dank scent of evening, the rich odors of old earth, they do. Her memory lives with the present as if it is all one, her village, the old ones, and this place, Ho Chi Minh City, Saigon.

But for now her father, too, is light-years away, and as she thinks of him she remembers more than she has told anyone. She was always one for memory. She remembers her life near the rice paddies and water. She remembers that he did not want to leave her. She knows that. She cannot blame him or be angry and so her feelings belong only to her. She remembers the day the dark machine came down from the sky. They'd been there before, but this time the men in uniforms showed up in the early morning at the funeral of Lin's mother, amid the smell of incense, the burning joss sticks. Strangely she does not remember everything about her mother's death, just the smells and the helicopter.

Always before when the machines arrived, they heard them cutting through the sky. There was time for her father to hide beneath the ground in one of the damp caved-in tunnels. She was afraid of the tunnels. She still smells them, sees the tree roots, the green molds and mosses growing. Underground, secret entrances known only by a few. Most of these had not held up because they were too close to water and the clay was poor. But some of the tunnels were numbered, mapped, and then later forgotten. The Americans never knew how much underworld the tunnels covered. They were known and forgotten by the North Vietnamese who had lived there, even cooked there. Later, the Communist Party with their insistence on a different kind of order did not even recall them.

Sometimes, too, before ambushers and thieves passed through, her father hid in one of the places where their food had been stored.

But that particular morning, her mother was dead. Her father had too much grief to think of hiding, maybe to even notice when they dropped down from out of the sky. The Americans were there to make him leave. To take him "home." When they tried to take him, he protested and fought them off, walking away from them. The village was his home. She still sees one of them reach toward him, her father's arms rising up out of the man's grip, his tight back as he walked away and back toward her, his child.

Lin doesn't know her mother was killed by a land mine while chasing Lin. There is no one left to tell her.

She doesn't know, either, that her father remembers the same day over and over. That he remembers how the old man in the village, the one who always smelled of lime and flowers from his meditations, postponed their departure. Maybe he thought Thomas would disappear if he distracted the captors. The old man put them off as long as possible, the blue cloth in his hand. The Americans were made to wait. Their impatience was obvious, a shaking leg, darting eyes, the way they exchanged glances. Thomas explained to them that this was how it was done on a day when everyone was grieving.

Lin remembers this now and thinks she is alive, but her mother, the maker of shoes, the onetime cashier, is not, and Lin forgets her at times. No one ever told her about the death of her mother. Whenever she asked why her mother would go into a minefield, they only said it was a mystery. "No," said Auntie. "Her favorite chicken went there and she was chasing after it."

The village people found ways to make the army wait. One man read a story. To do so was a gift, the soldiers were told. He did it slowly, translating to English. It was the story of the butterflies that had lived in the forests. The soldier-searchers were impatient. "It is a funeral," Thomas told the intruders again. His voice implied again how rude they were. "You must wait." He himself listened and cried. Now there were no more butterflies. No forests. Then another story was told. It was the story of a wise man and a wise woman who had survived the French. The wise woman always wore a red scarf around her neck. They called her Red. But then the wise man and woman were

taken into captivity by their allies and never seen again and
after they were gone, the village people, without the guidance
of these two, forgot to treat the world well. They neglected to
be kind to the birds, or greet the trees. They thought that was
why they were bombed by a fire god from the sky. Otherwise
the bombs would have turned into birds and flown away like
leaves in a wind. Soon there were no leaves, no birds except
one, and it dropped a red scarf over the village where the two
had lived, reminding those who remained.

Maybe, Lin thought at the time, this was why Grandmother,
the eldest woman, always wore a scarf around her own neck.
Later she learned it was to hide her scar.

Then some of the accounts of Thomas were recalled. At first
that included how well he fished for them. Lin didn't listen
well enough. She was still thinking of the story and the birds.
In her eyes she could see them as they once were.

And one man praised Lin's mother. Crying, he said, "Oh,
how well she made shoes. No one ever made shoes like Ma
did." Ma. Her mother's name. She, the girl, is named for her
mother's *real* name. Thuy Doc Lin had made shoes waterproof
by using the sap of plants no longer there, long since bombed.
Lin had a special pair. They were a bit too large for her so she
could grow into them, and she wore them anyway. Each one
had an artificial red flower on it.

But stories were their riches.

They even told the story of the horse that had come from
France and made it by boat to their village. They first worshiped
its beauty. Then the old man said, "I rode it everywhere I went.
I even rode it to Old Grandmother's house." Even though it
was a funeral, the people laughed because Old Grandmother's
house had been only a short distance away. Some remembered
the horse and how the man rode it in every possible position,
not by choice. In spite of themselves and the sad day, they
laughed. He rode it sideways, leaning over the neck with his

round face in the mane, thrown across the top, and he rode it
almost underneath, yelling as he went.

"What a scene that was!" said a tiny woman.

But it was a double sadness that day, a funeral and the taking
away of Thomas. The people were afraid they would take the
girl, too, and then afraid they wouldn't because they realized
the direction the war had taken when the Americans left and
maybe she'd live like a queen in America and maybe she'd be
killed in their world. So when she cried, "Papa," to him, they
told the Americans it meant "Uncle" in their dialect.

Oh, and they gave Thomas gifts to take back, a Mickey
Mouse watch—who knows where it came from?—a carved
box, a square piece of hand-dyed cloth, a bell, and even a
prized American baseball hat he didn't want to accept because
it meant so much to the owner. One by one, he was given
something small from each person there as the chicken still
boiled in the pot, the one chicken that would feed the multi-
tudes. Ma's chicken that was not killed by a land mine.

They set out the feast for the men, who looked at the food,
the chicken looking a little gray to them. Fortunately it was
only a tiny amount. The vegetables were sliced well but unfa-
miliarly. The rice was wrapped in what looked like leaves.

One said, "We just need to take him back. We don't have
time to kill. There's no time to eat." But they were talked into it
anyway and they ate little, mostly the rice which was less likely
to be contaminated because the water had boiled.

As they went to leave, her father turned and looked back
and as he did, they handcuffed him. "They act like he's a god
or something," said one of the Americans.

Then they left and Thomas watched until all grew small on
the ground. He wept. How could he not? Down there was what
he loved. His other world seemed dimensions away.

He cried the whole time even as he was taken up into the

wind. Lin remembers that, and the grasses moving in circles so hard, her hair blowing, the wind on her, a woman pulling her away. "Papa!" she yelled, crying. The noise was terrible.

"It's okay. He'll be back." Lin barely heard the words, but she believed them. All her life she'd been told she was the child of a savior, a beloved man, a man of great beauty and spirit, and that someday he would come back with the spirit they so loved. She believed them and waited with hope. She was certain each morning when she woke and washed her face in the bowl: *This day. This.*

For such a long time the small child, Lin, watched the sky for him to return. Her father the fisherman fed many villagers. One day he had come to Lin with a red koi from the river market and it was in a white bowl. She loved the fish. She stood beside roads. Waiting. Holding the fish in its bowl. Watching for him to come down the road. In her blue skirt, she stood outside in the rain and waited. It seemed everyone cried except for Lin who believed he would return and so she waited, smiling, watching. For nearly a year she watched.

Thomas, her beloved father, the man who had brought a red fish from the river to her, was taken away. This, the handcuffs, and the fish are her memories.

Right now she hates memory. She sees it often now, in the city, old men crying with their memories, and their memories so terrible, and they have to contain it all within themselves. Nevertheless, they sit together as friends and sometimes gamble, sometimes playing cards the Americans left behind, talking about small things, someone always saying, "You cheat!"

For her, memory always hurts. She has no memory of her mother. Sitting on the bench she tells herself there have been light-years since then, the days in the country by the river, but even so it is all here now like the light of a star traveling the night, and the bats catching insects in the light of the full moon.

• • •

Then, back then, they heard a new army was on its way and they had to leave the village. The old man, knowing he would die, sewed three things into Lin's jacket: the address of an uncle in Saigon, what is now Ho Chi Minh City, hoping the uncle was still there, and the address and photograph of her father now in the United States, along with a folded map. "This map. Be sure you keep it. It is important. It tells where we are."

When Old Grandmother set out, she took her chicken, a pot of flowers, and a teapot. It was more than she could carry and someone had stolen their cart. Lin carried the teapot and the fish her father had given her. Someone else took the flowers from the old woman. "Keep quiet," they were warned. At first they went down past the houses on stilts in darkness, thinking the water would be safer to travel, but then they saw the water was dangerous, too. Sampans burned and there was the sound of men shouting. "Hurry!" someone said, and they stepped into a boat and they tried to float away, but not far from there they came to a bend in the river. There even more boats were burning and things were floating where they shouldn't be, clothing on the water, shoes. It was so light from the fires, it was like daylight. Men and boys swarmed the little boats and rafts like ants that take over the other ants. She recalled hearing an infant cry, then suddenly stop. Its silence chilled her.

"Does it hurt when you die?" she asked her grandmother on the boat.

Her grandmother smiled and said, "No, and someday we'll all see each other again," because she knew already she would have to be left behind.

And then Lin was forced to leave. Old Grandmother said, "I will go back home. You go on. Go!" And Lin followed her orders, looking back at the small woman. It was just before her grandmother would be turned to light. The ant boys were swarming. They were like the ants she'd seen leave their hills to cover over an entire animal someone shot, or come through

a village in droves and enter everywhere while the villagers
tried to flee.

There was such confusion. A young man she didn't know
came and said to call him Uncle and she was made to go by
land. Already there was a trail, a train of people, animals, their
special things, their worn clothes and wagons and cages and
bottles, but they were walking again toward another loss. Lin
had only her goldfish now. The goldfish her father had brought
from the river market. She carried it in a tall glass now, one
she'd found.

On the way, Lin lost the young uncle who had warned them
about what was coming toward them. She lost him in a bomb
attack by the new boy soldiers. She looked back. Everyone
scattered. There were bombs with nails, with pieces of metal,
with fins. All around the girl, people screamed and bled in a
flurry of movement and sounds. There was confusion and running. She was certain her heart had been hit because it hurt so
bad and she cried.

The path had been changed from mud to dust and it rose up in
clouds as they ran. It would become mud again from the blood.
A young man picked Lin up to help her. He grabbed her under
his arm, but in the commotion and running about he fell and
she ran with terror after trying to pull him up and she couldn't
and finally she saw it didn't matter and left him on the ground,
another of her sins. Sins she couldn't have helped, like leaving Old Grandmother. Another young boy came. She looked
him in the face and waited for him to die, too, but he wore a
uniform. He looked at her with wide-open eyes for a long time,
then let her go.

She has told this to no one except now, later, to her husband,
older than she is by six years, and he becomes very silent.

Then she was alone. They did run. One of the new enemies,
as she then knew them, grabbed her, but she fell and escaped
and ran without knowing where.

Out of good fortune she believed given her by the shoes of her mother, she was thrown into a truck by someone. She, a child with no emotion on her face by then, no more tears, just unblinking eyes.

She stayed in the truck, curled up behind the others, and then began to cry as she realized her feet hurt. She wore the shoes but her feet hurt. Someone stopped the truck along the way and she smelled fear. Words were exchanged, but she didn't understand them from underneath all the human flesh. Someone was made to leave the truck. And somehow she was saved and traveled on, hearing gunshots, she, the girl with little legs and hands, the girl who wore her favorite red flowers sewn onto the tops of her shoes.

Later, even after the bottoms were worn out, she kept the shoes. They would touch the heart of a woman. Now, an adult, she still has them, in a cloth bag.

She was a child alone in the city, one of many such children. They walked in the city and back streets at first like ghosts. She had an uncle, but no one knew where he was. She unstitched her dirty jacket so carefully, leaving her father's picture and address and map still inside, removing her uncle's address, showing it to people, asking.

Most tried to avoid her as she seemed to wander aimlessly. A girl with a village face was bad luck. She was one of the Ugly People. She would be sent home or rounded up and reeducated or she would simply die on the street one night. Others who looked at the paper said they had never heard of such a street. Some said, "I don't read." Even the cyclo drivers who knew all the parts of town had never heard of this number or name.

Lin had a few coins, but at first she started her lost life in the city begging for food. "Please," she would ask a shopkeeper, looking at the soup or noodles or at the fried fish or a pastry wrapped in paper. Sometimes one took pity on her, but usually they sent her away, themselves too poor to give anything away, and too many beggars. Finally, she squatted down and thought hard and made a plan. She decided to stay on one street. Even hungry. She would make herself useful there. They would get to know her. She would make them want to keep her, to feed her, to give her small jobs. She used a broom that had been kept outside a shop which no longer existed and she swept the street made of old gray stones, the walkway, and picked up all the trash. After a while, she was noticed and recognized. Then, finding rags, old clothing, she began to clean the shopkeepers' windows. When the afternoon rains ceased, she wiped them dry, to a shine. "Hey," the woman at the florist shop called out. "Get out of here. Stay away from my window!" But this street was clean in a town half bombed and filthy. This one street where some of the communists had moved into the buildings upstairs and sometimes, when no one looked, one of them even tipped her. He looked like the young "uncle," the one who had been there so suddenly and then been killed. Later, she knew he must have fought for the wrong side then. There were too many sides.

Every morning, she woke from the tree where she lived, sometimes damp from rain. She combed her hair with a comb she had found that once belonged to an American. Then she went down on her short legs, already an ambitious girl, and swept the streets in front of all the half-surviving businesses. She was a small girl then, and young, with small dimpled hands. Those who saw her on the street and felt sorry for her didn't show it. They had their lives. And theirs were also sorrowful. She was a child among children and everywhere they walked were children. Sometimes they had an extra coin for her. Sometimes they didn't. There was no predicting when or what, if anything, decided it. They were all survivors there. No one thought about where she slept at night or what she ate.

The town had been broken and everyone was just trying to put their lives together again and even a child understood this.

Light-years away. This is what she tells herself.

She still showed everyone her uncle's address. No one knew of it. One kind man even searched a map of the city. Perhaps the street name had been changed. "To fit the regime, you know," he explained. "It's all changed."

And there *was* kindness. Daily the flower keeper's husband said, "Did you eat yet today?" He slipped her a piece of fruit, and down the street a grocer always gave her a hard-boiled egg. And the woman florist herself sometimes, in spite of herself, slipped her ginger candy, the woman with the square, angular jawbone, arranging the purple orchids, the flowers and green leaves, hurrying from the refrigerator to the ribbon, looking up as if she couldn't be too careful of the "new regime," even though the orders now were to renew their businesses. Most things that even hinted of the West had been destroyed and forbidden. Even haircuts and clothing, until it all changed again. But bread was still there. Lin longed for rice, but she settled for anything. The old man at the tea shop on the corner still kept different kinds of breads—the Americans had liked breads—and he gave Lin some of the sweet or still-fresh leftovers. She did well, she thought, with some of the businesses now encouraged by the new regime.

One day the husband of the florist gave her rice wrapped in a leaf. "Where do you sleep?" he asked. He wore a striped short-sleeved shirt. Behind him were flowers. The room smelled of hibiscus and plumeria. She sniffed the air, her eyes closed. She smelled the rice, then ate it, at first too quickly. In her memory was home, the aroma, the glint of sun on rice fields. And her mother.

But she told no one where she slept. She didn't want to be

taken away or found in the branches of her giant tree. Even those collecting the leaves for their own memories did not see her in her nest of branches. It was *her* tree, singing, creaking insects and all. She climbed quickly, like a monkey could climb. Still in the worn shoes made by her mother, she prided herself on that.

She only pointed in the direction of the park. And at night she walked to the other side of the street, the long way around, so he wouldn't know.

But he knew. He took this up with his wife.

"No," she said, a pencil always above her ear, her hair piled high. "No one is going to live in here. We hardly have room as it is. There are kids all over the streets. We would get caught. Who knows, we could be fined or worse. Here. Forget it and get on your bike and deliver these flowers. Here's the place." She handed him a map and note.

He held the directions, but continued to talk about the girl. "But on this street, who would tell? We all know her. She cleans it up so pretty and even that cruel boy above the grocery, he gives her a coin some days. I see him."

The woman set her jaw tight and waved him away.

Sometimes, too, a coin was slipped to her by the florist's husband who also stole from the money box for himself. Lin kept silent about this. They had a secret pact. He didn't tell that he helped her, she didn't tell that he went to the square and gambled with cards and dice. Sometimes he let her wash her hair so she wouldn't get lice like the others who lived out there on streets or alleyways. The woman herself was usually too busy to notice and perhaps, truly, she wouldn't have cared anyway, but the husband and Lin felt like conspirators and they enjoyed it. Nevertheless, the woman became suspicious when the man lost too much. The woman, thinking the missing money was because of Lin, said, "You give the girl money. Or maybe she takes it. I think she could be a thief."

"No. I don't. I give her nothing. She doesn't take it, either.

It was the boy," he lied. "He came in today. I had to pay him again not to break the windows."

"Ai, him again."

But Lin thought the woman knew more than she said.

And yet Lin had the soft palms of a child and a sweetness about her and the woman softened now and then, and gave her a meal with sweet rice and sometimes mango.

Because of the kindness and persistent pleading of the shop-keeper's husband, Lin was given a job at the flower shop cleaning. She cleaned the dark green doorway. She cleaned up the leaves and petals that fell on the yellow floor.

"Sometimes I think of her as a niece," the man said.

His wife did not smile at this. She thought of her own daughter, the one now killed.

Then one afternoon as it rained and while they were closed for their afternoon naps, Lin fell asleep on the floor of the shop in the back room and she had a dream and began screaming and she cried like a child.

The woman went to her. "It's all right. Shh." Then she saw her shoes, her feet showing through the bottom, cracked and scarred and looking sore. She began to think, for the first time, of the girl's history, and for the first time, that Lin was just a child, a very young child, not a threat or a problem. She considered where she might have come from, what she might have seen. One part of her thought, well, hadn't they all? But then, instead of thinking that the girl, like everyone else, was just another taker, a small contriving adult, the woman picked her up and held her against her heart, feeling a movement of her own grief, how small Lin was, a girl like her daughter had once been. Now only a picture on her altar. The man watched, his own eyes with tears, thinking of the child they had lost when the communists stormed Saigon and everyone tried to escape.

"She sleeps in the park," he said. "I think she came from the Delta. I think she escaped the Khmer. Maybe she's from Cambodia and not where I think. I can't be sure, but I think I see them in her eyes at times. I see the face of Buddha."

"Don't say that word."

Soon the flower woman decided to keep Lin in a corner of their space, "Over here. Over here." She sounded impatient. "You sleep there." She arranged a mat on the floor, a covering, losing her pencil in it.

One night Lin found a new pair of shoes beside the mat on the floor. They were only plastic and they were white, but they fit and she was happy. She tucked her other shoes in beneath her little pile of things and then one day the woman left her a pair of pants.

Yet Mrs. could change without notice. Again one day, she said, "I think the girl is taking money."

"No, no." Finally, her husband sat down and confessed. "It isn't her. I am the one. I take the money some days."

"What? You? You are just lying to protect her."

"No. I admit it, I go play cards. It's only a little money."

"You monkey! You idiot! You waster!" She picked up the broom as if to chase him away, but then put it back down. "Maybe you need to work harder. Now Lin will deliver flowers. You clean."

As a child, Lin grew too fast and her bones ached. The florist, wearing her hairnet, soothed her knobby knees with a Chinese liniment in a green bottle. When that didn't work, she used a Korean oil. It was a bottle that came in a tin because the cap leaked in every single bottle. On the front of it was a girl that looked like Lin, with black bangs. Still Lin hurt. And the woman decided it was chemicals from the war, or the poison smoke, because Lin was from the country. Again her compassion bloomed like her plants. Until she misplaced a ring or bracelet, and then she would think once again that Lin was a thief.

Eventually Mr. arranged a heavy cloth curtain and also a doorway with a deluge of green plastic beads hanging down to separate Lin from them.

Lin was paid a weekly amount. She delivered flowers and she cooked. At night she studied English.

As Lin grew older the flower woman, her back bent a little more, gave her a little more space separated by a piece of cloth the color of lilies and fine enough that a breeze carried the scent of flowers to her mat. The curtain moved and, as they napped in the afternoon, she watched the cloth in the air change colors like a cloud, and watched its soft movement. She thought, as she daydreamed, as she dozed, of her father. She lay on her side and sometimes took out his picture, quietly, so as not to be heard.

She went to secret classes at night. She had a hunger for knowledge. Because there were no schools, they met nights at the teahouse on the corner. Dr. Bread-baker, she called the man who had been a soldier once, taught English, reading, and writing, even algebra with the missing equation. Someday she would go to her father. They could not know who her father was. It would change their view of her to know that she was half American. She felt guilty about this. When she saw the other children of American fathers who had no place to stay, no food, she gave them coins and hard-boiled eggs.

She was bamboo, growing so fast, so lovely, so fluent you could read all of it on her narrow face, all her feelings and languages. There were old songs inside her, and the sound wind makes as it passes through the bamboo forest.

She remembered, later, on the afternoons she rested, some of them. She remembered the line of people on the road, having to leave with their babies and goods. She remembered leaving her grandmother crying in the boat, Grandmother with a pot of flowers and the chicken, something alive that she hadn't lost and thought she needed and Lin with her fish. She cried when she remembered this. But no one knew if they were "Yards" who assisted the Americans, communists, or ordinary villagers and whichever, they were threatening to any of the groups, as if there had been no such thing any longer as a simple human being, a villager. The child she had been was an enemy to someone. Everyone was one kind of enemy or another. Even a child, a little girl who carried a jar with a red goldfish in it.

The flower business grew. As it became more prosperous, they built a wall and even a door that opened and closed. Lin arranged her place just so, everything in order, a teapot and two cups, a jar of flowers, a pillow, her box of things, including her father's map and his name and address in America. Later the husband built Lin shelves for her things and added hooks for her clothing. Sometimes Lin made enough extra money at tips and small jobs that she could buy a Coca-Cola or, better, a silk blouse. Lin grew. She loved the returning forest and as she grew older she went there each day in the morning mist. Tall and narrow, with a single braid of black hair, she walked into the clouds. She returned looking radiant. Everyone noticed her. They saw her beauty.

"Isn't our Lin lovely?" said the old man to his wife as she lavished cream on her face.

"*Our* Lin." She snorted, unable to admit to herself her own feelings for the growing girl. And yet one day, a year or so back, she had gone to Lin's mat and put her arm around the sleeping girl and cried into Lin's hair. Lin heard her sobs.

In the hot afternoons after they closed down for a rest, all would bustle again. It rained. The streets ran with water. Now and then she'd still see an ox. Work lasted until night when everyone visited with their neighbors and talked about each other, how Doc Thin Yu's daughter had come home, and how well they had done for the day. Even if they lied about it, even if their business was on the edge of broken, they said, "We had an excellent day."

"Ours, too, was very good."

The bread-baker had been a scholar once. A professor. She learned from him, even when school was still against the law in the changed world. At his place she looked at the globe. She closed her delicate eyes and she pointed. Turkey. She wanted to go there, and she would because, above all, in her softness, her greenness, she was stubborn and willful. She pointed again. Midland, Ohio. Maybe not. But then perhaps it was exotic. Perhaps it was close to her father. How she wanted to see him. But for now, she was happy enough riding her bicycle through city streets, getting off and pushing it, seeing the look of happiness pass over someone's face when she delivered flowers for her boss woman, and looking at everything there was to see, women washing the windows of shops or cleaning the walk in front, green forcing its way through old stone.

Lin liked to watch the people mostly, a woman rushing by with a new haircut and a plastic bag of something no doubt beautiful in her slender right hand. Ho Chi Minh City, Saigon, had changed.

And then she'd enter the trees and stop, enchanted. She walked the bike through this world. The trees were her place. Jungle was her blood. Ocean was, too, but she didn't yet know it.

Lin had her father's map, along with his photograph. She didn't know that the dirty, folded, and rough-edged paper was a valuable thing. It was a book against the Americans. It told of those who crossed over into a country not theirs for war. It told of unlawful boundaries crossed, beliefs, places, and even bodies trespassed.

• • •

In class, it was easy for Lin to understand the dialects of others, as if some were a trace in her memory. And they also spoke English, from her childhood, but her own people had spoken many languages and dialects because they had to.

In her long-distant past old Uncle Song would gather them together and they would practice. "No, no," he would say. "Do you want to get killed? You pronounce it this way or they will think you are an enemy." They'd laugh. They couldn't cry. It was a world of many enemies, each with their own intonation of voice, of belief, of hatred.

"Ha! I am an enemy!" said Auntie with great gusto, a woman with a white streak of hair who hated all those around them, but she then looked vulnerable and her lip didn't hold as firm. Her face, the mask, would soften into nothing that hated, only what feared. Lin remembered this, even though at the time she was perhaps only five or six.

The older people already spoke French. "From before." That was part of their history. Some even spoke Chinese, she was certain. But the man on the corner taught her new dialects and better French. She was a fast learner. Dr. Bread-baker also taught her algebra, her favorite because she was always seeking the mystery of x. It was the important factor in her life where everything was missing, lost, and sought-after. She was always searching, this young woman, this very fast learner he favored.

She looked up the word *war* and found that it meant confusion more than any other one verb and it was not the noun it was thought to be. It meant hostilities, armed battle. She had never understood why humans did not live in peace, which seemed so easy, so simple compared to war. She asked Dr. Thieu, the baker, and he said he believed it was in the human's nature to seek power and to have greed. "Even a simple, peaceful woman or man will fight back when they see injustice or when something is taken from them," he said. "Oh, I have come to believe it is a necklace of skulls, a chain linked together with no clasp, and it is so strong it can't be broken. Humans are poor, unforgiving animals."

And so Lin wanted to learn a way to break the chain. Everything must have a weakness somewhere. She was young and she thought, What if there were no injustices, what if there were wisdom?

Lin still asked about her uncle's address, in vain. One man in English class said, "Oh no, I believe that's in Hanoi." It seemed so far away.

She saved her small wages and the tips given by those whose streets she still cleaned, even as a young woman, all the while watching the world grow back and be rebuilt, hearing the sounds of it, a nail at a time, a stone. This money, too, went in a small box and when she received enough coins she changed them to bills, and after a while she needed a second box. She spent little of the money, but now and then she gave some to the children of American fathers. She did buy a goldfish for her room, but soon it ended up sitting on the counter of the little shop. She thought it would be less lonely there. It attracted customers. It reminded her of her father. She could still recall him as he walked toward her, the red goldfish in a white bowl.

For a time after the war everything had been quiet. Too quiet. There were no birds. At first there was not even a breeze, as if the wind had gone to another part of the world. And when it was most silent, Lin remembered that her father became the wind. In every breeze that touched her.

Against the old woman's rules, Lin's body began to curve and swell. And now, whenever she could, she also worked in an office where people went to search for their families. At first she volunteered.

Her new mother, watching her study and read, said she was

too greedy for knowledge. "It is not a good thing. How will you live if you know so much? You will never be happy. You will be a poor worker. You will never be a good wife." But unlike the baker's wife, Lin had a hunger that wanted to consume something and what it wanted to consume wasn't rice in a bowl but learning, knowledge. Perhaps that was better because it kept her from remembering the burning sampans, the fires at nights, the sounds, her old grandmother floating away on the river to the unknown world of night and death, while she herself was pulled and pushed away to life.

"Don't worry," she said to Mother, her mistress of the flower shop. "I will stay here and care for you. I will care for you and Pa when you are old." Lin saw the relief in the woman's eyes. She had her losses, too, this mother did, too many to talk about. Lin must constantly reassure her.

And so, some days when Lin was called to help translate in the offices, at the desk where the terrible stories were told, this mother didn't send her out with flowers. She had a secret pride in Lin's success and so an overly tall boy down the street delivered the flowers instead.

Lin heard the stories: One small old man sat down at the table and opened a large bag and took out the bones of his ancestors, those bones that were left, and said how he couldn't keep them clean enough. He didn't notice if anyone in the room was disturbed by the bones. They weren't. They'd all seen worse. He said, "The Americans dug them up because they knew, we cared for them, and one man peed on them." He wept. The ancestors had been loved and buried with care. The bones were wiped clean with alcohol. He wanted to take them home. He cried and his hair was almost white. Lin understood him and translated what he said. This was a problem that could be solved. He could take them back, even if the place looked as if it was gone. They could arrange such a journey. Later, a scarred woman, a cut through her face, told about her lost children and she said she last saw them by a banyan tree. Lin said nothing, but she got up and went through files of children searching for their mother because she was certain she recalled a brother and sister saying something like that, and as she did a windstorm came up. They all went to the window and saw it rippling the water outside, some papers blowing across the streets and the people outside walking leaned against it, holding their hats and skirts to their bodies.

"I think I might have a lead," Lin said, looking at the file. "I will come to your house tomorrow." She believed this because it was a story told by two people who said they last saw their mother at the village tree just before there was a blast in the air and men came and took their mother away. At the time, they were just children left crying. She remembered this from the file. The tree was probably long since dead, but the children were now young people. She hoped she was right. She had the best of memories. It would be so good, it *was* so good, the few times she had seen people reunited with one another. She wished for her own father.

She went out in the early mornings while her new family slept, and took walks to where the forest was returning. She followed new roads and looked at the places people were rebuilding. After cleaning at the flower shop, after watching the owner make arrangements, after watering carefully all the plants, one day Lin made a beautiful flower arrangement with pale lotus blossoms and, instead of ribbon, she tied it with some of the wild green grasses, braided long and light, grasses from the forest. Surprised, the boss woman said, "Oh, it's so beautiful, it looks like angels made it."

One night, Lin met the man who would become her husband. It was his first night at the school. He was in the corner sitting on a crooked chair at their makeshift school. In one look she saw that somehow his eyes held her world or part of it. She knew what he knew. He knew what she did. Not in the way of school and learning, but in the world, in their lives and histories. Somehow he, too, had managed to survive. She didn't know he had been an enemy. That he had been on the other side. The necklace of skulls suddenly had another strand. She didn't know that he had wanted to be a doctor and then was forced to be a child-warrior in a child army. All she saw was the sweat on his forehead as he struggled over the words of English and his starched-collar white shirt was damp. Starch, she thought, he must have a wife or money enough to go to the laundry. Sweat. He must be having trouble with school. But in truth it was nerves from seeing her beauty and calm, like when the wind blows and water lilies fly across the water and onto the land, and what's on land is blown into the water. Lin said, "Doesn't that breeze cool you?" She pointed at the window and smiled at him to show that it wasn't an insult. She thought he needed help reading and he was struggling with the work. He thought she was reading his thoughts and knew they were all about her. He said, "No, but I like the scent of flowers." So forward he was being, but she thought he was a poet. What he meant was something with insight into her life, and it did have depth, as he smelled the scent about her as if he were a butterfly. Later they walked together and he said, "I am going to university. What should we do?"

She said, so bold she couldn't believe she had even spoken the words, "I think we should get married." Embarrassed, her face was hot and now she was the one in a nervous sweat.

"Yes. I know I have seen you before, but I can't remember where." Perhaps it was another lifetime. All he knew was that they were meant to be together. He didn't know she was the child, years ago, on the bloody trail, the one he had picked up that he was supposed to kill or injure and not help, that even then when he looked into her face and felt her tiny arm, he could not harm her.

But Lin returned to herself. She was a young woman who

had to hide her feelings. She wasn't a tree, she was a pond, and he would have to walk all the way around her to know her.

He was a man who would do it.

He had his back to her the next day when she came to school and she did what her father used to do. She put her hands around his head and covered his very deep eyes and said, "Guess who?"

No one had ever done that to him before. Again he was sweating. He liked her sweet manners. She liked his kindness. He had never been to war, she was certain. Not with his manners. He had lived in France at one time. He said he could help her with French. She could help him with English. Of course, they were perfect for each other. She even remembered a few curse words. "Repeat this. 'Oh shit,'" she said, and laughed out loud, a beautiful laugh.

Lin's ambitions now bothered her mistress, who had forgotten her own ambitions of the past, and Lin knew it, so Lin offered the woman gifts and brought her food from Dr. Bread-baker, and called her Mother and sometimes felt bad, as if betraying her own mother, the memories, and her father's fading photograph.

Over the years, the older woman's face, once angry and thin, suspicious of everyone, had grown sad. Lin never knew how the older woman often stepped out the door and watched Lin go down the street to learn, thinking all the time, She will soon be gone. And later, the pain was even worse when Lin rode her bicycle to Han Son to interpret for the others. Oh, Mother was never stupid. She always knew Lin had gifts and talents beyond the art of flowers and stems. She was a girl who was good at anything and everything. That was her curse. It would lead her to all roads, like the veins of a leaf, all feeding one plant. But when Lin returned she always brought the woman something special. This time when she returned, the night of

all the fretting and incense burning, it was sweet rice to make
her happy, and Lin said she was already paid and was going to
use some of the money to paint the counter and make it more
lively and bright and she was happy and energetic and alive.
She painted it the color of pale green with a hint of yellow. Lin
said the color was chlorophyll and she'd just learned this word
from leaves and school, and the woman who had known flowers so well loved the new word. *Co-ro-fiu*.

This time, too, when Lin came home she washed the woman's hair outside in a basin of warm water, pouring it over her
graying strands with a cup and noticing the thin back of her
neck, the protruding bones there, the birthmark so many have
in that place. A pale leaf fell into the tub of water and it seemed
so much a part of them both. Lin offered the woman human
comfort, the older woman who loved flowers and had spent
years hating being alive, while Lin was surprised to have lived
and had been thrilled when she remembered the bursts of fire
and the rockets like falling stars, thrilled she survived them and
proud of her abilities to live on streets, in trees, down roads,
but there were other consequences and she hadn't known
what they were at first. Now she who had been without a family helped those who were helpless families find one another,
and she swore upon the words of every dead and living savior
that she would find her father.

Her adopted father had a calmness, too, not like a pond, or
even a plant, not like Lin, but he had grown content with life.
He alone noticed there were times when Lin was a restless
pond underneath, not always a still one. He built things now.
Especially he built birdhouses and he imagined them richly and
elegantly. They were loved, pieced together by things he found
thrown out on streets, pieces of cars, but somehow they always
looked new and perfect. Lin loved him and remembered how
he'd slipped her extra money when he could, money she used
for books. He made a living room out in the back in a place

that had been bare. Now they had enough, unlike before, and he grew flowers and ginger and he cared for the stone basin he kept filled with fresh water to attract the returning birds, and he even bought a TV.

"What would our ancestors think," his wife said. "I won't watch it. Ever." She crossed her arms over herself the day he brought the square box home and turned it on.

She held out for three weeks and then one day she sat before it on the floor and watched so much he had to call her to her duties at work even in the daytime.

"Shh." She waved him away with her narrow hand. "They are having a fight. She is sleeping with her doctor."

"I had your future read by the woman who burns leaves on stones," Mother told Lin one day.

"I heard she charges too much. Did she overcharge you?" Lin was a skeptic.

"Yes, of course she did. But I had to know." She had a crease between her eyebrows which had disappeared. Then she kept silent, tempting Lin until her curiosity was too much for her. More silence. Until Lin couldn't wait. "Okay, what did she say? What did you ask?"

"She said you would go a long ways. You would marry a man who was somehow an enemy, but the fights are over. You will grow even taller. How can you? I don't know. She says you will always come home to flowers even if you go to school. You are meant for *co-ro-fiu.*"

Lin smiled without laughing. "And what about you?" She knew the woman would never ask only about the girl.

"Oh, I will live a long, long life and my hands will still be beautiful," but she shook her head as if she had sad news she didn't wish to tell. That was her way.

Lin wanted to go to a university. She didn't need school, though. She already was finding her share of work. And she studied maps. The teacher, Dr. Thieu, over the years watched her with love that grew as Lin grew. Now he watched her grow into love with the young man who would become her husband.

Once, the two young people went to the park and, despite the others, they sang together. They knew all the same songs. Another time, they danced to the band that was playing there, a few men with instruments, a singing woman in a tight dress who lifted her arms like in a movie and sang in English. "You're stiff," he said, stepping back, looking at her gently.

"I'm nervous." She felt embarrassed and again she was the one sweating.

It was a French dance. The air smelled of peach blossoms.

The streets were busy, but many had come to the dance and sat around on folding chairs or squatted on their own legs. Some of Lin's people were there, the Ugly People, the tribes. No longer do we have or love nature, Lin thought when she saw those from places like her own. Now we just try to get by, like everyone, or to make money and build. After the reconciliation, comrades were forgotten, and everyone strove in new ways to survive. Some left to work on oil rigs in Thailand. Some worked for peace. Some built businesses. Some lost them.

When Lin and Tran married, they stepped on the pathway of flowers. All was flowers because Lin's adopted mother insisted. It was a day of still ponds and plants. It was a day of baked food and a night of sweetness, even in the rains that fell.

Now, beneath the full moon, as she watches the bats, she is a young woman and she has done well with her life. She tells herself that she has made for herself a fortunate life. And it is true; this life was not given her, the girl who was once shoeless even though her mother had been a shoemaker. Now, she thinks, it is time to find her father.

RED FISH: HUMAN

Lin still remembers her father. How he'd made yellow paper into something that flew on a string and looked like the birds that once lived there. She held the string and ran with the kite down the hill toward the now-murky water and he'd say, "Not too high," afraid of attracting attention. She remembers laughing at his monkey imitation, although she had only seen a monkey once and it had stolen her grandmother's pearl hair comb. The soldiers had seen to it that no monkeys were left.

Mostly she recalls the day he walked up from the floating market and the houses on stilts with the red fish in a white bowl. He carried it proudly. He had earned the money for it himself, paid by Old Grandfather Uncle for his labor. And he brought a lotus flower for her mother that same day, sweet-smelling and with white petals, slowly opening. But she remembers only pieces. She calls them fractures, the way her life has been fractured. And some pieces have fallen away like the petals of a flower. She knows that her father, the American who didn't look like one, was one of their many secrets. Her people had nothing but secrets. Now, as a woman, she understands the careful line they walked to remain alive, between alliances, enemies, politicians of low order, and boys with a desire to kill. She'd heard all the words and, even young, she asked, "Are we Minh? Are we allies? Are we communists? Did we help the Americans?" Her grandmother, golden-skinned, tall then and not yet broken, said, "You are too young for these things. Anyway, now it is the past. We live for tomorrow." Lin could tell by her eyes, a closed look, her hair back in a twist, that she would never tell. The past had to be put in its place. Not so for young Lin.

Behind her grandmother she could see the fields of rice, the water almost invisible, hidden like everything waiting both for rain and the next wave of history. A sudden wind blew the rice and the field bent and glistened as the last of the sunlight moved like waves of water. The sunset over the fields glowed red.

Everyone was convinced that he'd never return. "Huh! The Americans would never let him." She lit an oil lamp. The old woman knew. She knew the Americans. "They could do anything. It's worse than the raw nerve in my broken tooth to think of these things," her grandmother said. And so it had to be enough that he loved her, her mother, the village. Her grandmother kissed her forehead. "You are alive because of him. That is good enough, my girl." Moist with the humidity, her shadow falling on the wall, she rearranged the comb in her silver-black hair, this comb unlike the one with pearl made of carved bone. Lin heard that she once searched the jungle for the one the monkey stole until her husband put a stop to it. "You'll get killed over a hair comb."

Later Lin understood about her grandmother not wanting to think about the past. Auntie, Grandmother's sister, told Lin how the old woman had been raped and left for dead, cut at the neck. Auntie said she found her, the woman's long hair red with blood all about her neck and shoulders. Auntie grabbed her and lifted her. "You! Sister, wake up! You are breathing!" Auntie yelled. By some miracle, the artery was not cut, even though Grandmother thought she was dead, wished she was,

and lay back weak and limp, but she was yelled into life by a
woman almost too thin to have a voice.

Auntie squeezed the skin together, using sticky sap to hold
it, the very same sap Lin's mother once used on shoes. "Okay,
now, let's go," she told her sister, wrapping her neck with a
sleeve from her blouse. "Hurry!"

"What else was there to do?" she said to the girl about the
sap. "But it worked." Still, it was why Grandmother always
wore one of her two scarves. It was why her eyes saw only as
far back as they would; not far. All this accounted, also, for her
grandfather's—"Uncle," as he was called by everyone—scars.
They were symmetrical, not the result of an accident.

"That's enough now for a young girl to know," Auntie said,
combing the tangles out of her own long gray hair.

Lin buried her head against her great-aunt's chest. "Is it
human?" Lin asked. "To do that. Is that human?"

"Such a question." Yet Lin had been born as a different child.
They knew that. She saw everything. She learned quickly. She
had watching eyes as a baby. If they were still tribal, she would
have been set into a special place in the tribe and trained for a
future. But perhaps she got this from her father. They thought
him a man of compassion and great strength. The aunt remembered him. She had been off selling American beer when she
came back to the village and found him standing there like
a statue, before he collapsed into a deep sleep. They ran off
with him and hid him when the helicopters came to take the
bodies, knowing they'd be blamed and killed for the deaths of
the Americans. "Yes. I think it is human. There is so much to
a human."

"Does it have to be?"

"I don't know." She braided the child's hair. "But that's
enough for now. There's only so much a girl can hear." Just
then there was a gunshot in the distance.

Later, when they were down in the reddish sand by the
water, she held Lin and said, "I'm sorry." Crying.

Lin studied her face, to see what she meant. She looked at her fine nose, her cheek that seemed dented, her eyes. Lin said, "I know. You're sorry about humans."

Auntie nodded, hiding her face.

The rains began. It was the beginning of the monsoon season. First a light mist, then a rain, then the downpour. Lin had time to think about what was human as the land turned to brown water and the air smelled thick and rich with mud. Clouds gathered darkly in the sky and water covered everything. The roads were filled and people stood with their legs in water as it poured down the hill. One poor man with one leg walked by on crutches. Another tried over and over to catch a fish from a lake now dead, throwing the line in again and again. "Well, at least the rice is happy," her grandmother said, her grandmother who told Lin a story about the great river and how there were a large number of white animals that had to cross over it and when they reached the other side they had all become black. Lin always thought of the animals crossing the water.

Across an ocean, her father had also changed. No more kites. No more presents. He carried the family's fading photos in his worn leather wallet and took them out to look at them, fearing the day their images would fade away completely and he would lose everything he had left. *Everything he had left.* He thought of the irony, the strange double meaning of those words. He could return now if he were able, but it wasn't a simple matter of human will. That, too, is human.

He remembers the air was quiet. No birds. There was tension unfelt by the food-buyers who had grown attuned to all things left unsaid and would force them to be spoken. He worked in the rice fields. He kept his back to the Others when they passed. After a while he was the only one not questioned by any enemy because he was an ignorant man who neither heard nor spoke nor understood the things happening around him. He wore a band around his head and his blue-black hair was the color of the hair of the others. Only in the way he moved could you tell he was an American; he disguised this by limping as if he'd been wounded. But when they'd gone and the work was done he and Lin sang on the road. They sang a song about the great frogs with golden eyes. She and her father sang and he carried a stick in each hand and beat a rhythm. He lived this life whole and fully, always knowing it could end at any second with a wrong step or movement. She looked up at him when she was too large to be carried on his back. They smiled.

Now, in Ho Chi Minh City, Lin's husband, Tran, is thin and wears a white shirt. His black hair is neat and combed back. He has a beautiful face, made more narrow by his soft dark eyes. He drives a motorbike. He always seems strong and confident even though he is narrow and slim in the way she is. No one would notice at first that he is missing an ear. Right now his eyes are worried. He has been left before. In so many ways: death and betrayal. He is thinking, What if she doesn't come back?

"But you have decided," he says, looking into her face. He knows her. He sees the determination in the way her face is set, the need, the decision, as if it is written in law. And it is. Blood law. Father-and-daughter law. Still, they are both full of unspoken words and fears.

"I will miss you until you come back." He moves closer to her and runs his hand down her hair, the back of her head and pulls her face against him. He smells like lemon, she thinks. And she always smells of flowers, as if her life in the presence of them has become her flesh. In the green and yellow light of their place, with the one wall that looks lavender because of the evening light, she is sweetness. She is soft and kind. She is sensuous. He presses his body against hers, into hers, then they sleep in the last of daylight, sweating in the heat before the rainy season, not even bothering to close the shutters, almost forgetting the veil of mosquito netting. She reaches for his hand and entwines her thin fingers in his and sleeps. They don't talk about fixing the rice. Besides, now they have electricity and a rice cooker.

They each have their own fears, lifetimes of them. He'd been forced into the same army that had once attacked her people. She discovered this information at her new job. He never wanted to tell her. He put his narrow hands over his face and cried when she asked him about it. "I was only eleven and hungry by then. When I tried to leave, they shot at me."

"What have we here?" said a commander who was his cousin. And so they only cut off his ear and the blood ran. He got off lucky, he told her. He lived. His ear at times still aches. He used to cover it with longer hair. When they had gone through her village they'd taken the young men and boys away. The women had hidden in the trees and down in the water, breathing through reeds. He never said where the young men and boys were taken. He tells her he doesn't know. Maybe they were killed. Others joined willingly, but war wasn't part of his hopes for the future. He'd had other dreams, of being a doctor, a professor, dreams he could tell no one after the revolution because he came from the other class. He'd even been to school in France at one time.

And Lin, she was used to escaping, hiding, running, he knew. Both of them knew in their skin the loud explosions, the bright lights in the sky at night, the smell of cordite that stayed on clothing. Red narrow lights and smoke falling, crossing earth, the sounds at first like ghosts calling down the sky.

But love is not held back by the lines and bounds and fires of war and they found love for one another. He knows that love has always been her constant search. It is part of Lin's cell structure. It is why she wants to find her father.

"It's so far away. You are very brave," he says, holding her in his sweating arms. He knows her story in the way lovers talk. "You always were."

Even so, she keeps a light burning all night. There are nightmares. He sleeps with his narrow arm across his eyes.

So, the plan is made. Lin will fly to San Francisco. She already speaks English and several other languages. She calls it the gift she inherited from her mother. She has the gift of flowers but she is also a translator and studies the archives of the lost. She remembers the joy she felt, finding the children of the mother who was taken from beneath a tree near where she once lived. She could sit for long hours at a clean wood table, looking at papers, orderly files, talking with people who haven't known order, who haven't slept, who have miraculously, as she knows, survived. It is comforting there for a girl who loves organization and cleanliness. The room itself is straight lines, neat and clean, papers filed away. But she also has compassion. It has always been her nature. She expends energy finding documents, as if each one is personal to her, a search of her own, sometimes working late hours. When the occupation and then the Party came, papers were gone through, torn, used against people. Some files were scattered and missing, some wet and difficult to read. Words have great power and she knows it and now she looks for words to put together. Sometimes she sits beside a person or family who has lost everything, where she can see the speakers and the emotions on the faces of those who understand nothing being said and have no choice but to trust her. She softens the direct questions. She looks at them openly. They might not know it to look at the gentle, steady young woman, but she has seen what they have seen, the wounds, parts of bodies, fires, the lost families and villages and crying children everywhere. She was one of them. She wonders what her father thinks of her.

. . .

Thomas remembers how on the day she was born he was sent outside the blue wooden door to wait. It was a door he and her mother had found and carried from a bomb site and added to their makeshift place. He used wood and leather for hinges, replacing them often. He thinks of her mother. He'd first seen Ma wearing the pants and tunic traditional to the women in Vietnam, silk, not work clothes. Later, Ma was so gentle with him, giving him water and rice when he could not stand up. And then she was having their child on a mat, on the brushed floor of earth. His child. He sat on the ground outside and it began to rain. He thought about, of all things, love. There were those who would have killed him, but now he forgets them and thinks of love. Out there, Ruth came to his mind like someone gone, a ghost he'd once held, and later, when he opened his arms, she had disappeared. He lived in another world then. He loved her still, but he was no longer an American. The village was his place and he was happy there.

At first he hadn't thought to ask why there were no young men. He didn't think they were dead or soldiers in another war than his. Even after the Americans left, the war was not over. He'd heard about the many who came to power. Whenever some of them passed by he was hidden, or, if seen, the questioners were told he didn't hear or speak. He looked like the village people. He worked with them, with the women in the rice fields, or at the river. When the enemy came by they thought he was a dullard, a stupid man, and even those who liked to hurt the vulnerable left him alone because he was a strong worker and they needed him. Otherwise he would have been teased to death, not by words. But they needed rice in the city. They needed workers.

He could still see Ma carrying the baskets of rice to them, walking up the white path, moss growing across it now because it had not been used for some time. Even the followers of Ho were hungry.

And then, the baby cried.

• • •

Lin looks like her father, yet she has her mother's gentleness and narrow shape. She was a reed as she grew. She was a willow. She was a deer. Nature is her place, though she now lives in the city with traffic, motorbikes, phones, noise constant, in a city once called "The Pearl." Saigon. Ho Chi Minh City. Yet there are still the country vendors, old-fashioned, hitting their sticks together, calling out their wares. There are street foods, and buyers.

From the plane, her seat at the window, she looks down at the world below, Vietnam, then the many green islands with the light blue water of coral reefs. Lin opens the map of the continents and looks again. Inside her mind is a boat, overloaded, sinking in the ocean, and people trying to swim, one young man being taken up, wet, skinny, by someone from a ship. She doesn't think of what happens with the others. The stewardess now brings her a soda and saves her from her memories.

Just as her father would have done, she studies the map of the continents, always having to check and recheck the flight path, the world as it should be. She looks down at everything as if the world could vanish, and then it does. There is only cloud.

She had investigated as much as possible before she left. She found the map of America, his reservation, the nearest towns, where he was born. She looks at it now, as if she can see him, a tiny figure on the paper. He was born at home, like Lin, if she could call her only place home. When she had visited it once, after working near the region, nothing was there except rice fields, remnants, trash and a faded blue door lying on the wet road near a collapsed tunnel entrance. She didn't know she was born behind that door.

It was easy to find information about her father's location, since she works with the papers that help connect people to whoever and whatever they had lost, or to families in America or France. Sometimes it is as if she is restringing beads of a

broken necklace, not the necklace of war, of skulls, but one of
beauty, pearls, and as she does, she hears Song's voice saying,
"Okay," that part always in English. Then he would say, as if
it meant nothing, "The government has changed again." She
continues stringing the necklace until it is complete, the clasp
in place. It is made of pearls with a dragon claw to hold it. She
closes it so it will not come undone.

After the plane lands she is sent through customs, thinking,
My father came to this very place. He walked here.

She walks through the long building, following the others.
They take away her fruit. Purpose for visit: Personal. Then she
picks up her bag and, looking around, finds the place to rent a
car, feeling good to be able to do all this.

Driving, she sees that America is strange, the places all the
same bright stores. Then she turns off and she drives into the
mist curling about the hills, sometimes seeing the ocean, its
waves and swells, the odor of the water not like the water at
home, a different air. Not swampy so much as fishy. At home,
water is the color of tea, yellow, almost brown. Here it is deep
blue, green and gray. The waves remind her of life and history,
enormous and without end. She stops the car and watches one
wave come in after the other.

When she reaches the last coastal town, she turns into a
shop in the last mall before the reservation and purchases a red
goldfish in a plastic bag and a glass bowl. It is an offering to her
father, to show him how much she remembers.

"You want food?" asks the woman with frizzy red hair who
sells her the fish.

Lin looks at her, thinking she means to feed her. She had no
idea they fed customers in America. She looks at her in amazement. How kind.

"You know. For the fish." The woman's voice is louder now,
as if Lin is deaf or does not understand English, because it seems

clear from her calm face, the way she moves, that Lin is not American. "Fish food." The woman's skin is thin and white. She wears a ruffled collar. She points at the container that holds the dried contents.

"Oh," Lin puts the fish down. "Yes. Thank you."

Lin purchases the food. Back at her car, she places the fish and bowl on the floor of the passenger side, but before she drives away she sings to it. She sits in the busy parking lot, cars moving behind her, and she remembers the old song. But it is more than just a song. It praises the golden scales and the red flowing tail, its beauty. "Oh, you swam the river of perfume, the river of my mother world in the current. You could hold still and not be swept away. That is why, for a while, you were strong and free." The song praises the world it came from, the egg it once was with only an eye and a heart visible in it, the direction of water it followed. Then she feels sorry for it, wondering if it is lonely.

When she arrives in her father's world she sees the striking beauty of green land. Not as green as home, but green. And black rocks. Dark mountains in the distance, mist around them. She looks at the map and drives all the way past the reservation, past the old houses on the hill, looking at the pier and marina. Mobile homes sit down on the lower road with cars parked beside them, a fence made of buoys and other plastic parts, a canoe planted with flowers. Some of the trailers and houses have flowers planted around them. She doesn't recognize whalebones. Most of the places are dark and worn. Some trailers have bleached plywood nailed along the bottoms to keep the heat in. At the waterfront is a gray warehouse. There is the long skeleton of a pier, just the pilings exposed, this one unused, left over from some past, but not far from it is a dock, a marina, although only a few boats are in good condition. She stops at a pull-off. She watches the horizon, her eyes moving from one side to the other. A mist is over the bay, a cloud. A blue fishing boat moves across water, leaving a path behind it. Then the water closes, as if nothing had passed. On one side of the land a forest is cleared. Elsewhere, it is moist and rich. There is a river in the distance. The green banks of the river flow into the sea. She likes the water running seaward and the sounds of the seabirds. Behind her, to the east, is a forest of great trees, a ray of late afternoon sun.

Lin realizes she is nervous. She turns left, driving along the damp road close to the ocean. She stops at a large square building. Inside, it looks like a hardware store, but disorderly. In a case are knives, ammunition, but also wood carvings of faces, painted masks, some with hair. The man who stands before her in overalls smells like fish. He sees her looking at a mask. "That one's whalebone. It's very old. You don't see them much down here, at least not these days," he tells her, as if she is a potential buyer.

She looks up and smiles and asks where Thomas lives. She realizes when she looks down at the address that his last name is worn away by humidity and her own hands. She gives the number and the street by memory. She remembers it by heart. "Thomas Just," she says. She doesn't know the name was given by an Indian agent who signed the people up for registration on the rolls. Some were given the name "Only," some named "Little." She doesn't know it was to demean the people, the namers of the Indians. She thinks "Just" means he is the balance of a scale of what is right, that America was built on fairness and justice. She doesn't know it shares the same history as hers. The people in this place were once massacred, infants bayoneted on these beaches and mounds. The land is full of the blood of their ancestors. She has read of this country, America, but she has read another history.

The dark man in overalls remembers Thomas and Ruth, then only Ruth and her boy. He says, "He hasn't lived there in, oh, maybe twenty or more years." Since before the war.

Lin looks at him and blinks back the tears. For some reason, she hadn't considered this, that her father would be gone.

A woman in the building stares at her, then steps forward, a kindly woman, a mop in her hand. She sends Lin next door to the gas station. "Really, they'd know more about it there, sweetie. They know him. Don't worry. It's a small place. Someone will know how to find him." She watches Lin leave. "Don't you think she's the spittin' image of him? Her nose, her forehead?"

The gas station smells of tires and oil and smoke. One of the men is pulling the slot of a candy machine. Almond Joy. Lin asks if they know where Thomas Just lives. She gives him the address.

He takes a long look at her. "That was a long time ago." He yells over his shoulder, "Hey, anyone seen Thomas?"

"A real long time ago."

There's a rumor Thomas is at Witka's, but no one's gone out there because they stay away from the places where the old ones lived. They think they are still inhabited by ghosts. Some even hear them, and of course that is true, but what they really fear is being seen. As if the spirits of old bent men or women will walk out the door, come out and look at them, deep in the eyes, and see what they have become, what they have done. Or they will slip into them and take them between worlds or down beneath the layers of earth to an older time where untouched objects of bone are dwelling; hooks, fish skin smoothers, needles. It's the same reason they don't go over to the once-white houses place. But no one has seen any lights on at Witka's dark gray house. "He could be at his father's, but they dislike each other, so I don't think so. Besides, old senior likes to be alone, to work." He laughs. "And they plain old don't get along."

She stores the information in her mind like paper in a file. On a piece of dirty paper, a man with short fingers makes her a dirt-stained map. It is to Aurora's. "Here, this woman and her girl know where everyone is."

"Thank you," Lin says, grateful, but she feels like crying. She is exhausted and it is getting late. "Is there a place to sleep near here?" she asks. He points her toward the town motel. "It is the only one, the Midtown. You can't miss it. You'll just wish you did." He laughs at the same old joke.

When she leaves, the men look at each other. One says, "Hot."

"Why do you think she's looking for him?"

"Who cares? She can find me anytime." Dwight shakes his hand and blows on it like it's on fire. "It puts me in a good mood just to look at her. Hey, are my tires ready yet? I've been here all afternoon."

"They're too big. We told you we had to go get some."

"I like 'em that way."

Lin drives to the motel, locks the car door, and walks past the puny flower beds. The screen door has a hole in it. She rings the bell. Al comes and sizes her up before he gives her the key to number eight. She pays with cash. She checks in and looks around her room. It is not very clean. She goes to her bag to get a paper clip to hold the patterned curtains together. Threads are coming loose from the cotton bedspread. A hair is on the pillow. It smells of cigarettes. The heater is at the bottom of the window. She can't get it to work. She is tired and hungry. Her hair is moist from the ocean air. She brings in the goldfish from the floor of the car and sets it on the table. She sprinkles the food in and watches it eat. Its fins are like the red silk scarf of that strong woman from the story she heard as a girl. It reminds her of her grandmother's scarf. She falls back on the bed and it squeaks. She's hungry and there is nothing to read. The light is bad anyway, almost yellow. She lies on her back and tears fall down into her hair as it all catches up with her. She is not as competent or as strong as she seems.

• • •

News travels fast in Indian Country. After a phone call from someone's wife, Ruth, at her mother's, hears about the girl. Sure as an electric current, she feels who this girl is. "Mom. It's his daughter. The one I dreamed about. I'm sure of it. Remember?"

"Oh? What are you waiting for? Go get her."

At the motel Ruth asks Al which room the young lady is in. "What's her name?" She knocks on the door. When Lin opens it, Ruth stares at her. She looks like Thomas, only slender and tall for a woman, and with an expression that says sweetness but also says she has seen a world broken to pieces. A feeling of knowing comes over Ruth. Also, she sees the younger woman has been crying.

"We're related, you and I," she tells Lin. It's true, in some odd way they are, but she can't say how. It confuses even her, but she wants Lin to stay with her. "Our family will help you. You can stay with us. Here. You haven't even unpacked. Let me carry your things. I'm Ruth. Are you Lin?"

Lin nods. This other woman has taken over so easily, so smoothly, and she lets her. Ruth takes the key back and rings the bell at the desk. Al comes from the secret rooms behind. "Hey, Al. Can you give her a refund? I'm taking her with me." He doesn't want to refund her money. "It's my policy." He points at the sign.

"Well, she didn't even use the sink. Besides, I see the receipt here and you overcharged her to start with. I know your rates. And then, Al, the room wasn't clean. The heater doesn't work and you put her in the smallest room you have when the rest are empty. In fact, I don't even know when you made it into a room instead of the closet where you used to keep linens, and I want to know, are you going to give her back her money or am I going to make a public scene and publicize this?"

Always the same threat now, Ruth going public, but he can't imagine this in a newspaper: "Man Overcharges for Motel Room."

Al puts out his cigarette. Slowly. He pushes his dog out of the way with his foot. He has a fifties hairstyle still. Ruth thinks he sprays it. Aurora swears he keeps a stash of Brilliantine behind the counter. He says, "This is why everyone here hates the hell out of you, Ruth." But he goes back and gets the money for the little "gook foreigner." His eyes reveal how much he dislikes her.

Lin looks at Ruth. Lin has a smile in her eye. She's only heard a few women talk that strongly. At home they have other ways of getting what they want, not so direct. Ruth is dressed in a T-shirt and jeans. Women at home in Vietnam wear skirts and blouses these days, but it's changing there, too. Ruth has brown strong arms, not at all dainty. She picks up Lin's things. Lin, usually strong, carries the fishbowl gingerly and walks like she is once again a girl, her heart afraid, but also trusting this woman who is called Ruth.

Ruth stops at the door. "You know what they hate, Al? They hate that I am honest. They hate that I believe in truth. Ponder that awhile, why don't you?" She lets the screen door slam.

There is something calm and steady about the woman with strong arms, and in spite of what she has said to the man, she has a gentle nature. Lin can see it in her warm dark eyes.

As they drive, Ruth smiles at Lin. "I see him in your face." She also saw her once, in a dream, on his lap. She has seen her running about the green fields as a child. She has seen her surrounded by flowers without knowing the meaning of it, but she can smell them now, as if Lin's skin is made of flowers. She has known Lin for a long time, in her dreams, even in brief waking moments, but she doesn't tell Lin that. "You want to find your father."

"Do you know where he is?"

She hands her the money Al returned. "Yes."

She doesn't say that he is a wounded man and you don't

ever know what you will find with him. She only says, "We'll go there. I'll take you."

Lin looks at Ruth and thinks of her father and feels her heart beating quickly in her chest.

At the little house with flowers outside, Ruth and Aurora offer Lin fruit, bread, and tea. "Wait here! We'll get your room ready. Eat. You must be hungry."

The two women make up a bed for her in the back bedroom. "Oh my God," says Aurora. "What do you think he'll do?" She pats down the bed and turns down the sheet so that it is welcoming.

Ruth takes things out of two drawers. "I have no idea. He'll probably deny everything. But isn't it so strange how I always dreamed her?"

"Maybe that's why she's here."

When they go back to her, Lin is asleep on the couch. Ruth covers her with one of the knitted afghans her mother made, then looks at Lin's face. No matter what Ruth's life has been, she can't imagine the life of this girl, not even the country with its stone water-bowls in the streets, the many old bicycles, wheels blurring. She has traveled far. She has a hint of lip color. Ruth kisses the top of her head lightly. It has a human smell. It smells of hair that hasn't been washed in a few days. It reminds her of Marco when he was young.

Ruth loves the girl already because she is the child of Thomas. She looks at her and sees him. She's not the kind of woman who would be bothered by the other woman, the mother of Lin. Thomas, she realizes, was never her own. She tries to think of how to deal with Thomas and all of the pain that is about to hit him. Then she thinks, It is time. He has been protected too long.

Above them a night bird flies, calling out names, talking to the ocean and all the other currents moving within life: hope, need, desire, like being human.

• • •

The next day Ruth and Lin first go to the small gray house out on the rock. The trail there is steep, but it is beautiful. Lin looks at the black rocks protruding from the water like dragon teeth. Ruth clears her throat, then knocks on the door, announcing their presence. Usually people here whistle as they approach, or they hum. Sometimes the older men will drum. But Thomas knows Ruth's voice and he is accustomed to her invasions.

Lin, who had been a girl afraid of nothing, then a woman with courage, is afraid when she arrives at her father's small dark house on the black rocks. Will he remember her? She carries the fishbowl in her hands, worried she will drop it. She is now dressed in a pale pink American tee.

Ruth knocks first, then opens the door herself.

"Look who is here," she says into the shadows. "It's Lin."

Thomas should reach out and pull Lin toward him right away. He should hold her and love her. He should say to the young woman fighting back tears, *I'm so proud of you*. Because she lived, if for no other reason. He'd spent years thinking of what he'd left her to. The boy-warriors from the Thai border. Cambodia. He stands up, but as soon as he sees her, Thomas thinks Lin looks like her mother. His chest aches, but he does not go to her. He says nothing to her except "Hello." Even hello is a struggle for this man who should be so proud of this surviving girl. In one moment, he remembers too much. As the two women walk inside, he sits down on his unmade bed.

Lin looks at him and thinks, He is a small human being. All these years I thought so much of him, so large, so strong, but he's only a man and we're the same size.

"Lin. This is your father. Don't mind him. He's shy. This must be a shock," Ruth says.

"Here, sit down." Ruth pulls a kitchen chair out for Lin. "I'll make some tea." Ruth strikes a match and lights the black stove. As the water is heating she goes outside to leave them alone.

Lin speaks to her father. Softly. "I brought you this." She reaches out to offer him the bowl with the goldfish, dark red, swimming in a glass bowl. "Do you remember?" He does. It is so bright a color it reflects on the inner walls of the bowl. She doesn't know it will make him remember the war, and the death of the whale and the red water. His son. She thought it would remind him of the same gift he had given her so long ago, one of her first memories. The American. Papa, she called him, with dark skin and black hair, had once brought her a goldfish. She didn't know he was a deserter. He was present and kind and sometimes he cried. At those times her mother would take him in her arms and tell him how good a man he was, how he had saved her life and that of her mother and aunt, even the old grandfather of the village. So Lin thinks of him in that way. When she sees him, she is surprised. He does not look kind. He does not look like he saved a soul in the world, not even his own. He looks weary. He even looks old and nearly American. He sits down at the table across from her, speechless but full of words. He only nods.

When Ruth comes back in, the breeze blows Lin's hair in her eyes. Thomas can't touch anyone, but he wants to push her hair back. He does say, "Thank you," for the fish, even if he hasn't really looked at it except from the far past, and from that past he smells the lotus blossom the day he carried gifts to his wife and daughter up the narrow pathway.

"I am proud of you. My grandmother said you were a hero," Lin says. She looks around old Witka's place. She has lived in huts, in pieces of wood put hurriedly together, in bamboo forests, grasses, on streets, in trees. "This is a beautiful place."

He is silent, but his eyes are moist looking at her, wondering how she survived, thinking of all the ways she might have lived, how she may live now. But he says nothing. He looks old and tired and sad.

She and Ruth exchange glances. They drink tea. Then Ruth stands and says to Thomas, "I'm sorry. We should have let you know we were coming. Anyway, feed it every day, your fish. It'll keep you company and we'll come back."

As they leave, she says to Lin, "It must be quite a shock. We should have let him know ahead of time." Lin and Ruth walk back to the car. Ruth leads her by the hand. The tenderness makes Lin want to cry.

"I try to imagine his life," Ruth says. "But I never can." Then she says, "Oh! Wait here, I left a key." She goes back in. He is staring at the fish. She walks straight toward him. "You bastard. I will never forgive you for this. I can forgive you all your other things. Your rudeness. Your lying around feeling sorry for yourself. But you pull yourself together and treat your daughter like a human being! Here is something back in place. Where's your heart? Where is your soul?" She slams the door as she leaves.

Lin hears it and thinks, Wow! This is the second time. What a door-slammer.

When she comes back out to Lin, she says, "He's not a bad person, I promise, but he's been like this since he came back. It's been worse since our son died."

"Your son?"

"We were married once. My son was older than you. Your brother, Marco, was from before the war."

Before and after, those were words that described people on both sides of the water.

"Your father was my husband then."

Lin doesn't ask what happened. Ruth doesn't tell. She takes the girl back to her mother's house.

"So," says Aurora. "You are already back. He was himself, I take it." They sit at the table where women have always sat together and shared more than food and that night they have a beer, even Aurora, and they cry with her.

Lin's expectations and hopes are gone.

"No. He'll come through. He just needs time."

He, Thomas, is all that Lin has left from before.

That night Lin is awake in a bed in a foreign country. She remembers one night when her flower-shop mother lay down beside her and pulled her close with one arm and softly began to cry into Lin's hair and how she felt loved and cared for.

Old Mother still makes baskets, as does Ruth, who has won awards for her dogbane and grass baskets. "Ruth still has a lot to learn," the old woman, Aurora, tells the girl. She forgets Ruth's hair is turning gray. "But she's come a long way." She doesn't mention that the men stole Ruth's baskets off the boat. "Oh, my, I'm rambling on. But here, look at this basket." She goes to the sink and puts water in it. "It doesn't even leak. There's a story of a woman who made a small fishing boat for her husband by weaving it. He was safe in it, safer than in wood. But the other men were jealous and they set fire to it."

Old Mother, Aurora, takes care of herself, but gets confused. She forgets last week. Like Ruth, Lin soon helps remind her of things.

"You won fifteen dollars last night at Bingo," Lin tells her. "Here, let me fix your hair." Lin takes off Old Mother's glasses and washes them for her. She arranges her soft white hair in a beautiful style, a French twist, but soft at the face.

"My, you have a talent," says Aurora, looking in the mirror. "Have you ever thought of going to school?"

Lin smiles. She never boasts of her accomplishments. "I've thought of it."

A few days later, it is time for Ruth to prepare the boat for fishing. She and Lin go out first in the rubber Zodiac, the engine roaring, the two of them puffy round with life jackets.

They pull up to the boat and climb to the deck. When Lin first steps onto the *Marco Polo*, she looks around in surprise. "Oh, it's like a home in here. There's even a bathtub."

"In the bow. Yeah, it used to be a horse tank."

Lin looks around at the table, the cracked leather chair, chained down, the bunks, the built-in seating. Ruth has made it comfortable. There are rugs on the floor, braided out of old clothes that belonged to her mother, her grandmother, and even herself. They are clean. Paintings are on the walls, an octopus, women dancing in red dresses. There are black-and-white photographs in black frames against a blue wall, the face of a young boy, young Ruth with an infant, older Indian people dancing, standing together by a fire at the ocean. Even plants.

"Yes, it's been my home."

Ruth already fixed up the bunks. She gives Lin the top bed because Ruth's back hurts. This is better anyway, because Lin needs a light all night or she feels nervous. Ruth can barely make up either bed any longer. Even making up the lower one hurts her back, bending.

After watching Ruth work for a while, Lin says, "Let me do that. You work so hard."

They have just carried in groceries. Ruth bought condensed milk for Lin's coffee. Ruth carried the heavy box of ice for their trip out fishing. Then there was some maintenance, cleaning, lifting, bending, coiling ropes, folding nets, putting them in place. Ruth is constantly at work, in motion.

They motor out. They pass an old cemetery, which appears to be under a soft layer of moss. "It's where I hope I will be buried one day," Ruth tells her. It is the one the archaeologists dug up for bones and artifacts so many years ago against the will of the people. The bones came back not long after. "They came back because they heard them singing and grew afraid." The employees wouldn't work in the rooms where the bones were. She tells this to Lin and Lin sits down and listens.

"Ghosts have great abilities," Ruth says.

"Yes. I am with them every day. They wander everywhere."

Then Lin tells Ruth about the American soldiers digging up

the ancestors and urinating on them. But not about the old man who opened the bag of bones.

Like Ruth, Lin loves the sea and stares into it. She doesn't know ocean, but she loves the small white jellyfish, the occurrences of tides that speak of the moon. Then, when Ruth starts up for business, Lin learns how to fish. She screams when a line begins to unravel. Ruth laughs and Lin hangs on and pulls. But soon Lin works with her length and graceful, smooth motions. Later she writes her husband about the different ways the people here fish. Trolling. Longlining. Netting. The tall poles and lines of the boats, the lights at the top when they move out or in at night. How once, out at sea, they caught a fish so big they used a winch. She sends him some Kodak pictures Ruth took of her with a fish. She has red eyes in them. He laughs when he sees them later and calls her his demon. He writes back and asks when is his demon coming home.

"Watch out for the hooks," Ruth tells her. "They are ruthless and painful to get out if you get caught. The only way is to push them all the way through."

When they use the net for some of the salmon coming down from the river, they sit back and wait at the river's opening. Lin drinks a root beer. They take out the many red salmon from the net. They don't keep them all. There are other fishers around. It is an easy catch, too easy. They keep enough to eat and sell and for Aurora to smoke.

"I don't want to kill them," Lin says. Ruth is handling a fish that hasn't given up. "I can't."

"I don't, either. But one of us has to, so turn around." Ruth, as soft-hearted as she is, hits each one at the back of the head in just the right place, praying, apologizing, then goes to work as fast as she can. There is much to be done. Fish to be put on ice. To be delivered. Ropes to coil. Lin helps wash the deck afterward. Fore and aft, she writes her husband.

They go farther out to catch the fish coming down from the

north. It is not so easy when they go far out for king salmon that come down. The boat is not easy. It rolls and seems to tumble. Ruth always has to watch the weather, the moon, the tides.

The two women are easy together, able to be quiet and alone. Ruth keeps a journal and Lin makes sketches. "Those are good," Ruth tells her, looking at the drawings of the sea, the dark rocks, the precise sketches of salmon.

At night, far out, there are the lights of phosphorescence, animals of the sea. One night nautilus shells come magically to the surface with their own gleaming. "Look," Ruth says. They are shining and nearly round in the dark water under the moonlight.

Lin leans over. "Oh, they are beautiful."

It has also grown colder, so that night Ruth says, "Here, use this comforter." It is soft, filled with down. Lin has never slept so well or felt so safe except that night she remembers when the woman finally put her arms around her in the flower shop. Then, waking, she recalls the night with her grandmother on the boat when she was a girl and the boats were burning, even the little sampans where families and their dogs lived, and she had to leave the old woman in the bright lights and take to land. "Go." Her grandmother was weary. "Go. You are the new. I am the old. It's only natural," said the old woman in the light of many fires and their reflection on water, and it seemed also that the old woman turned to light as Lin ran through the water. The whole world was burning. Lin left, sobbing, wet, but somehow still carrying her fish.

Sometimes at night she and Ruth talk. Lin, full of memories, begins talking about her father. "All my life they spoke of him, my father. He was a king. Now I find him and he's a common man." She thinks for a while. "He's not even good at that."

Ruth laughs. "It's true."

"They always called him a man of beauty, a loved man. Even Thuy Su Linh gave him the prized jewel in all the town. Why? I ask now."

The water is seamless tonight and still. It is listening to what she has to say.

"They say once he even tamed a mean dog. He saved us. I used to think it was because he stayed and he caught fish for food and he worked all hours in the rice fields. But that wasn't how he saved us." She sounds so matter-of-fact.

Ruth doesn't see the vast expanse of rice, the water in it like a mirror, the people bending, but Lin does. "He said he'd come back. He never did. I remember him. But I expected a different man. The way he used to be.

"I always waited for him to return. I looked across the burned old forest watching for him. I looked out at the water where the market was. I thought he would step out of every boat or come down any path whistling just before he arrived. Even in the city, I looked for him around every corner."

How often Ruth had done the same thing before she was told Thomas was dead. Even after, because she didn't believe it in her bones. Something in her knew what the army didn't. She had looked around every turn in the road, watched every door that opened, knowing he was alive somewhere.

Lin tells how she had traveled by water partway to the city, then had to walk, finally running. "I rode in the back of a truck, behind and under other people, maybe even dead bodies. I don't know because it was hard to get out from under them. There was always yelling. Somehow, in the confusion, I slipped away.

"When I left my grandmother, I touched her arm, her hand. She was narrow as a grain after all has been taken from it. 'Hurry,' she told me, but I didn't want to leave her."

On the water, Lin's cheeks are rosy from the sea air, the fog. Her eyes, Ruth realizes now, listening, are still those of a village girl born closed into a small world, a sad girl showing through all the education, the appearance of a young woman with a profession. She was a lost girl, motherless, fatherless, placeless, alone in the midst of turmoil and war. And she was also an old, old woman who had seen and lived too much.

• • •

The next night, as they stand on the boat watching the sea, Lin says to Ruth, weeping, "My mother, she is the dream in my cells, and him, Papa . . ." She can't finish her sentence. The word sounds strange to Ruth. "I have felt all my life the blood I come from. Even this place I have always felt. It is like I know it here.

"On that terrible day he was taken away we all cried. And my father, the old men and women told him stories and sang to him."

She can't help remembering. It has been a long time, but it is only yesterday. "Then when he was gone, they said he was air. He was wind. He went into the sky and blew away. He was in every wind. Maybe my hope was only in my head like a light, incense burning with a prayer to make sure it gets to the sky.

"Even if Papa went back, he never would have found us. I returned once. The place was nothing but moss-covered ruins." She recalls that day. There were a few men and women with one leg on the bus, people walking on the road. "Not a sign of us was there, except a once-blue door. Later, I remembered it. It must have been indestructible. He *was* the wind, even if he now seems like a rock.

"They took him away. Then there was no one but Old Uncle, nearly blind, and Grandmother and the old people we had to leave behind. There were other children, women, but I don't remember where they went." The words fell out of her.

"We all left because the old man said the government has changed again and this time you have to leave. He said, 'you.' Not himself. He stayed behind. Without a word we packed up a few things, tea, rice, a pot. We had to try to live, but the whole world said to me, *I am the dying fields of poor planters. I am the fallen people, the ruined land, the blackened trees with no leaves.*

"I was afraid to die at first, but here was so much that after a while it didn't matter. I was also afraid of life. If I felt life too much I would miss it even more when I didn't have it. I would break like a glass."

She remembered her father standing in the fields or paddies working, bent over. He smiled when she brought him a jar of water.

He caught fish from the river for them to eat. He worked hard and made the field safe from land mines. He was everything. She still remembers the sweaty feel of his clothing, warm, his long black hair and the thrill of being pulled through the air by his arms.

"I chased the helicopter. I saw him crying as he left."

At Witka's place on the rock, Thomas opens his window, the side where the seals groom and talk and wrap about each other. He has been watching the north where he can still see the fishing boats despite the wall, watching for Ruth and Lin, thinking, She is here. Lin is here. And I am locked in, a key turned somewhere in my heart.

He sees the *Marco Polo* when it comes to shore. He knows they will tie up the boat and deliver the fish and return to clean the decks with scrub brushes and mops. They will pull together the floats. *Do you do this all the time?* Lin will probably ask Ruth or at least wonder. He even knows that. He knows it suddenly, as if he can see them and hear them, as if he is again close to them. He knows they will shower and dress before they come to him.

This time he is reading. So when they come back, he opens the door. He has opened a few windows. They can smell the sea and feel the air from inside Witka's place on the dark rock.

"Where do you live now?" he asks Lin. He has put on a clean shirt.

She is surprised he has addressed her so directly and suddenly, and her face grows red. "Ho Chi Minh City," she tells him. "Saigon, they used to say. I work there. I am married now."

"Married?" He has shaved. His eyes look surprised at the new name of Saigon, always it surprises him. He didn't see, as Lin did, how it became a sell-and-buy city so quickly. *Saigon.* His eyes see far away.

"Yes. I am a florist, I think you call them here, part of the time, and also an interpreter there for people searching for their loved ones." And the interpreter in her knows that in their absence something has changed in him. Every night they slept on the boat she thinks he must have dreamed or remembered their past.

He fixes coffee, letting it drain through a paper towel. His hand shakes when he hands some to Lin. She is beautiful, he thinks. She looks like Ma and she is tall. How did she survive? Someday he will ask.

She looks at the fish, remembering how she had loved the fish her father gave her. She didn't tell Ruth that one of the boys with guns threw it out of her hands. The fish lay on the ground, twisting, flopping. She would always remember the eyes of the boy. They were filled with a hatred of life as he stepped on it. And now she thought more, that maybe the boys and men had a fear of life, for to hold it dear and to lose it was a burden to carry, vulnerable as a fish in bottle and water, carried by a little girl in the middle of a war. Maybe it has been that way for her father, too.

"I almost forgot," Lin says. She opens the large bag she bought at the airport with a Frida Kahlo face on it, a real prize. "Look! You're in this painting." She has postcards of a painting one woman in the village had made, a picture of people working in the rice fields. "It is in a museum now." She hands several to him, a few to Ruth. Thomas studies it for a long time.

Lin laughs. "No one knows it is an American there! It's you, and every time I see it I remember." It had been their village, their put-together dwellings and the blue door to the shanty where Lin was born.

Ruth looks at it, too. She is silent. She recognizes him in the painting, though he is different there, his body, his looseness. It is part of the mystery of his disappearance. They sit without talking. But Ruth feels it is like the old days when the traditional people came together. They would sit for days in silence and decisions would be made in that way, knowledge passed, relationships renewed. Now it is like that. In silence, much is said.

He thinks of Ma. He loved her when he first saw her, even if he never told her or spoke with her. He never knew that she spoke several languages, including Hmong, French, and English. He never heard her speak. She took orders in the make-shift bar and always spoke to the others in her own language.

Then one day he said, thinking she didn't understand English, "You are the most beautiful woman I've seen. You are like a candle burning. You are a woman I would like to carry over the mud when it rains. You are a woman I would sing to."

She said nothing. But the next time she saw him, she said, "There's a mud puddle outside." She smiled and put down his glass and ashtray and he carried her across the mud.

It was the beginning of Lin.

She also made shoes, the finest ever seen, the most comfortable, and people came to her from other villages to have their shoes repaired. On the day of her funeral, that was all they could say except that she had made the shoes waterproof by using the sap of plants no longer there after the war, long since bombed.

He doesn't know that Lin learned the same languages, that she had gone secretly to school at night when it was against the law. And the new people would come to the flower shop where Lin stayed to lecture and be certain they were all reformed. "Yes, yes," the old man would say. "Our daughter is shy. She doesn't talk." But at night she learned to read. And as an adult she has just translated her first book, but she doesn't tell them.

So, Thomas thinks, she has gone to Ho Chi Minh City. Ha, the world has changed. Life is always changing. He puts his hand on her arm, his fingertips, really, lightly. She puts her hand over his. She looks down, though, suddenly shy. Something has come to fullness.

. . .

At Aurora's, Lin falls asleep that night thinking of home, of her husband. Gesturing, the husband had said to Lin one day after she was learning to read in English, "You win the prize. We give you a certificate, a pen, a flashlight so you can read in the dark when the generator stops!"

Lin laughed at how well he knew her, except that she never kept it dark, always a candle.

"And paper, too?" Lin asked.

"Anything." He pulled her head forward. She let him. "You should write our stories," he whispered, and she put her hand over the missing ear. "Does it hurt?"

"Always."

Now she looks forward to seeing him again. She sees him standing at the door in the late day, greeting her in the brilliant color of their world. She sees him at their little altar, bowing to the ancestors and the gods of compassion that they also pray are real and true. She knows he once denounced them, but a man has to believe in something.

Then the day comes when Lin must leave. Ruth stands beside the door of the rented car. "Come back."

"I will." Thomas comes walking. Lin sees the village behind him as if in a photograph. She will remember. She gets out to meet her father.

The next week Thomas is gone. Ruth looks around his place and notices his clothing missing. The fish is there alone and unfed. Damn it! Ruth thinks. She takes it to the small lake at the edge of the forest to turn it loose. It is not a long drive. And she marvels that after the drought the plants have returned and some are blooming. The sweet smell finds its way to her. The water has other fish in it, even other goldfish and koi, as if they had gone under the mud and waited the return of water. The grasses are there, the marshy beauty where birds nest.

She carries the fishbowl in her hands, walking carefully and talking to this fish Lin sang over. "You will grow and become large. You should see the others in the lake. There are many." The lake, really a large pond, is calm and surrounded by large trees. Green plants at the bottom. Ruth empties the bowl, knowing she will see the fish some days coming, red, to the surface. Ruth says, "Look, you are so beautiful."

From behind her a man's voice says, "Do you always talk to fish?"

She stands up quickly, embarrassed. Dick Russell is smiling at her.

"Yes, always. It's how I catch them on the boat."

"I figured that." He smiles at her.

"Did you catch the fire-starters?"

"It turned out to be easy. One was burned and hospitalized up in Layton. His friend complained about his ruined jacket. Say, do you eat?"

She thinks he means she's lost weight. Then says, "I think I've fallen for that one before. Yes." She laughs, suddenly shy. "I eat a lot."

"Good, then let's go get some dinner."

HOME

When Lin returns home, her husband greets her. She holds him and won't let go of his thin shoulders, feeling with her hands the rib cage in the back. It's night and he takes her home from the airport.

When they reach home she leans into him. A light rain begins. "It's too soon to tell. But I think he's coming here." Inside, she opens her suitcase. "Here, a present for you." It is a mask carved of wood with raffia hair, a perfect face, painted with color. "It was made by my grandfather."

She also has a carved wolf, yellow cedar. It is becoming the moon and the moon is becoming a whale. He studies the wolf, not the mask. "Transformation," he says. "That is your father."

He pulls her to the bed. "You must be tired. I won't bother you tonight." He kisses her stomach. "But watch out!"

That night she doesn't keep a light on. She has new ghosts, but they are far away.

She laughs just before falling asleep. During the night she holds on to him as if he will disappear. She dreams a helicopter, black as an insect, will come and take him away. She dreams he leaps out before it gets high enough to keep him in.

In the morning, she wakes and in their place the light is

beautiful and almost green. The smells of America are gone. She is peaceful and she bows in front of the ancestors on the altar. Over the thick rich coffee she loves, she leans back on the wall behind the bed and talks to him. "It's so good to be home. I didn't like America. There is a shadow there."

"There are shadows here, too."

"Yes. But we know what they are. The shadows of rubber trees. Our loved ones. Our stolen ancestors. Our living."

"When is he coming here?"

"I don't know. It is just something I know he will do. He is very handsome," she tells her husband. "But not as handsome as you." She kisses him lightly. He grabs hold of her.

They laugh. He kisses her lips. "I had forgotten how much I could love. I missed you." She feels her body, cell by cell, wanting to step into, walk into, that of her husband, that close. They lie down. They become the same. Her nipples love the feel of his skin, her stomach against his, his body moving into hers until they are one person.

beautiful and almost silent. The whirr of speeder are gone. She is terrified and she says instead of the shadows on the short time that real only she puts she... she something in the with being fulfilled and tells him... it mattered to be human whether he wanted. "Don't I ache for mercy?"

"That are shadow's liberation."

But we know what that air the shadow of white... ... One of those are... evil...

... he said I love...

... and ... she puts her hand on his shoulder... ... She felt so still but unless he would decide to be outside ... She remembered how he... he had to her ... that at last she put... I had forced many angry ... Time came when her... that, told by all what little untidy tresses have forgotten the past. The become ... meeting the place that people have the heart of ... But that stopped again, but at least I would devote into her ... would have... for herself.

PART THREE

PART THREE

THE WALL: THE NAMES

There are many kinds of walls, like the wall Thomas built in front of the water. There are walls of history, and the secrets of history. There are ones no one can breach or climb, the invisible boundaries of humans. Some walls seem righteous instead of ruthless. They don't claim property or hold something in or out. They keep things separate, but now, in the District of Columbia, it comes together for Thomas Witka Just.

Here in this Washington is a wall of revelations. A strange word, Thomas thinks, like the end of the world in the Bible. But at The Wall, it is the ground he sees first, as if it is not possible to look up. So he sees a box of donuts; some boy's favorite food. On the ground, a baseball sits before this portion of the wall. On it is written, *For Dad*. A batch of carnations sits, still in its wrapper, leaned up against the heat of it all. There is a letter to a soldier, even a gold button with a rhinestone on the ground as if to signify a blouse this man's hands once unbuttoned?

Mementos. Poems are engraved on plaques. Someone took such care to write them, to preserve them. There are now nearly sixty thousand names and the reflection of light on one whole side of it. In the place of America it shines. The whole crying light of it.

243

Three single roses. People walking already feel the heat of black stone as if it holds the fire of yesterday and not today. Thomas feels it in his body, remembering the heat of another country.

The world of this shining black stone is shaped at an angle, a chevron, really, like the stripes on a military sleeve, an army shirt.

The black heat from the wall is powerful as he stands near it, then begins to walk.

One old man traces the names of many men. He couldn't have known them. It is his existence. He is there for who knows how long. He has grief for the whole war, maybe for other wars. A woman visits the name of her man and presses her lips there. The Wall is a world, a time, a place. A young man in uniform walks about to see who needs help, the man in the wheelchair or a person searching for the name of one of the many gone.

Someone is reading the names in the background, but Thomas hears nothing. The names are anonymous, even his own. The grass has been replaced in patches as if someone has taken away part of the earth as a memory. Something, he thinks, is always covering up, hiding what is taken away. That's part of the purpose of earth and walls.

Somehow he walks right toward the day of the plane crash. He stands up straight at attention before the names of the many killed in that crash, the one thing he survived. His name is not there, where it should have been. He didn't know the others in that plane, but they were a noisy group; part of their noise was excitement, part of it fear. It was long ago, lifetimes. It feels like a century. He remembers the man who sat beside him, one eyebrow higher than the other, as if he knew something he wouldn't tell. Until now he barely remembered this man took his hand as the shaking plane dropped, the overheads opening and everything falling, cameras flying, jackets falling, drinks rising to spill. The lucky bastards, Thomas thinks, all of them. They never even reached the war. The date; so long ago now. Some of those years he wished he'd been among those killed in the plane. And what did they do but put him on another one right away. He had swallowed his fear, just a boy still, and gone along with it when he should have walked away and said, *The hell with it, what kind of people are you?*

He moves slowly down the way, seeing the tall building reflected in the black stone. He sees an old president behind him, before him, but he carries his own reflections as he reads the names that withstand the elements long after the flesh and bones of the men and women are gone.

Then he looks up and down and all along the shining black wall and it is nothing but names. He follows to where they are constant, one name crowded together with another, and there is no break and everyone was killed at nearly the same time, just before the end of it all.

It is the dark wall of this country. It is a black hole, some name enters and is gone from the universe. Some people cry here, some talk. Thomas would never find words for what he is feeling. Anger, fear, guilt. But he'd had to live with what he did and return home. For a passing moment he thought about his world, his real world. Stone. In the A'atsika stories there is an account where the stones speak and tell a lost boy the direction home. So it is with this one. It says name after name of the boys and men of America, a generation broken, some now still lost, some who found their way home covered with a flag. He thinks of the song, "Can't Find My Way Home." For him, this stone is a direction home, speaking to him.

The morning light on it is reflection on water. The first name of one who died, and is remembered, is found by Dwight. Then he hears Dwight. "John Doe. That really was his name." He laughs.

Thomas thinks there must be a mixture of happiness and grief in finding a name. It asserts that at least the man had once existed, and there is also the sorrow for knowing what it meant, but in truth none of the men there on this day knows *how* to feel, *what* to feel. To see the wall is to witness numbers of the unmeasured sacrifice, countless more than ever should have been, and Thomas has a strange feeling in him, a mixture of dread and sorrow, love and hate. He watches a man touch a name as if it is a human being and cry and walk away. Everyone touches The Wall. Touching it you feel you touch a human being. A name is more than just a name. Thomas hadn't counted on that.

After all this time of solitude he begins to understand something. "I knew it," he says, feeling he is alone.

"What?" asks Dimitri.

Thomas turns toward the voice. "I knew what it would be like, I guess."

A woman holds a flower next to the name of her son and her husband photographs it.

He knew it would be memory: It was the monsoon season. There were walls of rain. He was pushed out of the helicopter to certain death. "I'm sorry, man," said the sergeant pushing him out. He spread his arms and tried to stay in the door. He thought he was a coward. He opened his arms to hold on for dear life. Trying not to cry, terrified. The man pushing him would have cried, too, but he had no more tears, and he would always hate himself even though he had to follow orders. He was trapped in his work, a part of the killing. If he quit, *he* would be thrown, maybe without a parachute. He thought each man he pushed fell to his death. He never heard what happened to them. The smell of chemicals was in the air. And on the way down Thomas remembered thinking, *This is it. This is it.* He wished he could at least hold Ruth one more time. He felt the reality of her body, the physical warmth of it, the length of her next to him all the while he knew it was the end.

She would at least be his last thought. Looking around he saw the fire ahead of him, the fire of what they taught in some churches. Fire and brimstone.

It was as if he knew already what he would find on the ground, fire, smoke, bullets, mines, grenades. He was afraid. On the ground, using a flashlight allowed you to see, but it allowed you to be seen. He wanted to die first and get it over with. To just be gone. The smells are still in him, he thinks now. The smell of war, of human flesh, chemicals, smoke, fear.

The others who survived that push, that first touch of feet, bend of knees, roll on dangerous earth, would stay together in the firmament of jungle law, in the darkness of the water, the earth. In all that destruction they'd say such things as, "You're a sorry excuse for a man," and laugh, blowing out smoke.

Then he remembers the bodies carried out and away, some in bags, some just thrown on top of each other until they could be carelessly gathered and their blasted remains sent away. Then, another bomb. They may have been good sons and brothers, good to their wives at home, but a disease traveled through them in war. It was a fire of fear, excitement, hatred. There was no trust of anything, anyone. Everything alive was destroyed, as if all life but your own was dangerous and yours was the only one that existed and it wanted only to live.

"There is a reason everybody cries when they are first born," he says out loud.

The others all look at him.

They returned to camp sometimes. They were given real coffee and even heard a radio, but half the time even they didn't know exactly where they were. Thomas always kept a map. Thomas was crazy about maps. He studied them, watched directions. He even wore a compass around his neck. That was how he knew they were going to the wrong location, that world he would remain inside for how many years he didn't know until later. Once there, he lost track of time. As he does now, touching the map of names, touching it as if to be certain it is real, *they* were real, as if to touch them.

And so he reaches the place at the Wall. So. His name listed as one of the dead. Then a cross with a circle at the edge of it, which means he was resurrected. He wants to laugh. It is so crazy, but he wants to fall on his knees.

Dimitri, quick, finds the names and dates and, like everyone there, he touches them. There, there they are. Thomas's men. Murphy. Voight.

The sun reflects in it, the clouds, his own face, his own name.

Dimitri stands beside him. "Geez, you're not only a hero. You're a dead one!"

"Don't I know it." Smith, Anderson, and two others. They had been good boys at home. Wholesome. Once.

He wishes he could have touched their skin, held their sweaty bodies. He wishes he could have stopped it. He wishes. And in the mirror light his own face is reflected across theirs. He obliterates them with his life. He sits—no, he falls—on the ground. For the first time it doesn't matter if his tears are seen. A man comes by and touches him and says, "Hello, brother." He's Indian, too. It is too much for him, Thomas, the untouched man, the smell of the earth and hot stone, to think of their faces, the redheaded Murphy who at first was so innocent. It is too much for him to be touched, and he begins to cry.

One name is missing. So he survived, that boy, the one Thomas pushed out of the way. They, the only ones in that smoky place where they'd been dropped—no, thrown—from the copter, him arguing about them being at the wrong place. It wasn't part of the country. That day, he was not afraid so much as angry. Thomas is relieved the boy survived. The new boy shouldn't have been there. None of them should have. Thomas reads his own name. *Thomas Just*. His face reflected on it makes him wonder, when did he grow to look so haggard? He realizes he doesn't even know the date. He didn't over there, either. He lost track of time. But not his map. Some people tried to keep diaries, but those on special operations would eventually give up everything constant. They were called at any time, any place, any year, it seemed, because time was irrelevant when you were there. But it's engraved on the wall.

It began when Thomas was upset about the defoliation of the rice at harvest time. "What are you doing?" He saw the poor peasants broken, starved, running away from the orange cloud, bending over, weeping, and he said to the men, his men, "What are you doing? Are you trying to starve everyone? They are just poor people trying to live."

"Hey, we're just following orders."

"Who gave you that order?"

No answer.

Or maybe it began at the hamlet where he protested about a girl and then he saw an M16 turn slowly toward him, point at him, and he knew they would kill him. "You even look like one of them," Murph said. There was laughter. He knew they were no longer together, not a unit. He, with his black hair, dark skin. He was a man who couldn't lose his whole history of knowing that life was precious, sacred, irretrievable. That's what he'd been taught at home. It was in his blood. From his grandmother and mother all the way back in time. It *was* his blood. But he became silent even though the girl screamed because he knew at night when they breathed in tobacco or something stronger, that the M16 was more honest than anything else around him.

After that, something in him changed and he became the land, the life that was precious, the man like his grandfather who could feel the presence of a whale. He felt the presence of the land, the jungle, the bamboo, the rain, the pathways, partly to save himself from his own men as much as to save himself from the enemy. He became the man who could tell where the enemy was, could *feel* them, even if he still believed there was someone to be trusted, at least an infant four months old. He remembers Murphy killing the babies. "Hey," he had yelled. And Murph yelled back, "Those aren't babies. They're bombs!"

The bruised sky suddenly lit.

Or maybe it began with the planting of mines in the paths of villagers who merely wanted to survive. The rain already beginning. Him, scared, having to shoot at a sound only to go look and find it was a water buffalo and not a group of men making the sound, and he felt bad about killing it. The other men wrote on it with knives, words he hoped no one would read, all the while he felt terrible about killing it and tried not to cry.

And then there was a little old woman huddling behind a wall with her grandbabies. They were hungry. In a war, unlike now, a wall can be no place to hide behind.

He disappears inside this black stone wall, remembering how he feared some of his own men.

"What are you?" one of them asked him after he started to leave his things behind. The heavy things that made some of the men lose balance and fall. He was going to survive. It began this easily in the suddenly unholy world. That way he could slip into the grasses easily, the bamboo. He could hear the sound of someone moving in the jungle. He became the jungle. He knew by feel where things were and weren't. He knew if it was a trail they were on or if it was a trap because the *Cong*, as they called them, could make a weapon out of a tin can or anything. Soon he walked in front of them, not a point man; they were not that organized any longer.

He'd seen it coming and asked for a transfer because these men were not right. The organization had left them long ago. Then, he refused to kill a woman.

"Hey, she's probably got a grenade in her snatch!"

"Probably," he said, walking on, letting the woman flee from them, his own vulnerable body in the way to protect her. She was small and he could tell by her movement, her face, that she had lost everything. It was as if he had become awake in a new way, able to see into the heart of things, the place, the people. Those who vanish into the trees silently. But he could never be too sure and it was not untrue that a child could be a bomb, the Cong had seen to that, had created fear in the American boys. But him, he got into the minds of everyone in order to live and to save his own comrades.

At The Wall a man takes off his glasses and weeps, his face turning red. It is a place where a person's allowed to be overwhelmed by the names of the dead and the overwhelming language of the heart. The men come together as if they know one another, but mortality is what a person really knows here.

Thomas's fists are clenched. He looks at this wall as if it is a living thing, not only names carved in stone, but the silencing of a jungle, the sudden flare of deafening bombs, every sense attacked. Ordinary people. American men and women whose mothers sang lullabies to them when they were children, who had been boys with bicycles, handsome young men, ordinary women who wanted children, boys who once stole apples, whose mothers and fathers read them stories, as Ruth had surely done with Marco, the boy named out of his mother's desire that he would do what she never did, travel and see the strange and beautiful world. He thinks sadly of Ruth and his treatment of her. He carries her in his thoughts, the vision of how she stands straight and has cared for his own daughter better than he has. He wonders if there are times when she falls to earth and weeps, if she looks for Marco when she is out at sea. He thinks, out of all the warriors he has known, she is the true hero.

. . .

The names prove history. They prove lies.

"Where were you then?" Thomas asks.

"What about you?"

It was the end of the war.

He thinks of all the men with stripes and bars and shining medals. He thinks of seeing the fire of a village burning. Shapes in silhouette in smoke and fog. He thinks, for some reason, of a human nerve, the way it branches off, the way you see it in your dilated eye, a tributary that makes all the difference between pain and no pain, memory and no memory, vision or none.

On this night the fireflies come out in a familiar, humid jungle smell. DC is built on a swamp, a jungle where you can watch the plants grow. Oh, they are beautiful, the insects lighting up between the leaves of trees, a reminder of the light still remaining in the world.

A wall is to keep things out. A wall is to keep things in. Here are the names of all the gods who have left the world. It is a map, right, wrong, changed, earth opened to geographies of other kinds.

Humans have carved on stone throughout all their brief existence. Here, instead of these names, should be handprints, spirals, buffalo, horses, or whales like the stones in sacred places.

Back in the motel he doesn't recognize himself but knows he is Thomas when they call to him in his own room. He goes over the walkway to one of their rooms. They are subdued, drinking beer from the cooler, turning on the TV, changing the channel, sitting around in T-shirts, making jokes as if they are uncomfortable with silence, with their memories.

He thinks of the boy he'd thrown out of his way. He had saved his life, the boy whose name was not on the wall, and Thomas was thus decorated and also wounded, but he had taken his medals and ribbons from his father and pushed them into the back of a drawer behind screwdrivers and wrenches. Ruth would never see them. No one ever would have known he had them if it hadn't been for his father, who showed them to everyone.

Dwight is now in the room putting down a Bud. "The men in my platoon stole food from a truck going to a camp for villagers. We ate cheese!"

Someone laughs. "Yeah, like it was their traditional food."

They are drinking beer. They don't see the despair on his face. Just as with the others years ago, they don't know Thomas any longer. But he knew them and he knows Dwight too well, the liar, the thief.

"She looked just like my sister. How could I kill her?" Dwight says this in wonder. "But I did it. More than once. But you know those gooks. Hey, I hear one came to see you, Thomas."

He is quiet a moment and so is everyone else.

"Well, it's not worth thinking about it anymore, is it?" says Dwight. "It was just a dream. That's what I tell myself. Who decides fate? It's you or it's Charlie. That's all." But Thomas sees his ghosts all around him. The old man ghost. The infant ghost. The girls. Dwight is heartless. The man without a heart. The liar about the whales.

Dwight sees Thomas looking at him. Nervous, he gets up and he takes off his ring and places it by the TV. "Come on. Let's go swimming."

But Thomas doesn't hear this. He looks at the ring. He remembers Dwight always wore it for special events. He hasn't worn it until now, this journey. Thomas looks at it carefully. Suddenly he knows. Milton saw it, saw the hand with this ring hit Marco on the head, hold him in water, underwater. Suddenly Thomas knows what happened to his son that day of the hunt. Milton never lies.

Marco is like Thomas. He was the one who said what was wrong. He knew it was not a whale to kill, that the time was not right.

Thomas picks up the ring and puts it in his pocket. He feels love for his son, and quiet grief.

From his room, he hears the others down at the pool.

Vietnam. It was so green there, another world, as if he dreamed it. The humidity and the many shades of green and the rich dank smell of mildew. He opens the box and looks at his medals. Like Dwight's ring. So proud a medal, a decoration, an identity of some kind. Thomas has a Silver Star for jumping in a bunker to save a wounded man.

Dimitri knocks on his door and Thomas pockets Dwight's ring as if he is the guilty person. He puts the medals inside the box. Thomas still remembers their grandfathers. Dimitri's grandfather was a whaler with Witka. Thomas still can see them walking together.

Dimitri comes in and sits in the worn motel chair. "You're lucky you survived."

"Yeah, lucky."

"What did you do over there all that time?"

"Take care of the dead, cover their faces, smell them."

"What everyone did, huh? But I mean what happened to you all those years they thought you were dead?"

"I don't know. I grew rice. I fished."

"You what?"

"Yeah, I worked."

"Were you like a prisoner or something?"

"I tried not to be a prisoner. I just pretended to be someone else."

"You must have been good at it."

"I guess I was. I still am."

"At least you survived it."

"No. I didn't."

"What do you mean?"

"Think about it. My name is up there. Among the dead and the missing."

"Jesus. You're right."

It's late at night. They've had too much to drink. Thomas wants silence. He can hear them down there at the pool until management or someone silences them. They argue a moment and then he hears them come to the door and enter their rooms.

"Hey." Dwight opens Thomas's door without knocking and drips pool water on the dirty carpet. Dimitri is already there. "What's everyone in here so solemn about?"

And Thomas says, "I'm a killer." He says, "Hit me." He stands up from the bed.

"Naw. I'm not going to hit you."

"Hit me."

Dimitri and Dwight look at each other. "What brought all this on?" asks Dwight, pushing his wet hair back.

"I killed my own men. I looked at their faces, I looked at the children they were going to kill, the women they were going to hurt, and I shot the Americans, those men. They looked so white. It was like it was happening to us Indians. They were going to kill the children. One of them was going to rape a little girl. It was like us, our history, like one more group of murderers." Crying now. Breaking the rules again. "I shot them. I had to."

Dwight hits him. "Shut up!"

Thomas stands straight and wishes he'd been hit harder. "Go ahead," he says. "Hit me again."

But then Dwight looks at him again. "You're not worth it." But then, later, Dwight says, "I might have done it too, Tom."

"You did."

"What?"

"You killed your own."

"What do you mean?"

"It just wasn't over there."

Dimitri says, "I did. I killed our officer. I had to or he would've killed all of us. He was sending us straight into a trap. He had no idea."

Thomas thinks of the graves of the old people at home, marked by whalebone, the shrines that belonged to the whalers and the women, the sky that isn't European. Its constellations are a great whale, a sea lion, a tree of life, and he remembers this; this is who he is; the man who stands beneath *those* stars, *those* planets. He's A'atsika. He comprehends the immensity, the pathos of the tragedy that shaped him and all his actions— and theirs—forever after.

He was one of the breakers, as Ruth called the men after her day sitting out the storm on the water. And she was right. He was still afraid of living. It took courage to live. It took courage to have happiness. What are inner walls made of but memory and forgetting?

"Yeah," Dwight says, thinking backward in time. "I would have done it."

"Like I said, you did. You killed my son."

"What? You're crazier than I thought, man." He throws an ashtray. It breaks.

Thomas looks him directly in the eye. "You killed Marco. My son. Dwight, Jesus."

Dwight looks up. "Hey, you know me, Tom. It's me, Dwight. What's the matter with you? You've been crazy a long time, bud, and everyone knows it."

"Yeah, well I want to think of how I'd be remembered if I died today." He'd been thinking that same thing on the day they killed the whale, the day his son died. "I'm not going to be remembered as the one who poured beer on the whale to say fuck off, America." As the others leave the room he grabs Dwight and pushes him against the wall. "I can prove it. You lied. You killed for money. What could be worse?"

"Shut the fuck up. Let me go."

"I'm not going to be remembered as an American who killed children and women." He comprehends the immensity of all his decisions, the long line of American tragedies that had shaped him.

He passes through a door, not the kind that opens and closes.

RUTH WATCHING

Ruth knows that on the day the whales went away, the blood of the whale and that of her son must have been mixed together. Marco and the whale were related once again. He was the boy who went to live with the whales. He left to travel far distances. He learned the bottom of the sea. He began to see with the whale's eye.

She wraps a shawl around her. She stood years ago in the same shawl watching the ocean, the wind blowing her sleeves and hair, light on water. It was the same shawl she had wrapped around baby Marco, and now she cries. Now ocean and tears become one. It is the same element.

The whales have left them since their hunt. The whales Ruth loved to watch. When she is far out, she still sees them rise and turn, open the water like new stones, new planets, breathing their eyes wiser, older, than her own. She thinks that now all she has in common with Thomas was giving a child to the sea, and where has he gone?

Over where the round rocks are, where the river comes into the sea, and the kelp forests farther out, Ruth watches.

Many of the men are now gone. She thinks perhaps the men have taken a trip together, or perhaps to visit whalers up north, or to piece together another way to hunt the whales, which of course she would fight.

Thomas was the young man who had once followed her prints in the sand to the large dark rocks. They made cairns and left them as messages on the beach. Some of these were elaborate in their balance, more than a message, but something beautiful and full, large-seeming, even as limited as the two young people were in truth and experience. But it was years ago.

Now she comes back inside her mother's house and the sound of the wind is sometimes like singing.

She sees herself. She is a shadow on the wall at her mother's house.

Her mother says, "They'll be back. As for Thomas, did he ever sweep the floor?"

He didn't. Ruth only shakes her head no.

"Did he eat the food you left him?"

"No."

"Did he go to the water?"

"Only at night."

"Did he cry at night?"

"Yes, I think so. I think I heard him a few times. Or it was the wind."

"Good. That is what matters in these cases."

Ruth thinks, We are in the town where everything is stolen from the sea. Most of the people have always lived here. A few mobile homes behind and among the houses now take away the old feeling, but where do you put a growing family? And everyone knows each other's business, who drinks, which man yells at night when frustrated by day. No one even bothers to close their curtains at night unless they are fighting or making love, and they look into each other's windows and then they can tell which purchase they must next make or how to arrange their furniture.

The sunset is like gold as Ruth watches it. On the windows are beads of light, the ones after a rain. And some nights they have a good strong moon reflected.

The ocean is a landlord here. Everyone pays the sea. Only some pay more. Even the seals have to pay to remain there.

DOA: DEPARTMENT
OF THE ARMY: *ROOMS*

Dear Ruth, he'd tried to write, early on in the war, *the birds here are noisy and the jungle is a place you would love.* But then, even as he wrote it, it was gone. That quickly. From flame to nothing. What could he say to Ruth? And so he is in a room of fire and all night he watches red walls rise up and fall back and he thinks of the creators of his own world, how unlike the Americans they were. The A'atsika creators punished humans who weren't peaceful. They sent them traveling, like Adam out of paradise, not for having knowledge but for having a lack of peace. They were sent from one world to another for being like the human he had become and he wondered what his next world would be.

In the next room Dwight sits up in bed, disturbed by the sounds next door. He thinks he needs to keep a watch on Thomas. He lights a cigarette. He has heard Thomas showering, then opening and closing drawers. Hell, the first thing a man learns is never to unpack, Dwight thinks as he listens to Thomas's every move through the paper-thin wall, not knowing that in the next room the walls are red and burning.

. . .

Thomas stands up straight and puts on his dress uniform. He carries the medals in his pocket. He opens the door. Outside is rain upon rain. He goes back in and puts the plastic cover over his dress hat before he leaves. He puts on his GI issue raincoat and ties the belt. He looks perfect. His boots are shined but he doesn't care to cover them, to keep them from being wet. He has already called the cab.

Dwight has heard all this, the door opening, closing. He goes out. "What are you doing? Hey, where are you going all spiffed up like that? Hell, you're even spit-shined."

Dwight follows a ways, asking Thomas questions, but Thomas ignores him. It is wet, even if it isn't cold. Thomas doesn't say anything. In fact, he doesn't acknowledge Dwight, not even his presence, let alone the questions.

"We're just different. It doesn't mean anything. We're amigos, you know."

He gets in the cab. "Department of the Army," Thomas tells the driver. The man looks at him, then opens a map. Then a phone book. "Sir, there isn't one. It's just a historical building. Is that what you want?" He looks Thomas up and down. "You might mean the Pentagon."

"I saw it on the map."

Dwight watches. He plans.

"That's not the department anymore. It's just the old building. The DOA. Ha, ha! I had one of those in here last night. Dead On Arrival."

Thomas doesn't smile. "Or maybe the White House."

"Which one?" The man is becoming frustrated, losing time, which is money.

"Okay, the Pentagon."

"Which section?"

"Hell, I don't know. The Department of War."

The cabdriver eyes the man in the backseat, dressed in his uniform, wondering why he is lost. "Where are you from?" He sees the other man still standing in the rain as he drives away.

"It's a place called Dark River. No one ever knows where it is. It's out West."

When they pull up and he gets out of the taxi, he gives the cabdriver a large tip.

There are doors and doors and an underground tunnel and somehow Thomas wanders through it all. Security. He thinks of how good he looks today, in his uniform, newly cut short hair, good proud looks. He looks right. He feels the way he did when he first joined, getting his picture taken with the flag. But going into the building at first makes him feel smaller than he felt while he was in the cab, riding without being able to tell the man where he was going. He had planned in his mind what it looked like and not that it was like a prison of deep concrete, then wood, stone, a place of vast scale, not like the rooms he inhabited but one designed to make the army look like it was all clean lines, perfect in scale despite being full with the spirits of the dead. In here is a museum of wars. Files of war. He sees it in his mind like a room one enters underground, then up steps, elevated, but it is still overdone. He should have known there are no buildings here that are not imposing and official.

"Can I help you, Sergeant?" the voice is almost an echo. "You don't look well." He can barely see the man behind the desk.

He himself thinks he looks official in his dress uniform, but for a while he is speechless, vulnerable. Of course, he is being watched. There are small cameras. He looks for them as a criminal would, before he enters through security without so much as being questioned, showing his ID. Then he goes into a room where a major sits behind a desk and he tosses his medals on the desk and says, "I want to return these. I want it noted that I am giving them back."

The major looks up, expecting to recognize anyone in the vicinity, but finds a stranger in their building. "You want to return them? Whose are they?"

"Mine." He drops them, bends down to pick them up, not at all with the dignity he wanted. He hears Dimitri's voice in his head. *No one gives a damn who killed what, who didn't. We all did it.*

"How did you get in here? This is a secured area."

He looks suspicious and he knows it. "They saluted me through." He laughs. "It must have been the uniform." How far a few silver things, a few bars, a pair of spit-shined shoes can carry a man. Oh, he forgot: "Sir."

"You have to go through two checkpoints."

"Yes. I did that."

"Just a moment, sir. I will direct you to the person in charge of this." The major backs out of the room, careful of Thomas.

Men appear as if from the air and they push him down and keep him down and he smells the floor wax and sees what could have been his life in so many ways, if he hadn't joined up and had remained home with Ruth and learned, himself, the old songs and ways they had started to teach him when he was young. Or if he'd gone along with the others and killed the children and women and the old man who was left behind and gone on to another village and done it again and lived or died with his troops, burning things behind him, keeping a souvenir here and there. And he could have gone home with them, found a job or two, drank a beer together with his buddies, watched a ball game, run for tribal council, the state legislature, or some other branch of a government just like this one where he is held down.

When his records come up on their computer, a voice from out of the sky like god's voice, says, "Hell, why do you want to turn them in?"

"I didn't earn them."

"Weren't you wounded? It says you were wounded."

They already have his information. He thinks about the scar across his middle, the bleeding leg he'd thought was an artery and tried to hold together, the impact to his neck and arm which he didn't even know about because of the blood on his leg. It made him sweat now to think of it. He kept it out of his mind, in one of the corners in a bundle he made called shrapnel and suddenly he weighed so much. "Yes sir, I was wounded."

He is moving closer to words, to truth. "But I wasn't killed or missing. I killed the wrong people. I stayed." Tears began in eyes that had forgotten to dry. "I killed Americans. It was supposed to be a raid. It went wrong. And we were in the wrong place. I tried to tell them. I had the map in my hand. And we were supposed to kill the children and I said no."

Time passed even if it didn't seem to. He was sitting now. By then the doctor was there. "They say that a lot, you survivors. Did you know that? But your records say you already told the doctors. They told you that what you did was right by military law. The simple rules of engagement. But it was common then, you know. It also says you had a head injury."

"But I did it. I knew what I was doing. They were going to kill innocent people. I left my own tags there so everyone would think I was dead, too. I ran away. I didn't go home. I couldn't. It was a choice, don't you see?"

The two looked at each other. One of them said, "Well, maybe you weren't wrong. The war is over, son. We have to let the past rest. Also, in my book you did the right thing. Get up. Walk out that door. Walk down those steps. Cross the street. Go home. The war is over. You don't have to go on trial. You don't have to give back your medals."

"I don't want them. The past doesn't rest. They were smoking dope, they were killing the people's pigs, they were planting land mines all around the place, killing innocent people. They shot at anything. The . . . cries, they were going to kill children. Rape and kill them. I looked at their faces. I looked at the children. I turned and shot them. There wasn't even a look of surprise on their faces. They weren't even that clear. I hated them. I hate myself."

"You only won this war if you stayed alive. You should have left well enough alone. You're more a hero in my book. Sir, is there anyone we can call to come get you?"

"No. But I'm trying to tell you I don't want the medals. They hurt my hands to touch them. They are hot. Like fire."

"You are free to go, Sergeant Just." He salutes.

He didn't know what he expected, but this encounter was as meaningless as the men who left their medals at The Wall to make a statement. Still, he left the medals, all of them, and walked away, merely walked away. Outside, looking at the Potomac, he wondered what Indian word the river name came from, where the tribe lived.

THE DAY OF TRANQUILLITY

He is a numb man. Flying back, almost home in the evening, he looks for whales in the ocean before the plane reaches San Francisco. He remembers when the whales used to pass by in great numbers. He would watch one, its great shining side, the eye with its old intelligence, the gentleness of it in the body covered with barnacle life and sea creatures. It was loved by his people. It was a planet. When they killed it, he thinks perhaps they killed a planet in its universe of water.

The next day he walks from the bus, wrapped in fog. He has left a part of himself behind. There are spiritual requirements to make up for all he has done. There are those that require offerings to the ancestors. You offer food, your body, your service, your heart to open and fill. Sometimes you go up to the rocks that are carved with humans being born of the whales.

His ache is so great he would like to harm it by harming himself. They don't want that, the old ones, the ancient ones. This requirement is not that of Thomas Witka Just. It may be dark at times but the ancients live in a lightness, lighter than dust in air. They want him to open the pathway into the future, not to fast or starve or harm any part of himself but to be whole and nourished. They are there to take his human hand, its lines, its dark skin with pale scars from a never-won war, not that winning would ever have made a difference. In their world, there is only the hand to take, the human hand, to slide through time along its mysterious pathway sometimes called memory, sometimes called feeling. They travel through ancient knowledge and the movement of mountains, winds familiar and singing, and through the sweet water. He knows they can take him to the shoals on the other side of his life even if he feels lost. Or they can take him seaward, farther than a man can see or know, that's where the grasp of *their* hands lead. They can take you to the green mosses, or to places where creatures cling to granite walls above the ocean. Oh listen, the seagulls call, and the sound of washing water comes to earth. In his raw condition, he could break open and a new man filled with beauty would be there as if from a cocoon, soft and new, shining. The dead heart falls away and there is a new one, alive and beating.

He knows the horrors in his body will be there the rest of his life if he doesn't heal them. Maybe even then they might remain, but he would see them differently. For every inch of skin, there is memory. Devils are so made. Saints, too, if you believe in them. His humanity has been broken as an old walking stick that once held up a crippled man named Thomas. He realizes the stick and the man are one thing and he can fall. He has violated laws beneath the laws of men and countries, something deeper, the earth and the sea, the explosion of trees. He has to care again. He has to be water again, rock, earth with its new spring wildflowers and its beautiful, complex mosses.

The fog has fallen the night before and now its hand covers their world. Ruth watches it lift a finger and a man walks out of the fog, a ghost becoming real, taking on a body. Thomas comes to Aurora's door. Ruth stands behind the door, feeling him, not answering. She can feel his condition and it is full of voices. She hears them talking. Maybe they mumble, or maybe they are all talking at the same time, but she thinks it is A'atsika they speak and it makes a chill rise up her spine to hear a man's body speak so. She doesn't let him in. It is not the right time for them to meet and face one another.

Aurora watches from the roadway and stops and waits for Thomas to leave her front door.

Inside, she asks Ruth, "Why didn't you let him in?"

"It didn't feel right."

"There's water on the front step. Where did it come from?'

"Maybe it rained."

"I don't know. I was out here and it didn't rain." And then she tells again about the octopus. Ruth has heard it before but she doesn't tell her mother about the Rain Priest and the octopus old Gus saw leaving her boat when it was stranded far away out there in the water. She just listens and knows the water has fallen from Thomas's body. It is all of his uncried tears.

That night Ruth loads up the Zodiac with things she needs for the boat and makes her dark way out through the water, home to her *Marco Polo*, and as she travels the water and sees her boat it is a strange presence rocking there in the fog but the wind is rising and so the trees on the nearby shore are moving and if she could hear them, they would be creaking.

She knows it is only a matter of time before Thomas will want to speak with her some more. She could hear that, not just in his own words but in the many voices that emanated from him where he stood. He was waiting for something to open, but it wasn't the door. Nor was it her.

A few days later he comes to her on the boat. She's tired. She sold all her fish early and the price was too low. She is cleaning the decks. But she stands and she watches him.

This time his face is relaxed, his eyes not haunted. Our brave people, she thinks when she sees his face in the light and shadows. We have continued.

She rinses herself off with the hose and she invites him in and looks him over as she wraps her brown shawl about her and combs her wet hair. She dries her face and waits, watching him from where she stands beside the stove. He sits down, but then he changes his mind and he looks at Ruth and gets up and holds her, standing behind her. She is wrapped up in warmth, her hair down over the brown wrap, a black river of hair that could flow on out to the ocean. For Thomas, it all passes through his heart again. Remembering. Then he begins to sob. He thinks, And I'm a grown man, and she is thinking, Thank God, stepping out of his hold and turning to him. The boat is moving sideways and back. At last, at long last, the tears are there for him. She wept for many years. Now it is his time. She looks at him. She brushes hair back from his face even though none is there, as if he is her son, or as if they are children again and his mother has just died on the road, in the car, the father drinking, the other car, all the people in it. It was in the terrible times and his father, the man of artistic gifts, so highly treasured, the mask-maker, was never the same, yet he was alive. Still sometimes he made spirit faces, transformations.

Together they sit and look back at the green hills. They both remember how one generation took down a forest. They don't even need to say it. Thomas, who left his uniform behind in DC, says, "I have to think. How am I going to be remembered in the end?"

"What are you going to be remembered as?"

"What am I going to do? I'm changing history now. I am going to be remembered as the man who could kill but doesn't. As the man who one day said I'm going to be like the old people, I'm going to be like the ancestors. If I ever have to kill a whale I will prepare for a year. I will have good thoughts. I will love the whale.

"I was wrong about so many things," Thomas says.

She feels for him. "I know. Shh. Oh, look out at the water, Tom." It is beautiful shades of color, worked by the sun and water.

"I thought Marco wasn't my son. For a long time I thought

that. I can't forgive myself for that. I couldn't even come home. I went to San Francisco. I found a place. Remember Van Gogh's room, the one we used to look at in the picture I had? It was like that. That's why I moved there. And it was cheap."

He has traveled away from the subject. "Anyway, I came home and I went to look up the date of Marco's birth."

"Yeah. I know. The girl at records told me. Here." She pours him coffee, thinking maybe he'd been drinking with "the boys," as she's always called them. She doesn't smell alcohol, but then suddenly she's angry. She remembers the evening he came to the meeting, her excitement, seeing him finally, after all the lost and gone years, the years she had waited for him, then grieved him, that night telling him where Marco was, pointing out their son to him so he could at least love the young man, if he did not love her all those years.

"You're right. You've been wrong and you are a bastard." But she's not yelling, just stating what sounds true. "One hell of a bastard."

"It was Dwight. That's what he told me. We met at a landing strip in Da Nang and he said you were with my father."

"Yes. It's always him, isn't it? It was Dwight who killed my son. Ours. I feel it. I know it every time I have to look at him." She becomes fierce. "Everything was always Dwight. He was jealous of you. Always. First he wanted what you had. He wanted to be you. Later he wanted what Marco had because you know what your son had? Marco had the old ways. The thing is, Dwight could have had them if he'd tried, if he could have given up some few, meaningless things. You could have them even now. The old people want us to learn and know.

"And it was your father. He tried to rape me. Dwight and some of the guys walked by and they could have stopped it. I cried out for help. They were drunk. They didn't do anything. I was already pregnant. I said, Help me, and they didn't do a thing. I fought your father off. I attacked him with all I could muster."

"Jesus." Thomas is quiet, thinking of his father, but he is also a man possessed by his own offenses. He thinks of Dwight lying again. Then he remembers. He takes Dwight's ring out of his pocket. "Here. It's his ring. Just as Milton described it." It makes a hollow sound when he drops it on the table. "We can go to the police."

She looks at him long and hard. She wishes he would leave. He didn't even care about what his father had done. But then she turns to the ring. "Which police? The tribal police? The town? The FBI? Our word supported only by a retarded boy and everyone out there hating us for killing the whale? This whole part of America hates us. Even our children are attacked in school. Who is going to care about a dead A'atsika who was whaling? Me with only a mother's feeling and you with something you didn't even see?"

"Yes, but Dwight knows I know."

Thomas still fails to see that sometimes there isn't justice, that the world still is not one made up of black and white, right and wrong. How could he have survived a war, she wonders, without knowing that zone of gray, of being in between, of sitting on the border between lies and half-truths, between the goodness of some and the evil of others?

"Nothing is ever finished," he says.

"What does that mean?" She's almost sarcastic. "Some things are finished. Gone. Done."

"I don't know what it means. It is some kind of riddle of being human, being a man."

She sits down. "Okay. Do it. Get Milton to testify. Between the two of us we have a history of Dwight's betrayals, including the death of whales, the stealing of tribal funds, his lies." She knows it is futile, but at least Dwight would have to sweat it out.

"It's even in the fact that Marco said no that day."

She is silent, taking it in, taking him in. Sometimes she wakes up thinking Marco is alive. She talks to him out loud in the floating darkness. She tells him, "Good morning," or "Oh, look at the whales pass by." But now she looks at Thomas in wonder. "He said no? You mean about killing the whale?"

In the long silence that follows, Thomas thinks about how, with surprise, he could have been the first to fire a shot and he blamed it on history, his history, and he hated himself for it, but that day it was like war all over again, the copter above, the men in the boat yelling, the Coast Guard boat, the excitement akin to fear. He remembers the men, them firing, too, the barrage, the sound, the whale coming to them in its pain from somewhere it didn't know, *to* them instead of away in its last fight, larger than they could have thought even though it was just a small one, moving the boat, and then it turned in its bleeding agony and the canoe was tossed like a stick and the Coast Guard rushed in with all the noise and yelling. The confusion, everyone with a different focus. Some trying to get the whale up from its descent down to the bottom of the ocean with lungs full of water, some trying to find the men who were lost in the water. Yet for most, the focus was on the whale, even with water all around them, the men trying to get out of water, afraid of the whale, of the great waves created by it and the Coast Guard boat, the spray of blood on them all.

"The thing was, he didn't want to kill the whale. It was friendly, he said. It was timid. It was young. the People taught him well. And then, Goddamn me, Ruth, I fired and we all fired. I had my own brother in my hand, that's what we called it, an M16. Hell, I'm surprised anything was left of the poor creature. It was like war all over again, and we were warriors, only then he tried to stop the men even if it was too late and the canoe overturned. I did stop them. In the war, at least. Then on the water." He is silent, mulling it over while she doesn't know what to think of this man she once knew so well, after just forgiving him everything. "Maybe I wanted to be Witka. I came back to prove something. That I could be one of us. But in truth, *he* was us. He was Witka. But how I wanted. How I yearned. I longed for something."

. . .

She stands, waiting for this man to shut up and leave. He had gone against her own son. Then Dwight had killed the boy.

She has no idea what is on his mind. She just sees his expression. She puts her hand on his. The boat slowly rocks. "Thomas." Again she speaks, "Thomas?"

He doesn't realize how his own face looks. They are quiet awhile. Then she says, "You should leave now."

"What?"

"You went against Marco. My son. Ours. How can you come here to me? How could you have touched me!"

He looks at her wide-open eyes, the flecks of red in them. "Ruth, you are my only family."

"I'm not. And Thomas, I am not coming back to you if that is what is on your mind." Her eyes are clear, disarming, as if she sees what he sees, knows what he knows. It's not about the whale. Not even about Marco.

He looks down. "I know it. I didn't expect you to. That's not why I came."

In spite of it all, she closes her hand around his, caressing it, the familiar hand she has known all her life, then stops herself. "There are all the years, the lies. The times I've had no money. I went to the army and they said our marriage didn't exist. It wasn't even on the record. There were times when there were no fish, no jobs, and you were gone. And now I want you to go."

He sees her dark eyes fill with tears. They come from nowhere that can be explained by anything but feeling. They come from everywhere, like the rain. "Ruth, I ran away from you. I never even asked for an explanation for anything. I never gave one. I just ran. From everything."

"You ran out of our lives."

"No, really, I *fell* over the edge." Suddenly he wants to explain everything to her.

He looks at her. "You must hate me."

The darkness is lowering itself outside. Rain. Ocean. Storm.

Evening. He sees the swaying of things underwater, how the fish hold their own in it and how he can't hold his own in still air.

"I do."

"I had to stay. I couldn't come home in the condition I was in. War is another world. Hell, Ruth, it's another universe. It's like one of those Brueghel paintings we'd look at." He puts his head in his hands. "I couldn't come home to you like that. Even now, after all these years, I can't explain it, the feeling. Then . . ." He pauses, looking out the window as if he'd find answers in the darkness where they sometimes live. "It was all lies. You know? The boys didn't even know what a communist was or why we fought them. And they were scared at first, thinking everyone was a communist. Then something else took over. They'd shoot at anyone or anything. The first night I was there I dropped down so scared I peed myself. I saw a beautiful forest. Suddenly the forest was gone. What about a little human?"

There are limits to what he can say.

But she hears the voices begin in him again.

"I am sorry to be a man," he says. "I am sorry to be a human being. I used to think it was other people. But I am one of them. I became one. I even killed Americans. I had to."

She has thought often about being a soldier. She thinks she would have killed herself on her first day in war just to have it over with.

"At the end, they dropped us outside the war zone. I had a map. It was all one fiery lie. I kept telling the pilot, Look, look where we are. We aren't even supposed to be here. I kept telling him we were off course."

She knew his love of maps, how he could follow them.

Then he is silent again. She thinks of how he used to show her the lines of demarcation, the legend, the way he used to show her sea monsters and how they thought California was an island.

"That was why you stayed all those years."

He only nods, swallows.

Suddenly Thomas seems to grow small. Bent.

"You didn't really have to tell me." She sounds tired. "I already figured it out. I know what happened. I had years to think about it and then when she came, Lin told me more. You saved a village there." She even sees them, the dirty American men, desperate, sweating, the way they moved, even their thinking. She knows how they approached the people. She sees the people about to be in a trench, some waiting to die while the men take a smoke break. The unborn Lin is an egg inside a woman about to be stabbed in the vagina. She loves Lin. She loves that Lin did not become a casualty.

She thinks of her own lone pregnancy. She doesn't hate what he did. If she hates, she hates the men who sign the papers. On their own land, too. She thinks, I am capable of hatred. Suffering is our history. Oh yes, there is singing down by the water, dancing, and joy some nights. As if it is a little gift wrapped in stars to make up for all the rest.

"I have practiced now, like Witka. I have gone beneath the water. I have learned to stop breathing."

"I know."

He looks at her. "What do you mean, you know?"

"I followed you to be certain you wouldn't drown. But you did, didn't you?"

She gets up and turns on the lights. Now it seems darker out. He says, "I loved you. I loved them. I loved. I tell myself that is what matters."

"It is."

"And at the end I loved Marco. No, I loved him before then. When I first saw him. I was a coward. I should have gone over and hugged him. But I talked to him on the boat. He was beautiful. He was one of us. An A'atsika."

"Yes. He was."

She'd been so proud of him, to see him paddle, to see his

strength and hear his voice singing the songs. "If you'd only known. And the way he moved."

She stands at the table, as if waiting for Marco to arrive.

She hears the splash of oars in water. The voices leave with him.

Thomas paddles on from there out to the white house people. He paddles, staying close to shore at first, passing away from Ruth's boat. Along the way he stops. He feels it in his muscles, sinew, where things meet in the body. It hurts at first. Not just tendons, but whole histories. He doesn't hear them speaking, but he follows what they tell him to do, as if now he, too, hears the voices inside him.

It is nearly morning. The houses are white again, now from rains and mist, but that doesn't mean that grief has disappeared. It has more staying power than weather. The people are busy. A man sings in a crack of light from atop a black rock, as if he were inside a clamshell. He stands with his arms outstretched and his eyes closed and he doesn't lose his balance. Thomas is invisible in the night, but it is as if the man is singing Thomas toward him, as if the voice leaves the man's body, travels outward, and is a path to their world. Thomas follows. His back and arms hurt, but he paddles and he closes his eyes and follows the voice. When he opens his eyes, two women are standing in the water, ready to pull his canoe in.

"Look," one says. "It's one of the old canoes."

He thinks it must be very late. He is surprised they are awake because he doesn't realize how long it has taken him to arrive, but they knew the man with many voices was coming. They summoned him. One has her hair down, gray and disheveled. The other is dressed and tidy. "Well, father of Marco, grandson of Witka, Thomas Just," she says formally. "So."

On land one woman with twine for hair steps toward him. She says to his body, "Be quiet, you are driving me crazy," and the voices subside. He feels calm and even laughs.

. . .

Ferns grow there in that place as if it is the first moment of
their universe. His bones are an eye through which the spirit
is looking.

The people are waiting, their faces like open questions. No,
Thomas thinks, they are answers to questions not yet even
asked.

They bring him inside into the old warmth and he sees
the stones carved with spirals. A fire burns. He sees animals
in the flames, as if he has walked into another world. He
watches the fire. Sea animals. A red otter, an orange seal. Land
animals, the forest deer coming from the woods where they
hide. A candle burns.

Old as some of them are, the people are still alive in the
body, laughing, talking, sweating. They are people who lived
through the starving times, the treaty-making times. And then
they watched the last humiliating kill of the whale.

And then they were completely silent, even the man with
the hurt foot.

They live near the wall. A stone wall. It has a whale carved into
it and the whale is giving birth to a human. It is their ancestor.
There are no names of humans on the wall. Few people know
it is there. Even fewer are allowed to go there. When Thomas
was a boy the old ones took Ruth and him to that stone wall
and told them about the mother of life and all that followed.
After the whale, the octopus in all its intelligence was next in
the line of creation, then the salmon, Ruth's clan; a spiral, and
then the other constellations.

They have already made a place for him as if they knew he'd
arrive. But first they set down a cup of coffee. He sits on a stone
which is warm from the fire. "Starbucks," the old woman says.

He smiles at her. "Thank you." He thinks it's funny and he
sips the coffee, trying not to laugh.

"They tell me you put up a wall," she says.

"I have taken it down and burned the wood."

"Good. You have gained some weight since your return. That's good. I knew your grandfather. I was younger than he was, of course. You are like him. He was always so quiet."

Thomas only nods. Inside himself the voices have stopped. He feels clear. It is right that he is there.

As if responding to his thoughts, she says, "We called you here. This is your home. You were born here. Did you know that? It was the time of the octopus. Then your mother went back across to be with her mother and she showed you to that octopus. It's your clan, you know. There are not many left. But we delivered you. And boy, what a head of hair you had, and we all said, 'He's so big!' We love you, son. This is your home. You came back like the salmon come back. We wanted you. We sang for you. We called for you. That is why you came."

The old singing man has white hair pulled back. "You will be here for a while." Outside the seagulls were waking and beginning to comb the shores. "You are going to learn. The songs. You are going to gain strength. Here, eat this." They place a meal of acorn mush before him.

The next morning, the man says, "Come."

Thomas follows.

They go over the dark rocks behind their houses to the freshwater pools in the rocks and bathe, the wrinkled old dry darkness of the older man and the almost newness of Thomas.

Then, afterward, they sit in silent council, meeting together for a long time, and much is said through the silence, more than all the voices inside him could have said.

As it has turned out, there is another plan to go whaling. Thomas doesn't know it.

Although Dwight had gone away for a while, to live up in Washington with a cousin, he had his friends and family still at Dark River and they made plans, connived and bargained with people from other places, other countries, other monies.

Dwight had covered his tracks. They were mere footprints at the edge of the ocean, filling in with water and disappearing, but they were there nonetheless. Though his house had fallen and his wife had left him and he had become something of an enemy to everyone, he only had to give it time. He only had to stay distant for a while. Everything blows over there. Everything is forgotten, at least on the surface, as if the people learned amnesia in order to survive. And so, he lets it pass over, like a fast hard wind across their bay. Then he will go back and start again, and they will whale.

In the meantime, there is a girl to consider. She lives in the apartment downstairs. He met her when she came to the door to complain about the noise. "Ho," he said. "We are Indians. We drum and sing and dance. Come in." She looked around, seeing they were all men, and said, "No, I have company, but maybe another time." He thought maybe she would have come in if they were white men, but then thought, No, she wouldn't. This is the city. She wouldn't feel safe. At home the women sit and talk to the drunks that live in the driftwood at the beach. The men tell them the same stories over and over. "I keep hearing the women and children crying," that's what the old drunk vet, Smith, who lived on the beach, told Ruth every time she saw him, Ruth good enough to take him food and coats, sometimes even beer. Smith Tiny was the son of a good man, the grandson of a great one. A mountain had been named for him. Once.

Smith's words are the reason Ruth doesn't blame Thomas for anything he might have done, even though she knows he blames himself.

Thomas remains at the white house place. His bed is near the fire and during the night he watches the flames, the animals swimming in them, the way they billow and flow. Sometimes they are like the waves of morning water he crosses over with the elders, singing as he paddles.

Over time, Thomas makes himself at home. He is helpful to the old people. He gathers wood. He splits wood. He lifts stones and moves them to where the elders can better see the water. He fishes for them. He takes their dinghy out and catches the daily supply. "You better not spoil us," says the man with his missing teeth, laughing. "Then we will forget how to take care of ourselves." And so the man goes with him, and the women clean the fish. But Thomas doesn't know that he will ever leave.

He says little. They don't care. He has come to them and now he is there paddling the ancient cedar canoe, he is singing at night around the fire on the beach. He is sometimes dizzy and falling from the movement of the earth. This is all good.

The day of tranquillity is a day he will never forget because this day he hears the ocean. He hears the seabirds. He is free because of truth. He wakes alive, as if something is happening in his life, something unknown. He wakes up and he is not a halfhearted man and he can't remember why he wakes this way, except that he hears the sound of birds and it is as if behind the human world something else is taking place. The ocean is peaceful, too, on this day, and he stands at Old Point and looks out at the light of morning, then with the excitement of a young man he puts on his boots and he walks from the rocks to the beach and he looks in the black stone for the creatures again. It is a still day, everything silent. Even the wind isn't blowing. There is just a breeze of something living, like the breath of the universe.

THE MAN WHO
KILLED THE WHALE

After that Thomas fasts. He scrubs himself with cedar boughs, scratching his skin. Thomas prays. He thinks of the story from the north about the whale that lived in the lake. It was a tiny whale. It gave the first hunter instructions on hunting and other details of living a good life. He places on the bow of the canoe an eagle feather and it does give him the power of wings to move through water, arms strong as wings, as if flying.

He goes into the water like his grandfather when women wore woven grass earrings and hats and shells and they all wrapped themselves in blankets. The man who killed the whale now holds his breath again.

Thomas is in the place where there is the only reef, in this place just before it drops down into the depths. And there is sand blowing like a storm in the water, which isn't clear. Even so he keeps his eyes open and sees the fish that remain and the starfish hanging on like purple and orange hands to the rocks and the feelers of other creatures, maybe crabs taking a measure as if they can tell things by inches or feet, fin or tail. Then he sees a young octopus float by, silken, one-eyed, beautiful, and he moves toward it, but it changes color to white and vanishes so quickly into the smallest place in the reef between rocks.

In all the green beauty Thomas recalls his purpose before he needs to rise and take a breath and he listens to the water because he doesn't know how Witka determined what needed to be done in the thickets of seaweed or the forest of swaying kelp and the school of silver fish all in a circle beside him, a marvel of fish, he hears the sounds of all the life in water, the clicks and ticking, and for a while time changes. It seems he was there listening, hearing what almost amounted to words and now he no longer needs to breathe. He hears a low rumble, the kind Ruth describes, the low rumble of a whale and it comes to him and it looks at him with its wise old eye and he knows everything in that gaze. He knows how small a human is, not in size, but in other ways. As he rises to the surface, it helps him, pushes him slowly and it exhales a breath as he surfaces, too, gasping for air. For a while he catches his breath, choking, the upper world reeling around him. The whale leaves. He is suddenly cold and aware of it and then he swims in a ways, floating with the current until he is butted up against the sand of the near shore and he stands, seaweed in his hair, suddenly colder, and he walks, no, he limps with the cold and his old injury no one had seen—one of his injuries—and with every- thing reeling around him still. He comes out of the water and sits down on the beach where things meet in the world between sea and land. Finally, with as much dignity as a bedeviled wet man with sticks in his hair and sand on his flesh can summon, he goes indoors and drinks hot water and later he meets with the people who are still waiting patiently even though it has started to mist outside and is growing chilly, and he says, "We are going to be better people. That is our job now. We are going to be good people. The ocean says we are not going to kill the whales until some year when it may be right. They are our mothers. They are our grandmothers. It is our job to care for

them." Then he sings an old whale song he has never learned.
He looks toward the ocean, and the song, it comes to him from
out of a hole opened in time. He sings it, a little embarrassed at
first, then growing stronger in voice.

"We are going to become better people."

"I've heard that song before," one old woman says later. It
was so long ago she can't remember where exactly except she
thinks it was her own grandmother's song, but then again it
could have been Witka who sang it or maybe the whole village
back when it was just a little place with old buildings that were
dark from the sea spray and rain and time.

Thomas knows there is a volcano out in the ocean. All the
world is changing and the ground is always moving. He feels
it, the ocean change, the sea change, shifting life. He is part of
it. They all are and he sees Ruth smile at him like she is still the
girl he once knew, a beautiful smile full of words.

The morning light is brightening and Thomas wonders when
the first sand was created from the wash of water on the mountains, or the first seabird grew feathers and wings, or the first
whale with inner legs walked on earth then turned back to
the water. He wishes he knew the real name of the world. The
beach birds walk away and the water fills their prints and even
the poor men who live on the beach feel rich today as if the sea
breathes and it is the exhalation of a conquered world and it is
being breathed away and the spirit of the place is breathed back
in and they are part of it all now, it is part of them.

So now the other men have said they will go to join the other
paddling nations. There is the announcement. "Ho, we go to
strengthen ourselves, not to kill a whale."

Thomas walks into the water like his grandfather, pushing
a canoe.

The women watch. They are thinking it is a lie. They are
waiting to see if the men are really going to kill a whale. There
are no weapons to speak of, none that they can see, but they

are suspicious now anyway. They wait to see what is the truth. Now, if they want to hunt, the women, even those who had been afraid to speak against their men, will fight them. All the wives and mothers watch and are wary. After all, they are people of the whale and this is history.

Even the man who sells his sometimes crooked homemade chairs to the tourists is on the beach, in the glint of light, watching the men disappear.

The endless vistas of water are shimmering and for a moment Thomas sees the women of Vietnam floating above the streets of the city in their cheongsams. He sees his daughter of flowers, Lin. He sees her surrounded by orchids and lotus blossoms, the sweet perfume of her life, but he doesn't know how he sees this far.

He doesn't see the old women in dresses of red with woven grass earrings and hats and shells, but they are there.

They live in a land where even at noon there are shadows. Thomas had been strengthened. Now his arms are firm, his legs are able to push against the side of the canoe, strong and capable. He is teaching the men to paddle. To paddle and to sing their names. He takes them out in the canoe. Men he has known. This time the men are quiet. He thinks they are all humble. But even at noon, they go out without telling anyone their plans. Thomas has a feeling of uncertainty about the endeavor, but he wants to practice paddling, to make a group of men who will go with the other tribes who have avoided them since their hunt, to journey the ocean north and soon to even travel at night by the old astronomy, by stars the old people know. They can stop at all the villages and feast and rest and make friends.

The others join him and drag the canoe into water. It is an older one, not as old as the ones over at the white houses, but old cedar and he is thinking how hard it was for his ancestors to bring in the large fish of any kind with these canoes, let alone a whale. They walk into the water with it and when they sit in it, he pushes it out. Then they begin, awkwardly, to paddle. He paddles the hardest as he looks at the beauty of the water, looking into it, thinking he would see the face so like his, Marco's, looking back at him, looking up. We are not the fallen, he thinks. We are suspended and we can take this turn and rise.

They are traveling to the old village and the songs come to his voice. He sings. The water is like mother-of-pearl. The men smelling like men, the sea smelling like sea. He sings.

"That's good," says Dimitri. "That song, I sort of remember it."

As for Thomas, he is whole. His mind, his heart, his being, all of him is in the paddles, the canoe, the water, and his song, too. He wants to live in the right way with the people, so he hasn't said anything about Dwight coming back for this journey. He saw him come, but they were going to be better people and so he had decided to say nothing. Dwight was looking for this path, too, and he was part of them. Maybe forgiveness exists for all their deeds and the actions of humans, but he can't stop thinking that Dwight probably killed his son. He couldn't prove it. There was so much happening, the canoe overturning, the confusion. Someone saw it, he is sure—someone besides Milton. But it is so hard with the conquered, having no one but each other. How much they want to thrive and watch the life grow back, and also how much they want what the conquerors have, long journeys to beaches and hotels, good cars, better boots, and then they want the other, longer journeys where they imagine the ocean and recall the constellations that guided their ancestors. Thomas has now become something else, not one of the conquered any longer but whatever was deep in him all along and precious as if it, too, crossed the water, the old world new in him, yet old.

They are trying to be The People, he thinks as they lose sight of the shore and head north. But Thomas is there with the games god can play on men. He feels the force of it hit before he even hears the shot. He sees Dwight with the pistol. He hasn't even finished the song when he falls backward as if through a door without a room, an anchor tossed down. He is still taken by the beauty of the world as he ages suddenly. His hair already is whitening with the salt. The spirit bones are all moving inside him. Dwight thinks, I killed him instantly. Thomas is thinking, Ha, there is no death.

His eyes see the crimson dresses of red all around him now and what hasn't existed for a long time is there again, the constellations, the human portions of water, the rapid waves soothing the cells, oh, a new world, one of changes, full and potent, and when he looks back everything, everyone but the spirits has disappeared.

And he knows the others will come to them, that they know his decision, that they know what he said about the kind of people they were becoming. Cedar will be brought, feathers, even flowers in the canoes. The crimson dresses come closer until they stand around him in the water, flowing the way blood does.

Out in the water the men are silent.

In water he, Thomas, sees above his head the points of the sea shining, the frothing water. At death, he feels, but doesn't see, all those moments of the past, beautiful and terrible. His senses are awake. He remembers even the unseen, the sweat of labor and love, the taste of the salmon from the river, hears the songs of the ocean, the loved ones singing, smells the garden in the first of spring, the green sprouts, he feels the cool taste of something he can't name, the sweetness and the physicality of the bending and working in the rice fields.

STIRRINGS UNDERNEATH

Like the water, the earth, the universe, a story is forever unfolding. It floods and erupts. It births new worlds. It is circular as our planet and fluid as the words of the first people who came out from the ocean or out of the cave or down from the sky. Or those who came from a garden where rivers meet and whose god was a tempter to their fall, planning it into their creation along with all the rest.

The red dresses he saw may have been his own blood growing, blooming about him in the water. But if he was too far from shore to see the women with his human eyes, there are other ways of seeing. And when they hear there was an accident, the women dressed in red dresses with grass belts and woven earrings and hats sit down in the sand, dismayed that things had once again gone so wrong. So do the women in jeans and T-shirts. Ruth falls, sinks down, with her face against the sand, sand in her hair, weeping. "Oh, what will ever help us now?" says Wilma. "We are beyond it. How could this have happened? It's like evil has been living with us." Even the way they walk. Even the darkness around them. There is evil in the world. It takes the shape of humans. Who want something small. Who want to distinguish themselves. Who want power to make decisions. Who think they want to change things.

Who want their own ends. It took the shape of the invaders. It
took the shape of the whalers. The men who killed things here.
The women who didn't turn away from them. The women
who fed them and didn't say, We are your hearts. We are your
conscience.

Nevertheless, like Jonah in the book written by many men
who heard the voices of their own gods, he washed up out of
the belly of the Great Mysterious that held him, washed up to
the old white houses, the houses that sat back from the shore
made of lava and rock worn by centuries into sand, the place
where the whale gave birth to the human and it was writ into
stone, like a commandment, back up behind the houses of the
old people.

There was surge and foam of ocean, the waves that rise over
a mere human in all their greatness, and he washed up the way
most alive men would gasp for a breath or double over in pain.
But did he come ashore without breath and did they find the
old person who revived him, the one, it was said, who brought
back the dead? It may have been the same one who lobbied
for the Rain Priest to come to them during the drought. If so, it
would have been kept a secret. Also, others would have feared
a man or woman with such great power and connections.

Perhaps Thomas had been enfolded by the large old octopus
that appeared at his birth, and he was taken down for a time
to its own magical world of shining things beneath the sea, its
walled world with the hoard of eyeglasses, necklaces of rhinestone, the emeralds dropped by a Russian whaler's wife.

When Thomas woke was he truly laughing at the stupidities
and frailties of mere humans, as it was later told by the people
to others?

When he arrives, he is carried by all that mystery to the old
land where they hold to what is valuable, perhaps by the whale
who heard his song and recalled it and knew his intentions.

. . .

Intentions are everything to the whale, older than the humans by millions of years. The whale, with its barnacles and wise old eye sees straight into the human soul. Through skin. Through bone. But perhaps, like some later would say, they saw an octopus lift him. Maybe the octopus took him to those who could help.

Now he is nearly naked, his clothes washed away, and he is newly born and so beautiful, this drowned handsome man who was loved and cherished by the people. They see him in the first blush of morning, newly arrived. He is a sleek branch of a man, muscular because they have been teaching him to paddle and swim and he has been working hard ever since he took down the fence and again faced the sea. They bend over him on the sand, the stronger ones kneel while the others marvel. Feather says, "Oh, no. It's Thomas," and he with two others get down on their knees over the body and lay their hands on him. Thomas is pushed and pressed and turned by their hands until the seawater runs from his throat.

When Thomas wakes he thinks he is dead. Then he laughs. A woman with her hair held by bone sticks helps him get up and stand and walk like old Witka, with almost no clothes, just rags now, with grime and weed, salt and blood falling from him and he walks into the white house place. He is as gray-haired as the rest. He is bent, hair hanging down. And old as she is, that one woman notices the man is pale as a fish and just as cold. She thinks, I am walking with a dead man. No one is more astute than she is. It was said at her birth that her soul was an ancient tree and so she leaves him to the one who revives the dead. Something secret is being done by the man who says he bought the gift of revival from an old man in a marketplace in Turkey, haggling about it over coffee that was the best in the world.

That man said he kept a human spirit which was a wind in a

bottle for just such cases as death or near death. This scared the people. But that was that. The bottle was now emptied.

While this is being done, Argentine walks away and out into the forest and gathers greens. When she returns she boils them and then she leans over the sleeping man and she puts a plaster on his terrible wound with forest greens and mosses, and with a candlestick and lantern she sits beside him and sings and spoons boiled herbs into his mouth at night. Sometimes he feels a hand on his chest, but no pain. He dreams that she can see his heart. He believes she can. It is a good heart.

When Thomas has his spirit back and can sit up and his heart has been covered with something like bark, they all sit in silent council for days. He understands what is being said. This is the way it used to be. The speaking is done through the eyes and through the soul and heart. A person can feel what is considered. Intelligence is passed all around, knowledge is shared. Decisions are made this way, primal, primary. Stories are told. For Thomas, he is emptied of all his stories and secrets, even his deeds, and one time he thinks, We keep nothing. What we are shows on our faces, our every move, our grasping, the way we consume others or ourselves.

The ceremony begins and it is never what those who are not Indian think, wish, hope. They want something more. They want so much, as if they have nothing. But now it is asked, What has he nourished himself with? What has he given the world and what has he taken? It is like judgment day for those who are questioned by a god in the sky or an angel who does the accounts.

For some time afterward all that can be done is to sleep. The room is full of his even breathing and snoring. No nightmares. Then the man named Feather wakes him and beckons to him. He gets up and washes and they go out, pull the ancient canoe into the ocean, and paddle, invisible in the light, as if they are ghosts transparent as dragonfly wings in the misty light and maybe they pass to the other side of something. All the clouds soon lift from the sky and the sun comes to their faces, glints off the ocean. No one can ever tell what it is, but travelers to other worlds return with special light.

In one world it all matters, the truth, all the many truths. In real worlds for those travelers, it is all the same.

The tribesmen and tribeswomen take him in, Thomas Witka Just, grandson of Witka. Even so, they are still questions, the people. Some are even shaped like questions, those who have bent backs. And there are the questions to be asked.

Thomas tells the old people he has learned to hold his breath for long periods of time. "Oh, just like your grandfather. Maybe that is why you lived."

"No, that wasn't all of it." But he can't remember. He is still salty. When he licks his lips even those days later there is still salt. And he doesn't know he is still cold.

Argentine tends to Thomas. Later she says, "How come Marco didn't wash up?"

"He had other places to go. But I always look out there, watching for him anyway."

After the silence and the healing and the tending, the people want to know everything about his life at Witka's for the last year or so. "How did you sleep during that time?" Feather asks him.

Though Thomas is healing, the water has swollen his hands and they will remain swollen. He opens and closes them. "Mostly by day." The dreams at night he didn't want to tell about.

"I see. And you practiced holding your breath at night."

"Yes." He sees it now, the world beneath, the particles in the beam of his light, the starfish holding to the rocks and pilings. He doesn't know that Ruth was ever there, watching him.

"And where did you stay?"

"Usually close to the pier."

"No. In Witka's house, I mean."

"Mostly in the corner of the house."

"Like a spider in its web, I think. With its silk. Out of your own self you made a new man."

They speak until all the words leave English and they exist then in their own language.

He is tired. Yes, he has shed a skin. He has worn it for years and he's had a weeping inside that only Ruth could hear when she was around it. It walked about with him like another person. Now there is silence, even peace, no more haunting. He is red in the eyes. They watch him sleep, coughing now and then. They think, Yes, he is equal to it.

Then one woman says, "He doesn't look like much more than a boy now. He's good-looking."

When he wakes he says, "Spring is coming. I smell it in the air. Dawn, too."

On the other side are answers. A few men have grown tired of their leader, Dwight, and walked straight as they could from near the fisheries, the marina, and went to the police. They walked up the single rotting wood step into a modular building. It was as if no one saw them at first. Because the police receptionist and the two busy men and one woman don't want to hear about the Indian problem. "We have another tribal 'thing,'" as the receptionist says, almost to herself, as she blows her red nose, cursing the weather that has spread a recent virus. She throws the tissue into a trash can near her desk.

But then the men show them the bullet casings and, standing there, tell their story. "A man was killed. A good man. And it was Dwight who did it. Dwight . . . he killed Thomas Just." The officers' ears opened to the mention of the hermit war hero. Thomas Just was missing for so many years and is now lost at sea.

"Okay," says an officer with a crew cut. "Sit down."

It has been told before, but none of them know it now,

when the whales were there years ago, at the turn of the century, when the Americans first came and made some of the Indian men believe they could take up another way and profit and win when *win* was a word that never existed in A'atsika. Neither did *profit* or *lie*.

And the other policeman looks up. One with his hair sprayed and combed like Johnny Cash gets up and brings the men back to sit on hard wooden chairs near him. They have a record on Dwight. For a while they are all bodies of silence. Then Dimitri talks. They listen for a while. The one with a crew cut runs his fingers through his hair. It feels good, his new haircut, like touching an animal, and the officer rubs his sore shoulder as he listens. The other writes it all down, then he pushes back his chair on wheels and says, "At last. Let's go," and they leave the men on the hard chairs and walk out the door to go pick up Dwight. "This time the witnesses want to talk." All of them, no longer afraid. There is something the men want deeper than what they know, beyond human law and justice. It is to go back to being who they used to be, to love, to the touch of a foot on earth as a sacred touch, to the whale mother, to home.

At Dwight's the dogs bark fiercely at the door. Outside, the policemen look at each other. They hope they don't have to shoot the dogs. They both hate shooting animals. Dwight gets up from the couch and the ball game and goes to the door where the dogs are barking. He opens it to see if there is a raccoon or skunk. He has his rifle in his hand to shoot the damned animal and hang it somewhere for others to see, hoping it is not a skunk because it will stink to high heaven. He is surprised to see the police there. "It's okay," he tells the dogs. "It's okay, Jake."

When they see him with the rifle, they think he is dangerous. "Drop the fucking gun," says the officer. "Call off the dogs."

The other tries to be more soothing. "Just put it down nice and easy and don't try anything. We don't want any trouble, especially with your wife here."

Dwight knows the routine. He's been through it. He lays it down gently on the floor. He has been to war. He has told many men the same thing.

"Here, boys," he says to the dogs. "It's okay." They go out and pretend to chew on each other's necks, growling, playing.

"What's up, Lyndon?" Dwight asks, feigning innocence. "Hey, man, you know me. Haven't we known each other forever?" He looks at JC, as he has silently called him behind his back. "I been buying you drinks for years."

It's true, but the officer hasn't been bought off like Dwight thinks, and he's not his friend. They went to high school together. JC remembers him. And he's been waiting for information on the whales killed, thinking a drunken tongue will sooner or later tell the truth and he'll find Dwight behind the wall of lies.

Dwight had brought the white woman back with him. She was so proud to be with the man who sings old songs and tells her traditional stories, even those not intended to be told and some he even made up, and he is a warrior and a paddler and such a good, proud Indian man. Her friends think she is fortunate and privy to tribal secrets. She watches Dwight at the door. "What's going on?" she says. They all ignore her.

Suddenly self-conscious, she goes into the other room and puts on the new robe she bought to cover her gown, a silky pink thing Dwight secretly told his friends about, laughing about her wiles. She stands at the door, watching his hair fall across his face as he looks down and they handcuff him, in front, not like on TV with his hands behind him, and they tell him not only his rights but also his wrongs and he says, "There are witnesses. I have my witnesses," meaning from the boat the day Thomas was shot, but he doesn't say a word, nor will he ever, about how he thought he saw the great octopus lift a tentacle and rise up and look right at him with a black, intelligent eye and become red with fury at the humans who were said to be similar to itself except for the bones that limit them so much they can't slide away and into safe, small places, and only two arms, oh, poor pitiful creatures. Dwight will never tell how the whale lifted their canoe from beneath or that he was jealous that Thomas had been the one that could hear the low rumbling of the whale that day and he'd said, "Wait. Listen." Or that Thomas had been the one who could paddle and sing and truly had been a hero and a man. Always, really, when they thought of it, as if he'd been born to it, even as a child.

"I do. I have witnesses."

"Yeah, your witnesses are the ones who told us," the policeman says.

Dwight hadn't counted on that, but now he is already figuring out what he might say. He wouldn't tell the truth if it was his name.

"What's going on?" the blond woman asks again, fear in her voice. "Dwight?" She hollers after him as they leave.

While Dwight is taken away and concocting stories, the woman who has been left behind, and worse, ignored, thinks and says out loud, "Geez, my mother was right. I've gone wrong with another freakin' man." She closes the door after watching them load Dwight into the car. She steps over the rifle, and, crying, takes out her new underwear and the clothes that no longer fit her pregnant body. She gathers things from the room, the slinky top, and she tries to figure out how to get home. She'll hitchhike, but she doesn't trust her own judgment, so she sits and cries until Milton hears her and goes to tell Ruth and send her over to see if the woman is being hurt by Dwight.

Outside, Ruth can hear her crying, too. When she goes in, the first thing she does is unload the rifle and put it under the bed. All the while the woman packs her suitcase. "It's okay. It will all be okay. I'll help you out," she tells the girl. "Here, let me help you," Ruth says, being kind to the woman she hadn't really acknowledged enough. "What can I pack for you?"

"They arrested him."

The woman named Angela wraps her arms around Ruth and sobs. "And I'm going to have a baby."

Ruth sits on the unmade bed.

Then Angela remembers where Dwight keeps his money. He always thought it was secret, but Angela has a keen eye, and while Ruth folds her things, she goes to the freezer to find the key to the safe-deposit box, the freezer out in the back room with the guns, It is in the freezer where he keeps meat he has hunted. She finds the box there and when she opens the box, she says, "Jesus!" Then she remembers Ruth and closes the box. She thinks she better go to the bank with Dwight's key, too. It is for the baby, she tells herself.

Ruth has already seen the cash in the box, but Angela doesn't know it.

"Could you drive me to the bank?" Angela asks the older woman. "I need to get what's left out of our account."

In the meantime, Ruth decides to talk Angela into staying in town until she has the baby, at least. There are the dogs to think about. "We could help you out. With the baby and all. You can fix up the place any way you like. The birth will be free here." There are a dozen reasons. And while Angela is in the bank, Ruth goes to the pay phone and makes a call to the police about the money.

Angela has money in her eyes. At the bank they know already she lives with him and she is showing. They guess she's his wife. Anyway, they don't care. She opens the box to find cash. Bills and bills of cash. Rolls. Stacks.

Charges are pressed against the war veteran Dwight, and he is not released because of his record. They were not minor offenses. One of the cops built a case against him with a tribal police officer and they thought they had him for sure and the feds were involved. Then, after the arrest, they saw him walking along the road just a few days later. It took the officer all he had in him not to swerve and run over the man named Dwight. But this crime, the newer one, isn't just a parole violation.

The other men from the canoe the day Thomas was shot hear what has happened. They are satisfied that justice is done, but they worry about whether they are accomplices or witnesses, men who will have to testify against the man who always gets off and can bring them down because they were part of it. But this time they believe something better. Because men can split and lie to themselves, one part to another, a part of them believes they are returning to better ways. Still, Dwight had promised them money from the next whale and the money would come from Japan, the eaters across the sea, and he still owes them from before and now they won't see that money, either, and hell, they'd made plans for it already, and the two with credit cards ran up large bills, but damn if it wasn't just like always.

Over at the white dwellings they could forget America almost, except they like their small conveniences, not electricity, which they do not have, not even running water, for they still want the fresh spring in the rock, but having their laundry done would be nice. They need their propane stoves on cold days, their umbrellas on the warm days, but even though they are great thinkers, they believe in, live in, the world of matter. The Great Something lives in matter, the trees with their mysterious fluid, their force, the green fuse of light, the orange with its inner crystals, the stones and their great and small beginnings. For centuries, maybe a millennium, their own ancestors carved stones, no small labor, with spirals. Then, over by the spring is the carved whale, mother of humans.

One day in the moss-covered stones Thomas finds other carvings. Not wanting to harm the mosses, he only traces these

by feel, the sea creatures. All things with more of a handle on
the world than a single, simple man.

Thomas, who has always loved consulting maps, now maps
their land by story and event and the old names. "We want
you to record all this on paper." They bring out a notebook and
pencils, but they have stories woven into sea grass, baskets,
and cloths. They take him from place to place, over rocks and
across streams. He wonders at the agility of the people.

One day of blue and calm ocean, he takes up the paddles
for the painted canoe and he has the muscle to pull himself
through the water. He goes to Ruth's *Marco Pollo* and up the
side and knocks on wood as if there is a door he can enter.

Dick Russell is there helping Ruth and she is smiling, looking
youthful, and even as feminine as she looks, she is still working ropes and twines and has broken nails, no gloves, when
her father always told her to wear gloves. She has filled out
in a way he hasn't seen before, but her hands are worn hard
and have aged and cracked in places. Still, he has never seen
anyone so beautiful. He stands and looks. The boat is badly in
need of painting.

Ruth has seen him but thinks he is a ghost, so at first she
looks at him, then looks away and goes back to her labor at
coiling the ropes and pulling over nets, heavier than you'd
think, no longer smiling. Her arms are sore. Then she stops
and turns and looks at him. "Thomas."

"They said you were dead." She is crying now, but looking
at him. His arms are strong and his body agile, more now than
hers, tired of her labor. He looks like an older version of their
son, Marco. She embraces him. Dick Russell at first feels jealousy of this man, their relationship, but Ruth says, "Let's all
have coffee."

"Shame on you," she says to Thomas, as she puts the coffee
in the filter, "for letting us think you were dead."

But things would have been different if he was alive. There would still be fights among the tribe and now things have calmed down. Dwight is in jail down in Lompoc and the world around them seems to have been growing right again. Thomas has been gone for many months. He looks so good! It's as if he's shed a skin.

"We had a wake and a great service for you. You should have been there. All your friends were there. They turned Dwight in. He's in jail. For murdering you. We had beautiful flowers at your wake, and even bamboo, for your time in the jungles. There was a giveaway of all your things, so now you have nothing." She pours the coffee into cups.

"Be sure to tell your mother I am thinking of her," Thomas says.

Ruth is quiet now. "She's gone, too," she says. She died shortly after you did."

"I am so sorry."

"She wasn't buried. She wanted to go out to the ocean with the whales. We wrapped her in the grass cloth. I wove it for her and stitched it together and sang for her. We had a sing for four days." Ruth goes to straighten things on the cabinet, the saltshaker, the sugar. "We won't have the memorial until next year. Are you going back over right away?" To the white house people, she means.

"Yes. But I have tickets to go see Lin. I am going to use them."

When he leaves, he says, "Ruth, you have always been so kind. I will be living with the old people now. I want you to take Witka's house when you go back. He left it to both of us. I know you love it. You can live there like you have always wanted. I can see that you are almost done with this fishing life."

"Yes. I will." She doesn't know what else to say. "Thanks, Thomas. I already have sold the boat."

"Who to?" he asks.

"I sold it to two guys from the village. One is Vince's son and the other is Dimitri's brother. Remember them?"

Ruth has always loved the house on top of the black rocks. "Thank you, Thomas." She is older now and wants solitude.

After Thomas leaves, Dick says. "I can see you love him."

"Yes, but not like what you think. I knew him as an infant. All my life." She leans against him. "He and I had passion once, the young kind, and we had a son but we never really shared him, but that kind of love has gone away. He's a brother to me now."

On the day Ruth moves into Witka's old gray house, she opens all the shutters and windows to the sea air and looks out. Three dolphins are curving above the ocean. The seals are napping in the shade of the rock.

At times she walks through the forest and it is a green lamp; sometimes with the fog weaving between trees, at other times with light shining.

Some say the day he died, the day Dwight shot him in the chest or heart, that they saw him moving above water, dead, as if it was his soul, carried straight out to sea. Others say his body traveled to land. Some are certain a wave took him under and there was a great stillness on his face that made them less afraid of death, therefore of life. They saw a whale carry him, and some saw an octopus tentacle wrap around him like a snake and hold him into the air.

Some just say the spirit world searches for us. It wants us to listen.

ACKNOWLEDGMENTS

With gratitude to all of my supportive friends and relatives. I thank especially Deborah Miranda, Margo Solod, and Peggy Shumaker for material help with this book during rough times. Thanks to Allison Hedge-Coke, a great human being. Thank you, Dave Curtiss, for being There. For Lisa Wagner and your creative energy. For Cathy Stanton and our long talks. For Kathleen Cain and your trees. For my student and husband, who talked with me about Viet Nam back before my accident. I apologize for forgetting names. For my Brenda Peterson, who also loves the whales, and for the Quillieute Nation and other paddling Nations with beautiful canoes and paddlers who do not kill. And last, for my brother, Larry Henderson, who went with me on part of this journey where we survived the "desperadoes" and their guns! This book has been a long time in the creation and I could go on about all the people and whales who have helped me throughout, but I hope you all know who you are.

PEOPLE OF
THE WHALE

Linda Hogan

PEOPLE OF THE WHALE

Linda Hogan

DISCUSSION QUESTIONS

1. When Thomas Witka comes home from Vietnam, he is no longer connected to the people in his tribe. One of the themes in *People of the Whale* is the significance of tradition, the glue that holds a community together over time. Why might Thomas Witka initially seek reunion, not with Ruth and Marco, but with the whale?

2. The A'atsika men who endeavor to end the moratorium on whale hunting suggest to their tribespeople that hunting whales "will bring us back to ourselves." Why does Ruth reject this argument?

3. According to A'atsika tradition, when one whale is killed, its spirit is reborn in another whale. Is this traditional notion of "deathlessness" reinforced by Dwight and Dimitri? Can you sympathize with their point of view? Is their argument valid? Why or why not?

4. Discuss the parallels between Thomas Witka's Vietnam experience and his participation in the whale hunt. How are his psychic wounds affected by the killing of the whale?

5. Linda Hogan borrows from Native American knowledge systems, stories, and myth to tell this provocative story of a man's falling away from and painful reconnection with his family, his tribe, and his history. Why do you suppose she blends myth and history with present-day Western notions of reality in her writing?

6. After Marco's disappearance and the killing of the whale, an old man tells Ruth that a drought will come. "A wrong thing was done," he says. "Maybe more than one wrong thing. . . . Get ready

for it. N'a sina." Native American lifeways, like those of other peoples, include sacred narratives *and* conventional wisdom. Consider the importance of the old man's words. Do you see his memory of the past as a particularly Native American attitude?

7. Ruth was born with gills. Marco was born with webbed feet. Animals figure prominently in the A'atsika people's environment, daily reality, and collective imagination. Analyze how animal symbolism fits into the past and present in Native cultures.

8. When drought comes, as the old man prophesied, Ruth senses that the sea is holding its breath, waiting for something. What does Ruth have in mind? How might the elders of her tribe elaborate upon this notion?

9. *People of the Whale* is concerned with loyalty to and betrayal of the natural world. Discuss how Thomas Witka's relationship with his two children, Marco and Lin, also illustrates the breaking of a sacred trust and the painful moral choices humans make. Does Lin's meeting with Thomas and Ruth offer new hope?

10. Linda Hogan ultimately offers a striking portrait of what it is to be a modern American Indian. Her narrative plumbs the difficulties of upholding tradition in the face of modern demands. What messages do think Hogan intends to transmit through her storytelling? Discuss the relevance of these ideas in your own community.

and forward to those we have yet to make. *Power* is a haunting, beautiful testament that finally leaves out nothing, including hope."

—Barbara Kingsolver

"Hogan has examined the brutal overlay of white society on Native American culture in her previous books, but none have caught fire as gloriously as this enthralling tale of a young Taiga woman's struggle to come to terms with her heritage. . . . Hogan, who is absolutely magnificent in one radiantly dramatic scene after another, compels us to consider all the forms power takes and how foolishly we abuse it."

—*Booklist*, starred review

"Its profundity is great: this is a book about losing and regaining the living world. . . . Hogan uses her skills as a poet here to cast a potent spell. Her sentences, full of vivid images and often composed of long, rhythmic phrases, have an incantatory, dreamlike sound."

—*San Francisco Chronicle*

PRAISE FOR *DWELLINGS: A SPIRITUAL HISTORY OF THE LIVING WORLD*

"Hogan exquisitely examines both natural and internal landscapes. She writes beautifully about animals without anthropomorphizing them and, in so doing, explores what it means to be human. Herself a Chickasaw, Hogan is able to bring a diverse cultural perspective to her analysis of how people relate to nature."   —*Publishers Weekly*

"Hogan brings her feeling for language and story to these quietly beautiful and provocative musings on the nature of nature . . . of the 'circular infinity' of life and death, of how air, earth, and water commingle and transform each other, how flowers bloom even in a place as blasted as Hiroshima."   —*Booklist*

"She encourages her readers to see themselves as a small part of the whole that is our ecosystem. The pieces come together to reflect the author's profound respect for the earth and prompt us to feel the same."

—*Library Journal*

MORE NORTON BOOKS WITH READING
GROUP GUIDES AVAILABLE

Erica Jong	*Sappho's Leap*
Peg Kingman	*Not Yet Drown'd*
Nicole Krauss	*The History of Love**
Don Lee	*Country of Origin*
Ellen Litman	*The Last Chicken in America*
Vyvyane Loh	*Breaking the Tongue*
Emily Mitchell	*The Last Summer of the World*
Honor Moore	*The Bishop's Daughter*
	The White Blackbird
Donna Morrissey	*Sylvanus Now**
Patrick O'Brian	*The Yellow Admiral**
Heidi Pitlor	*The Birthdays*
Jean Rhys	*Wide Sargasso Sea*
Mary Roach	*Bonk*
	Spook*
	Stiff
Gay Salisbury and	
Laney Salisbury	*The Cruelest Miles*
Susan Fromberg Schaeffer	*The Snow Fox*
Laura Schenone	*The Lost Ravioli Recipes of Hoboken*
Jessica Shattuck	*The Hazards of Good Breeding*
Frances Sherwood	*The Book of Splendor*
Joan Silber	*Ideas of Heaven*
	The Size of the World
Dorothy Allred Solomon	*Daughter of the Saints*
Mark Strand and	
Eavan Boland	*The Making of a Poem**
Ellen Sussman (editor)	*Bad Girls*
Barry Unsworth	*Sacred Hunger*
Brad Watson	*The Heaven of Mercury**
Jenny White	*The Abyssinian Proof*

*Available only on the Norton Web site: www.wwnorton.com/guides